VENGEANCE RUNS COLD

A Wally Morris Mystery

Other books by Joani Ascher:

VENGEANCE RUNS COLD

•

Joani Ascher

AVALON BOOKS
NEW YORK

Asa

Published by Thomas Bouregy & Co., Inc.
160 Madison Avenue, New York, NY 10016

Library of Congress Cataloging-in-Publication Data
Ascher, Joani.
    Vengeance runs cold / Joani Ascher.
        p. cm.
    ISBN 978-0-8034-9938-6 (acid-free paper)
  1. Morris, Wally (Fictitious character)—Fiction.   2. New York
(State)—Fiction.   I. Title.
    PS3601.S29V469   2009
    813'.6—dc22 2008031627

PRINTED IN THE UNITED STATES OF AMERICA
ON ACID-FREE PAPER
BY HADDON CRAFTSMEN, BLOOMSBURG, PENNSYLVANIA

This book is dedicated to the real Wally, a woman who never ceased her quest for knowledge, even into her nineties. She was a true inspiration.

As always, I am grateful to Deborah Nolan and Kim Zito, the members of my writers' group. It would not be possible to finish a book without their help. Thanks also to Faith Black and Erin Cartwright-Niumata for their insightful editing, and to my family, especially David, who always puts up with my being off somewhere in my head, even when he's talking to me.

Prologue

"Stay back, lady. You don't want to see that."

"Just tell me," said Paige Griffin. She was near tears. "Is it my uncle?"

"Lady," said the plumber. He himself was standing back. "That ain't nobody's uncle. Not unless he wore skirts."

Relief washed over Paige. It seemed so wrong, especially since someone was dead, but at least it wasn't Ted.

"I'm not a child," she said, holding her breath and edging closer to the corpse. She saw long blond hair surrounding a grotesquely desiccated face. The body in the disintegrating blanket wore a long, black skirt with a black turtleneck. Rope bound her wrists and three of the fingers on her left hand were missing.

"I think you'd better call someone," said the plumber. Paige picked up the phone. In the back of her mind she knew the man had meant the police, but the first number she dialed was that of Wally Morris.

Chapter One

Two months earlier

Wally Morris sat beside Paige Griffin, the daughter of her old college friend Marion, as she steered her SUV along the unpaved road to an enormous fieldstone house overlooking Lake Champlain. Wally had never seen the old place that belonged to Marion's brother, Ted Verrill, a world-renowned archeologist and author. She looked on it with the same fresh eyes as Paige's nine-year-old son, Mike, who had sulked in the backseat of the car during the whole ride from New York City.

His face lost some of its anger at being ripped out of Manhattan as he stared openmouthed at the mansion with its vast picture windows. It stood up on a rise, with a wide veranda in front, and was surrounded by a lush lawn.

The second the car stopped under the portico and Paige opened her door, Balto jumped out. The golden retriever raced around the lawn sniffing all the new odors that he had never smelled in the city. Mike zipped after him, his sneakers a blur in the grass, yelling for the dog to sit still so he could attach the leash. Paige was right behind them, laughing, looking happier and more relaxed than Wally had seen her in years.

"I don't think you need to worry about it, Mike," said Paige, stopping to catch her breath. She was wearing just a tank top and shorts and her brown hair was in a ponytail. She was an attractive young woman and to Wally she looked far younger than her thirty-one years. "There isn't likely to be much traffic up here."

The air seemed quite warm after the air conditioning of the SUV and Wally was glad she also was wearing shorts. She pushed her chin-length Sable Mist–colored hair behind her ears to get as much of it away from her face as possible and she looked at the huge house with trepidation. If she had to admit it, she'd say it made her kind of nervous that Paige and Mike were moving here. Tamarack, although it was a charming and quaint nineteenth-century-style village, was a long way from Manhattan and would be very different from Paige's life only a year earlier.

"Hello," said a voice.

Wally shielded her eyes from the bright sun and looked at the house. She was startled to see a woman, somewhat plump but all smiles, a few years older than Paige, just coming down the stairs from the porch. As she came toward them, she quickly wiped her hand on her sundress, then adjusted the brightly colored napkin in the big basket she carried. "I see the city girl has arrived in the North Country," she said, extending her hand to Paige. "My name is Jolene Valley. I guess you could call me the welcome wagon."

Paige introduced herself and Mike, then looked toward Wally. "This is my very dear old friend, Wally Morris, who has come for a few days to help us move in." She smiled at the galloping dog. "And that's Balto."

Considering the ages of the two younger women, Wally kind of wished Paige hadn't pointed out the old part.

"Pleased to meet you," said Jolene. Now that she was closer, Wally could see that she was not so much plump as muscular, and she was taller than Paige, which meant she practically towered over Wally.

Jolene gazed down at Balto, who had finally come to a rest and lay panting in the grass at their feet, and frowned. "Did you have any trouble finding the place?"

Mike rolled his eyes. "I thought we'd never get here. Mom got lost a few times. She even got lost right here."

"I missed the road," Paige explained. "And I don't know if I'm properly equipped to be here," she joked. "I didn't bring a canoe." Every third car on the Northway since they passed Albany had a canoe on top, Wally remembered.

"We have a lot of lakes up here in the Adirondacks," Jolene explained, laughing. "People come up all summer to use them. But don't worry about not bringing a canoe—your uncle Ted has two down on the racks."

"He hasn't come back, by any chance, has he?" Paige asked. "I thought he might try."

Jolene shook her head. "No. He hasn't been around. But we knew you were coming. I think the whole town does. That's why I came over, to see how you're doing and bring you some muffins." She set the large wicker basket on one of the Adirondack chairs in front of the porch. It looked heavy to Wally and the scents emanating from it made her mouth water. "But you weren't here."

"We're here now," said Paige, reaching for Mike, who was just running by again after Balto. "And thanks."

"Do you live nearby?" Wally asked. "I didn't see a car."

Jolene stared down at Wally. "Not far. But not walking distance on a hot day like today. I parked my car around the side of the house, in the shade."

Paige looked at her watch. "We should get unpacked."

"I'd love to help," Jolene offered.

"This is so nice of you, Jolene," Paige said. "If everyone else around here is even half as thoughtful, I think we'll like living here." She opened the back of the car and starting pulling out boxes, suitcases, and groceries. Wally took as many bags as she could carry and started going up the steps. When she got to the top, she turned around, realizing that the door was closed.

"This car will come in handy when winter comes," said Jolene, grabbing several more shopping bags. "It hits pretty early up here. And hard. You can expect the first real snow in October and it goes through May, sometimes."

Mike's face brightened, but he didn't say anything. He was determined to be miserable.

"It gets old fast," Jolene continued. "But Foster, the fellow down the road who takes care of the house, has a plow. He'll clean your driveway. There would be no way for you to do it yourself." Jolene picked up the basket of muffins with her spare hand. "By the way, his wife, who took all the dust covers off for you last week, will come in weekly, if you want."

The look on Paige's face told Wally that she wasn't sure this was in the budget. Not for the first time did Wally wonder what happened to all the money Michael, Paige's late husband, must have made.

Paige unlocked the door. As they stepped into the foyer, they all stopped for a moment while their eyes adjusted to the interior darkness.

"Wow," said Mike, looking around. Wally had to agree. The foyer was impressive. Beside the door stood a table made from the cross section of a large tree with legs made from the roots of a smaller tree. There was rough-hewn wood wainscoting on the walls, and at the rear a wide staircase branched midway up and became two narrower staircases leading to the second floor. A chandelier made of the antlers shed by scores of deer hung down over their heads from the twenty-foot ceiling.

The upper hallway that went from the steps all around the second floor had doors spaced evenly along it. Wally knew there were ten bedrooms and five baths in the house, which had been built as a summer home for a beer baron from New Jersey in the early part of the last century.

"Let's take these to the kitchen," Paige said. "It's through here, if I remember correctly."

Jolene, who was walking past them with the basket of goodies, jerked her head in the opposite direction. "That's the parlor. The kitchen is the other way, through there."

They passed through the dining room with its birch-bark furniture and bear skin rug, then went into the morning room, which had a fireplace with several pictures of Ted on the mantle. In most of them he wore a hat, sunglasses, and khaki clothing with many pockets, looking almost like Richard Leakey, and he was displaying some artifact or other. There was also an artifact in the one picture of him in which he wore regular street clothes. It was from his book jacket and showed his face clearly. He had black hair, light-blue eyes, and a smile that seemed to be hiding amusing secrets.

The kitchen featured an eight-burner professional stove, a walk-in refrigerator, and a huge sink with a stainless steel counter, all legacies of the previous owners, Wally had heard. The oak parquet floors gleamed as if just polished.

Balto came trailing in behind, sniffing every square inch of his new home. When he got to the middle of the kitchen, he suddenly turned and went the other way, finding a comfortable corner along the far wall to settle into and watch the proceedings. Wally shook her head and laughed. Her dog, Sammy, was just the same.

"Those muffins smell wonderful," Wally said when Jolene uncovered the basket. There were also several packages of coffee, as well as cookies and doughnuts.

Jolene smiled. "Thanks. They're from my shop."

Mike was wide-eyed. "You own a bakery?"

"Oh, it's more than just a bakery. I sell everything from sandwiches and soups and salad to coffees and teas and lattes and chai teas and pie and cake and cookies. All of it healthy." She looked at Paige. "All organic and all delicious. You'll have to visit."

"Can we Mom?"

"We sure can. And we'll take Aunt Wally with us." Based on everything in the basket, Wally looked forward to it.

"Where would you like me to put everything?" Jolene asked. "I'm sorry, but I need to take the basket back with me. I use it for my large take-out orders. The muffins would keep better if they were in an airtight container anyway."

"Of course," said Paige. "I'll find something." She started looking through the kitchen cabinets and came up with some plastic containers. She reached for the basket to unpack it, but Jolene waved her off.

"I'll do it," she said with a smile. "I certainly didn't mean to make more work for you."

Wally went to get another bag from the car and returned just in time to catch Jolene as she stumbled, falling against the stove with a thud and a clink while trying to catch an errant muffin. Luckily, though Jolene was shaken, she was unhurt and the muffin was saved.

"Thanks, Wally," she said when she'd recovered her balance. "I can be so clumsy." She straightened her sundress. "Okay then.

I'll be off. I hope to see all of you soon." She picked up her basket, waved, and left.

Paige and Wally set about putting all the groceries away. Mike started to look bored as soon as the snacks were stored. "Maybe you'd like to see your new room," Wally suggested. "I bet you'll like it."

"I'd rather be in my room at home," said Mike.

Paige frowned. "We went over this. We don't live in New York anymore. Not New York City, anyway."

"Why couldn't we stay there?"

"Uncle Ted told me about a job here. He was nice enough to let us use his house." She sat down at the round kitchen table on one of the ladder back chairs and got eye level with her son. "There really was no other way."

Tears welled up in the boy's eyes and his bottom lip quivered. "But he isn't even here. He wouldn't care if we changed our minds."

"We knew he probably wouldn't be able to get away from the dig," Paige told him. "But I'm sure he'll be back before long. And I need the job!"

Mike's tears spilled down his cheeks. "I'd like to see my room now," he whispered.

Wally saw that Paige was biting her lip and fighting her own tears as she led him upstairs. It was upsetting that Mike was whispering again. He'd gone through a stage like that after Michael passed away and only hours of therapy had him talking in a normal voice again. But here, in only a few minutes, he'd been set back months. And there was nothing Wally could do about it.

Paige put on an optimistic tone. "Let's go find it. There are a lot of rooms up here. We'll have to see which one it is." She held back, letting Mike go ahead of her up the stairs and along the hallway. He put his hand on a doorknob and looked at her for an okay. This timidity had also been acquired after Michael died, Wally remembered. Before that Mike had gone helter-skelter into just about everything, with a joy that was contagious.

"Why don't you turn it and see?" she encouraged.

But it wasn't a young man's room, by any stretch of the imagination. There was a canopy bed and the walls were lined with dolls. Everything was pink.

"This isn't my room, is it?" Mike sounded horrified. Wally had to stifle a chuckle.

"No, of course not," said Paige.

"Does Uncle Ted have a little girl?"

Paige shook her head. "I think the dolls were from the former owners. They were transferred to Japan and couldn't take very many of their old things with them. They left the rest behind, and Uncle Ted hasn't given anything away yet." She closed the door. "Let's try another one."

"Can I see Uncle Ted's room?" Mike asked.

Paige led the way along the balcony, opened the door, and stepped aside. Mike went in. "Wow. Look at all this stuff."

The room, which overlooked the lake, was filled with photographs of various digs. There were many pot shards and several bones, including one skull, on every horizontal surface. There was also a small oil lamp, with a tag hanging from it, in a little glass-enclosed box.

"Ted gets a lot of gifts from various governments," Paige explained closing the door. "But don't worry. None of these things are valuable antiquities. Most aren't even old."

She moved farther down the hall. "You room is right down here." They passed another door and Paige opened the next.

Mike smiled, delighted. The room was filled with old toys—some mechanical, some wooden, all antiques. Ted had been collecting them all his life, Wally remembered. And he'd put all his old toys in Mike's room.

"There's a note," said Paige.

Mike tore open the envelope and read it out loud.

Dear Mike,

I hope you don't mind that I put these old things in your room. I guess with all my archaeological work, I can't bear to throw anything old away. Would you please take care of them for me?

I'm looking forward to seeing you.

Love, Uncle T.

"Can I unpack, now, Mom?" Mike asked in a normal voice.

With a sigh of relief, Paige nodded. "Let me show you to your room, Wally."

Chapter Two

After dinner, Paige and Mike took Balto out for his final excursion of the day, and then they went upstairs while Wally cleaned up. Paige felt guilty about not helping, but Wally told her it was more important to spend the time with Mike.

Paige ran a bath in the long bathroom. It was the largest in the house, stretching from the window over the kitchen to the hallway, and had a claw-foot tub. While it ran, she took a bath towel from the well-stocked linen closet and set it out for Mike to use when he got out of the tub.

Their own towels were in transit along with their furniture, meager though it was and no match for the antiques in Ted's house. It, as well as their household goods, wouldn't be delivered for another day. The best deal Paige had been able to make to bring their things up here was sharing a moving van with another family. Everything would happen on their schedule. That was why she hadn't been able to come to Tamarack sooner. Sometimes it seemed to Paige that their lives were being lived on someone else's schedule, and it didn't at all coincide with their own plans. At those times, she chastised herself for her self pity. They weren't out on the street, after all.

"I want my Big Bird towel," Mike said.

Paige caught her breath. She had put it aside to pack, knowing that Mike would want it. But it had somehow gotten into one of the boxes that was put on the truck, as she had explained to Mike last night. "It isn't here yet," she reminded him. "This one is wonderful. You'll like it."

"But I want Big Bird."

He hadn't used that towel since he was four, but after Michael died, he'd gone back to it. Paige wished she had packed it with his clothes before the movers came. "I'm sorry, honey," she said. "It'll be here soon."

She turned and went toward her room. Once there, she unpacked her suits, hanging them carefully. She didn't want them wrinkled on her first official day as principal of the local K-12 school. It started at the beginning of next week so she would have no time to get them pressed.

Paige felt that she'd been very lucky to get this job, especially since she'd just passed her licensing exam. She worried that Ted had used his influence to help her land it, but she couldn't be sure until she spoke to him, which she hadn't since the funeral, nearly a year before. He'd been traveling extensively, so most of their correspondence had been by computer and it was extremely sporadic. She hadn't heard a word from him in over eight months. She might be worried, if he hadn't spent most of his life being out of touch.

"I'm out, Mom," Mike called, interrupting her thoughts. "You can go next."

"Thanks." She looked at her son, hoping this move wasn't too hard for him. "Get some sleep. Tomorrow we'll go exploring."

After her own bath, she put away a few more suitcases full of things and looked in on Wally. She found her just finishing a call on her cell phone.

"The baby rolled over," she said to Paige. "But he's only four weeks old, so I think it was a fluke."

Wally's grandson, Charlie, had made his appearance mid-summer. Now, as August drew to an end, Wally was forced to find out about him from three hundred miles away, rather than firsthand. It made Paige feel guilty that Wally was here helping her instead of at home.

But when Wally heard about the opportunity Paige had to move up to Tamarack, she offered to help in any way she could. She hadn't waited for Paige to figure out how, either; Wally just volunteered to help with the move and set up. She'd promised to stay for a week, until she had to go back to her home in Grosvenor, New Jersey, for the start of the nursery school year. And Paige was very grateful that Wally had come up with them.

"I'm sure he's adorable," Paige said. "When you get home, give him a kiss for me."

"I will. And now I'm going to get ready for bed. Today was a busy day."

Paige had to agree. She went to her room and read for a little while. But she knew she needed some rest. She had a lot ahead of her. So at ten, impossibly early until just yesterday, she went to sleep.

The light on her bedside clock said it was 3:15 when she woke up and went to the kitchen to get a glass of water. She slipped down the back stairs in the darkness, and from memory, she went down the corridor that ran from the staircase to the back door, then turned toward the kitchen. And ran smack into a wall.

Wally's good-morning greeting to Paige was cut short by the sight of Paige rubbing her nose gingerly. "What happened?"

"I ran into a wall during the night," said Paige, taking a bag of frozen peas out of the freezer and placing it across the bridge of her nose. "It'll be okay. I can't understand it though. It didn't used to be there."

"What do you mean? Which wall?"

Paige pulled the bag of peas away from her face and pointed. "That one. It wasn't there the last time I visited. I'll show you."

She led the way inside and through the rear passageway to the kitchen, or at least as far as she could go. It was blocked by a wall, devoid of the crown molding and wainscoting of the rest of the passageway, and when she knocked on it, it sounded like wallboard instead of plaster.

Wally tilted her head. "Well, it certainly doesn't look original."

"Take my word for it," said Paige, gingerly touching her sore nose. "It wasn't here. Why would Uncle Ted block this hall-way?"

Balto's barking drew Paige outside onto the porch where she saw a car coming to a halt in front of the house. "You must be Paige," said the tall, athletic man getting out of his car. "I'm Quinton Wyatt."

She shielded her eyes from the bright sunlight and looked at him. Quinton wore neat khaki shorts, a navy polo shirt, and docksiders. He was just a few years older than she and seemed to have spent the whole summer in the sun, considering his golden tan. After looking back toward the road, he came up onto the porch and gestured at a truck coming into the driveway below.

He'd been driving through Tamarack, he explained, when the

driver of the moving van flagged him down and asked for directions. Instead of telling him, he led them up the long bumpy dirt road, past the Fosters' place to Ted's house at the end.

Balto started barking at the truck. He'd been running around ever since he'd finished breakfast, and he'd jumped into the lake and run through the kitchen, only pausing to shake himself off in front of Paige. She caught him by the collar and handed him off to Wally, who had come to see what the commotion was about. "Keep him out of the way," she said to Mike. "We don't want him tripping anyone."

Mike took Balto from Wally and came up to the porch. Paige started to make introductions.

"Please call me Quin." He looked at Paige, then Mike. "If that's all right."

Mike looked up at him. "Are you the handyman?"

Quin shook his sun-bleached head. "No. Actually, I own a hotel in Lake Placid. But I came to say hi, since Ted is a friend of mine." He leaned closer to Mike. "I'll bet you never drove on a lake. In the winter, you can drive from right here to Vermont."

Mike's eyes, which were a warm hazel color like Paige's and framed with the same long dark lashes, got big. "No way!"

"Absolutely. Look over there, across the lake. What do you see?"

"It's kind of fuzzy," said the boy. "But it looks like a mountain."

"Those are the Green Mountains of Vermont. And when the lake freezes, you can drive on it. Or you could just go sit in your ice shanty on the lake and do some terrific ice fishing."

"Ice shanty?"

"That's what we sit in when we fish through a hole we cut into the ice. We can squeeze all kinds of things in there, even a portable TV, and it's a lot of fun."

As the driver and his helpers chocked the wheels, Quin straightened. Paige saw that he had deep blue eyes that appeared to reflect the lake over his shoulder and at the same time they seemed to be assessing her.

A voice from the vicinity of the front door called out. "Hello? We need some instructions here."

Paige went to tell the driver where to bring each of the boxes. She'd already decided that her furniture could go into one of the spare bedrooms. "Wow, ma'am," said the truck driver, who had picked up her furniture from their two bedroom apartment in New York. "You sure got yourself a nice place up here."

She felt silly thanking him, since the house was in no way hers, but Paige couldn't ignore the comment, nor did she feel the need to explain that it belonged to her uncle. She smiled, feeling embarrassed, until he moved away.

Wally went upstairs with the movers to help supervise so that Paige could stay with her guest, as she put it.

Quin's blue eyes studied her.

"Oh," said Paige, taking the semithawed bag of peas away from her nose, "I should explain. I ran into a wall that wasn't here the last time I visited." She took him inside to where the new wall was in the hallway.

"I don't remember this," said Quin. "Although to tell you the truth, Ted and I usually hung out in town, not here."

"Can I offer you something to drink?" Paige asked, leading the way into the kitchen, where she threw the bag of peas into the sink.

"No, thanks." Quin glanced at his watch, which looked like a Rolex to Paige. "I guess I should be going," he said. "I've got to talk to some wine merchants. I'm taking them out on the lake to persuade them to give me a good price."

"Do you have a boat?" Mike asked, as he walked into the

kitchen. He carried a small box marked *utensils* and put it onto the table. Balto, right behind him, stopped halfway into the kitchen and went back out, coming in from another doorway. Paige could only shake her head—clearly the dog knew his way around better than she did.

Quin smiled. "Yes, I do."

Mike's eyes lit up. "Could I go for a ride on it sometime?"

"Mike," said Paige, "you shouldn't invite your—"

"It's okay," said Quin. "Sure, if it's all right with your mom."

Paige liked what she saw. Her son was perking up. "We'll see."

Mike's smile fell upside down and he hung his head. "Oh."

Quin gazed over him at Paige and raised an eyebrow.

Paige looked at each of them. Mike's scowl showed that in his opinion, "We'll see" meant "No." And thinking back to the last several months, he was probably right. She turned to Quin, willing to try to change. "When could we go?"

"We?"

"Do you mean it, Mom?"

She looked at both of them, her son's ecstatic face and Quin's pleased one, and felt happy with her decision. It would be fun.

"Come down to the dock when you're done," said Quin. "I'll be finished with the wine people by then." He told her how to get there and left in his SUV.

Suddenly Wally was standing in front of Paige. "Oh!" she said, jumping back. "Where did you come from? Are you telling me you just came through the doorway that I thought was over there?"

Wally smiled. "No. Not exactly. I just came through a door, but it wasn't that one. I did, however, figure out why it was blocked off. Come back this way and I'll show you."

She led the way through the other doorway, this one closer to

the main hall but narrower. While Paige tried to figure out why
anyone would put one there, since it had meant moving the
kitchen table to the middle of the room, Wally took her around to
a closet. "This is the other side of that wall. Ted must have wanted
a closet here, near the back door, for his raincoat and boots. This
way he wouldn't have to track mud through the house."

Paige looked at it. In contrast to the rest of the house with its
six-panel doors, the doors to the closet were louvered and
pulled outward, folding up as they did so. The closet within was
just deep enough to hold a rubberized army-style raincoat on a
hook and high boots, as well as some umbrellas. Several empty
hooks looked ready to hold Mike's and Paige's rain gear.

"I guess that explains it," said Paige, rubbing her nose again.
"Although it's kind of odd, since Ted never did a single thing to
the house, as far as I knew." She shrugged. "I think I'd better get
some night lights."

When Paige, Mike, and Wally got down to the dock, Quin
was standing on the deck of his red speedboat. Wally was unfamiliar with boats and knew little about them, but she did notice
that on the stern it said *Marissa, Lake Champlain, New York.*

"Wow," Mike said.

Quin climbed down to the dock. "Wow, indeed." He lifted
Mike up and put him on the deck. Paige followed. Wally held
back. She had never been on a boat like this. A rowboat was
more her speed.

"Come aboard," said Quin. "You'll love it."

Wally tended to doubt that, but she didn't want to transfer
her fears to Mike, so she plastered a smile on her face and
stepped gingerly onto the boat.

The deck had a nonslip surface, but she still didn't feel comfortable until everyone had put on life preservers.

Quin cast off and edged away from the dock, then revved the engine. "Do you want to see your house from another view?"

Mike looked at Quin. "What do you mean?"

"From the lake. We can take a ride past it."

Mike smiled. "Okay!"

They took off, with Wally holding on to her seat for dear life. They raced out of the wharf area into the open, swinging in a loop toward Ted's house. When they were fairly close, and looking right up at the house towering above them, Quin turned abruptly away. Wally saw a buoy in the water in the direction they had been heading.

"What's that for?" Mike asked.

"There are shoals there," Quin told him. He must have noticed Mike's furrowed brow, because he added, "Shallows. The water over there isn't deep enough for this boat."

"But it's not near the shore," Mike said.

"That's right. But if you were to swim out there, you might almost be able to stand. I've seen people do it."

"That must look strange, as if you're standing in the middle of the lake," said Paige.

"It's hardly the middle," Quin said. "But it does look funny anyway." He looked at Mike. "Are you ready for some real speed?"

Wally and Paige's protests were drowned out by the wind.

Chapter Three

Whۅen they pulled into the driveway back at the Griffins' new home, tired and happy from all the fun they'd had, Wally was looking forward to nothing more than starting dinner, then stretching out while it cooked. She'd planned to make Mike's second-favorite meal, macaroni and three cheeses.

But Balto had other plans.

He came out of the house through the doggie door built for Ted's old dog, and greeted them when they drove in. Then he dashed off after one of the cats that seemed to patrol the property. A moment after they got into the house and put down their things, they heard a yelp. It was followed by howling. Paige and Mike raced off to find the dog. Wally was right behind.

They followed the sound into a clump of bushes and around the other side, where they saw tall, white wooden boxes. The top of one seemed to be missing.

"What're those?" Mike asked, momentarily distracted.

"Beehives," said Wally. "Don't tell me—" She broke off when

she saw Balto. He was furiously licking his nose, alternating between using his paw to rub it, writhing around, and crying out in pain.

"What's the matter with him?" Mike cried, running toward the dog.

"Stay back!" Paige stood between her son and Balto. "Run back to the house and get a blanket and my cell phone. Hurry!"

While he was gone, Paige made soothing noises. Wally saw Balto tiring and hoped he would allow them to take him to the vet. Kicking off her shoes, she yanked off her knee socks and tied them together to form a loop, which she slipped over Balto's poor nose, so he couldn't bite. Ordinarily she trusted him completely—he was as gentle as her own dog, but now he was in agony. She spoke soothingly to him while getting her shoes back on, although she was anything but calm.

Mike came back with the phone and a quilt, which Paige wrapped around the whimpering dog. With tremendous effort, she and Wally struggled to get him to the car. "Dial 411," Paige told Mike. "Tell them you want the number for the nearest vet."

Mike did as she said and had the call put through. He held the phone to her ear while she got directions, all the while dealing with Balto's unwieldy bulkiness.

Running ahead, Mike opened the back door of the car and they put Balto in. Wally hoped the vet was nearby because she had noticed that Balto seemed to be breathing in short, shallow rasps and she was getting really worried.

"We've got to hurry, Mom!" said Mike, running to get in the car. "Here are your keys."

As Paige turned the car around, she went over the directions she'd received.

"Turn left at the end of the driveway and go toward town,"

she said. "When you get to the fork turn right. The animal hospital is on that road, about a mile down." Wally acted as lookout and after what seemed like hours she saw the shingle: Noah Oliver, DVM.

As soon as they pulled in, the door opened and a tall, rugged man with short reddish-brown hair, a trim mustache and beard, wire rim glasses and wearing a white lab coat, ran out to the car. "Hi. I'm Noah," he said. "Is this my patient?" He opened the rear door, lifted out the eighty-pound dog effortlessly, and ran into the building. Wally, Paige, and Mike followed.

"I see you've found a beehive," Noah said, talking to the dog as if he could understand. "Well, then, I think one more sting is going to be necessary. In the meantime"—he handed Mike an ice pack—"your little buddy here is going to make you stop feeling like your nose is on fire."

Mike looked up at Paige with a big question mark on his face. But Noah answered, "Don't worry. It'll make him feel better. Just be gentle."

While Mike held the ice pack to Balto's nose, Noah filled the syringe he held in his large hands. "He's going to need an antihistamine. But he'll feel a lot better soon."

Wally hoped he was right. Balto's breath had become even shallower, and he looked awful. But a few minutes after the shot he seemed to relax. He took a deep breath and sighed, gazing at Mike sheepishly. Since his nose was double its normal size, he looked ridiculous.

"You're quite a fella," said Noah. "Now I hope you'll pardon me while I talk to your mother."

He was looking right at Balto when he said that, Wally noted. And he called Paige the dog's mother with a straight face.

"You're new in town, aren't you?" he said, holding a clipboard with a form on it. "I'll need some information. Name?"

"Paige Griffin."

"Not yours. The big guy's."

"Oh. Balto."

"Ah, the dog who inspired the Iditarod." He picked up Balto's paw and shook it. "Pleased to meet you."

Mike looked at the vet. "Huh?"

Noah handed the clipboard and a pen to Paige, indicating that she should fill it out. He stroked his full beard thoughtfully. "Didn't your mom explain why she named your pal Balto?"

"No, I don't think so." He turned to Paige.

"It was his dad's idea," she said softly.

"Oh," said Noah. "Well, the first Balto lived a long time ago. And when there was a diphtheria epidemic in Nome, Alaska, in 1925, people organized dog teams to race to Nenana to get the medicine serum so that lives could be saved. Once they got there and got the medicine, twenty teams relayed the medicine from dog team to dog team to get it back to Nome. They went six hundred and seventy-four miles in only one hundred and twenty-seven and a half hours." He paused while Mike took in the information. "Now here's the important part, at least as far as your buddy is concerned. The lead dog on the last team to mush into Nome was Balto and he became famous."

"Wow," said Mike. "I didn't know all that."

"Pretty impressive, huh?"

Wally was impressed, not so much with the story, which she knew, but the fact that Noah had been working on Balto that whole time, pulling out the stingers and cleansing his wounds with bicarbonate of soda while keeping Mike from worrying about what he was doing. By the time the story was done, Balto was all ready to go.

"Your dad is going to be pleased to see that Balto is all well now," said Noah, with a big smile.

"Uh," said Mike, staring at the linoleum.

Noah looked at Paige, who shook her head. "Mike's father passed away last year."

"I'm sorry," said Noah. He squatted in front of Mike, getting eye to eye with the boy and put his hand on his shoulder. "I didn't mean to upset you."

Mike shrugged. "It's okay. You didn't know."

"I'll have to come back to pay you," Paige said. "I forgot my purse. Unless—" She looked at Wally. Wally shook her head. She hadn't brought hers either.

"You remembered all the important stuff," said Noah, smiling. "Have I mentioned how impressed I was with the muzzle guard? Too bad about your socks." With an appreciative glance at Paige's bare legs, he handed the torn, filthy socks to her.

Wally felt her face flush and decided against pointing out whose socks they were. Paige stuffed them into her own pocket.

"Look, don't worry about the money," said Noah. "You can pay me next time. If Balto gets into any more trouble, and my guess is this city boy just might"—he pointed at Balto's dog license from Manhattan—"we'll see a lot of you. Okay?"

Gratefully, Paige accepted. "I have a question though. How are we going to keep this from happening again? I mean, I didn't even know I had beehives."

Noah laughed. "I guarantee it won't happen again. Balto isn't stupid. He has learned his lesson, at least about bees."

Paige shook her head. "I wonder what else is hidden on Uncle Ted's property."

Noah looked at her in surprise then down at the clipboard with Paige's information. "Oh, you must be the folks who moved into Ted's house. You're his niece."

"How did you know?"

"I've known Ted for years. His dog was a patient of mine. Also, he and I have some common acquaintances, and I heard he was expecting you." He paused a moment. "Gee, that's a big place for this guy to get into trouble on. Maybe I should come over there and take a look around, build some barricades or something."

Wally was astonished by his generosity. Before Paige could protest, Mike had accepted. "When can you come?" he asked.

"Very soon," said Noah. He looked at Paige. "It'll be my pleasure."

Wally found herself sucking in her lips. This was getting interesting.

Mike had been up since 6:00 watching cartoons, and he'd fed both himself and Balto, whose nose seemed much less sore, allowing Paige to sleep in on Saturday morning. But she'd felt guilty once she heard Wally downstairs and had come down to help.

Paige was just reaching for a mug to pour her first cup of coffee when the ringing of the doorbell startled everyone. Puzzled, she went into the front hall and pulled open the heavy oak door, screening her eyes against the bright sunlight outside.

Noah, wearing jeans, a work shirt, and work boots, held up a paper bag. "Bagels," he proclaimed. "Isn't that what you people from New York City like to eat on weekends?"

"Uh . . ." Paige pulled her robe closer around her.

"I went to Saranac Lake for them. I heard they have the best ones. I hope you have cream cheese. Oh, and I brought a big chocolate-covered doughnut for Mike."

"Um, sure, come in." Paige yawned. "I'm sorry I'm not more awake." She led the way toward the kitchen, then stopped short and turned to her visitor. "Did you say you went all the way to Saranac Lake for those? Isn't that around fifty miles, each way?"

"Not quite."

"Thanks. That was so thoughtful of you."

Mike came running at the sound of Noah's voice. Noah gave him a high five that had Mike grinning from ear to ear. When they were walking through the dining room, with Mike trotting right behind, followed by Balto, Noah pointed to the stack of Paige's paintings she had been trying to decide where to hang. "What are those?"

"Some of my paintings. I thought my uncle wouldn't mind if I hung a few."

Noah raised an eyebrow. "Watercolor or oil?"

"Mostly watercolor."

"I'd love to see them sometime," Noah said.

The welcome aroma of coffee lured them into the kitchen. Paige groggily took a mug and poured automatically, barely stopping to offer it to Noah before it reached her lips. "Would you like some coffee?" she asked, longing to take her first sip.

"Yes. But you go ahead and have that one." Wally, who had an odd smile on her face, poured a cup and handed it to Noah. He dubiously sniffed it. "What is it?"

"Vanilla macadamia nut," Paige said, savoring the aroma. "Do you like it?"

"I don't know." A tentative sip and discarded cup gave Paige her answer. She looked at Wally in confusion.

"Nate is the same way," Wally said, referring to her husband. "He refuses to drink anything but plain coffee. It's a man thing." She turned to Noah. "I can make you a cup of regular blend," she offered.

"No, thanks. I'm alright." He took a seat at the kitchen table right next to Mike and opened the bag of bagels. "Now where is that cream cheese?"

As the coffee began to infuse itself into her brain, Paige pulled the cream cheese container out of the refrigerator and found a bread knife and spreader. "Here you go. Can I get you anything else?"

"What's this?" Noah said, in mock horror. "Strawberry cream cheese? It's pink!" He turned to Mike, who was eyeing the doughnut. "You let your mother give you girl food?"

Mike looked at Paige, hiding a smile and acting bewildered. "What are you trying to do to me, Mom?"

"You tell her, Mike," Noah encouraged the boy. "Tell her you're a man."

"I'm a man, Mom. I need man food."

Paige giggled. "I thought you needed Cap'N Crunch."

Noah turned to Mike. "I'll tell you what, man-to-man," he said. "You go upstairs and get dressed, and we'll go take a manly look around the house and grounds. We've got to protect Balto from himself."

"Thanks, Dr. Oliver."

"Call me Noah."

Mike beamed. "Can I, Mom?"

"Sure." Paige had expected to take Wally and Mike exploring again to find her way around the area, and maybe even go to the Adirondack museum in Blue Mountain Lake. But she knew that plan was out the window, now that they'd be spending the morning with Noah. Somehow, she didn't mind at all.

"We'll go over every inch," Paige told her son, "so Balto won't get into any more trouble."

"Great!" He dashed out of the kitchen and up the back staircase, calling down to Noah that he'd be right back.

"Make sure you wash up," Paige called after him.

Noah munched on his bagel. "This will be a good chance for you to see all the buildings. Ted has nearly fifteen of them."

Paige nodded. "I appreciate it." She was about to take a bite of her bagel when the doorbell rang again.

Puzzled, she went to see who it was. Noah and Wally came along too. She had that funny look on her face again, almost as if she had heard a private joke. Paige was still too groggy to try to figure out what it was.

She had to shield her eyes against the glare from outside again, but this time Paige saw that it was Quin, dressed for another boat ride on the lake. He took a look at Paige in her robe, with Noah and Wally behind her, and scowled.

Paige struggled to keep her composure despite her intense embarrassment. "Come in."

Balto came bursting out of the kitchen and ran to see the new visitor, wagging his tail furiously, before going to sit beside Noah. Noah bent down for a moment to rub the golden retriever's ears. Balto licked his glasses.

Paige started to introduce the two men, who towered over her. "We've met," said Noah, who had removed his glasses to clean them with a handkerchief.

"What brings you here, Noah?" Quin asked.

"Balto."

Mike came bounding down the stairs, wearing jeans. "I'm ready, Noah," he said.

Without waiting, or asking Paige's permission, Quin said, "I'd really like your company on my boat today, Mike. There aren't many more weeks left before we can't take the boat out." He glanced at Noah. "Couldn't you do this some other time?"

Mike looked torn.

"We can go explore that inlet you asked about the last time we were on the boat," Quin added.

"I'm sorry," said Paige. "I don't have time to go and Mike can't go without me." She looked at Wally to see if she'd go but it was clear that the one time had been enough.

"Aw, Mom," said Mike, scrunching his face into an angry frown.

Quin's face looked nearly the same, but then he smiled. "Some other time. Maybe I can help here."

She noticed that Noah was now scowling. She turned to the two men. "If you'll excuse me?"

Noah said, "Come on Mike. We'll wait outside on the porch." He waited while Quin, who had hesitated, walked out the door.

Paige went upstairs and jumped into the shower. She was back in ten minutes, in jeans and a long-sleeved tee shirt, although her long hair was still damp. She twisted it into a knot and went to the door.

"That was quick," said Quin.

Noah looked like he wanted to say something, too, but his face just turned red. "I'm glad that Balto is better, Mike," Noah said finally, looking straight at Paige. "And I'm going to have a good look around, with your mom's help, to make sure there isn't any more trouble lurking on the property. I hope you'll help."

Mike was annoyed, Paige could tell. He seemed to want to go on the boat, and nothing else would satisfy him. "I'd rather watch cartoons here with Wally."

Paige was about to say something, when Noah put up his hand. "Let me know what happens on Scooby Doo."

A grunt was the only response he got.

Quin suddenly didn't seem ready to leave. "I can go along with you. Maybe I'll notice something you'd overlook."

"That isn't necessary," said Noah.

Quin frowned and seemed to be trying to come up with another reason to help out, but he finally went to his truck. He waved good-bye to Paige and Mike, gave a last look at Noah, and pulled away, leaving clouds of dust flying in his wake. The tension that had Paige's hair standing on end began to subside.

Noah turned to Paige, smiling broadly. "Are you ready?"

"Don't be angry at Mike," Noah said as he and Paige set out. "From what you've told me, he's been through a lot."

"He really wanted to go with Quin. But I don't think it would have been right to let him go by himself."

Noah nodded. "It's a beautiful lake."

"Quin said it's polluted."

"Then maybe he should stop using his gas-powered boat on it so much. I like rowboats and canoes better. What was he complaining about now?"

"I think he mentioned zebra mussels."

"That figures. He ignores the six-legged frogs and focuses on something which might harm his precious boat. Meanwhile five hundred small lakes here in the Adirondacks have been killed by acid rain."

"If there is something wrong with the lake, isn't it irresponsible to keep letting people drink its water and swim in it?"

"There is nothing seriously wrong with Lake Champlain," Noah insisted. "It's tested constantly."

"But the frogs . . ."

"It happens in other parts of the world that aren't polluted." Noah interrupted her. "You don't need to worry."

An hour later, they were sweaty and dirty. Noah had gone over every inch of half the buildings but he needed the keys for the rest. Paige went back to the main house to find the keys and check in on Wally and Mike. Mike was happier, or at least less unhappy, and he seemed interested in exploring, so he and Wally went back with Paige to help with the safety check.

They crawled under the outbuildings and around the boathouse, and looked into the chimney of an old glass furnace. Noah showed them where Ted planted imported trees, bushes, and edible plants in an effort to reconstruct the diet of an ancient people in Europe, before becoming bored with the project. They didn't go all the way through the groves, though, because Noah said they were choked with weeds. "It's unlikely Balto would go in there," Noah said, frowning at what looked like grass-covered ruts just outside. "Let's skip it."

They walked toward the one remaining structure on the property that they hadn't inspected, with Noah leading the way. It was a small, windowless hut, little bigger than a toolshed. To Paige's surprise he went into the building without needing a key and came right back out, holding up his hand to keep them from coming closer. "Don't go in there," he said. "Some animals must have broken in. It's a mess."

Mike moved up to see, but Noah's look had Paige pulling him back. She got the impression that something nasty was inside and it would be better if they didn't see it. Wally seemed to understand and she started up a conversation with Mike about the possibility of someday finding some Native American artifacts right on the property. Noah took his hammer from his tool belt, some nails, and a nearby board and shut the building permanently.

They walked back to the main house in the peaceful warm

sunshine. Paige felt a sense of contentment she hadn't felt since they'd arrived. Maybe it was because the unfamiliar was becoming familiar and the strangers were becoming friends. Whatever the reason, it was an improvement in her life.

"Can I offer you something to drink?" Paige asked when they reached the porch. She felt awful that Noah's clothes were now filthy.

"Thanks." But after another step, Noah pulled his beeper from his belt and looked at its display. "No, thanks. There's an emergency and I have to get over to the clinic. I'll take a rain check."

On Monday, Wally went with Paige and Mike to look around the little village of Tamarack. Wally found it charming. The business area near the post office and the library had several antique stores and gift shops. The attractive window of Dyna's Paper and Unique Gifts pulled them inside, where Paige and Mike received a warm welcome from the proprietor, a friendly woman about Paige's age.

"Are you meeting people yet?" Dyna asked.

"Do you know Quin Wyatt?" Paige asked. "He has a hotel in Lake Placid. He took us out on his boat. And I met the vet, Noah Oliver, because our dog got into a beehive."

"It's interesting that those are the two men you met."

"Why?"

"They've known each other forever," said Dyna, shaking her head. "Yet they couldn't be more different."

"Those two men don't get along, do they?" Wally asked.

"You could say that. All the years Quin spent away in boarding school didn't get rid of the way he feels about Noah. And the feeling is mutual."

"Did something happen between them?" Paige asked.

"I guess you could say that. It used to be just the usual stuff, when they were younger. More recently, though, Quin was engaged to a woman whom Noah liked, as a friend, but still. Anyway, she disappeared."

"What did the police say?" Wally asked.

"Oh, it wasn't that kind of disappearance, I don't think. I heard something about a note. But Ilke left, and Noah seemed to be the one who cared more that she was gone."

A customer came in and Dyna went to take care of her. Wally, Paige, and Mike waved good-bye and went across the square to Jolene's café to sample her delicious food. The shop was cozy and inviting, and out back there was a small deck overlooking the lake. They could see Ted's house from the railing.

Jolene came to sit with them while they ate and asked how things were going. Paige filled her in.

In turn, Jolene filled in some gaps about Quin and Noah. "I used to be good friends with Quin's grandmother, Marissa. Being her assistant was my first job after college when I moved into my grandmother's summer home here.

"She told me that Quin and Noah never got along as boys, although I sort of knew it from spending all my summers here. She said it was one of the reasons she was glad he decided to go to boarding school after his parents, um." She looked at Mike and seemed to decide not to finish the sentence.

"Oh, the poor guy," said Paige.

"How long was he gone?" Wally asked.

"Ten years. He didn't come back until after college. I thought Quin would move away and start a life somewhere, but he wanted to come back here. I guess it worked out because shortly after he did, Marissa died, leaving him the hotel."

Wally munched on an orange-and-dried-cherry scone. "This is wonderful, Jolene," she said. "I'd love to have the recipe."

"I don't give out recipes," Jolene snapped.

"I apologize for asking," said Wally. "You're right. They're your livelihood and you can't give away your secrets." She took another bite of the scone and tried to think of a way to revive the conversation. Jolene's reaction was so unexpected, and odd, that it took a moment. The best she could do was, "There are lots of stores and businesses in town. Do you have any tips for Paige?"

Jolene nodded. "The gas station near the train depot has the best prices, but don't let them fix your car. You'd be better off at Al's."

"Thanks," said Paige. "I'll take your advice. And we'll be back here soon, I promise."

The time came when Wally had to leave, on the Amtrak rail line that ran from Montreal to New York, stopping right in Tamarack. Suddenly Paige realized she wasn't so calm about the whole thing after all. She could never have come this far without Wally's help. She stammered out a thank-you and looked to Mike to add one of his own.

"Call me if you need anything," Wally said. "I can be on the next train."

"That won't be necessary. We'll be fine."

Wally gave them each a hug good-bye at the train. Mike and Paige watched as Wally boarded, then drove home in silence. When they got inside and Paige closed the door, the reverberation in the hall was like a shot. They were alone in this big house, miles away from neighbors, or so it seemed, and completely out of their element.

Wally was in heaven. For the first time in a great while, her whole family, including the newest addition, was together for a

Friday night dinner. Rachel, Wally's eldest; her husband, Adam; and their children, Jody and little Charlie; along with Debbie, Rachel's younger sister; and her husband, Elliot, had come for the final dinner before Mark, Wally's youngest left for graduate school in Philadelphia. Wally had the same sense she'd had when the children were little, of counting her ducklings. Tonight they were all here.

She made the usual dinner of roast chicken, roasted potatoes, asparagus, and a freshly made challah that she had taken out of the oven only minutes before dinner was served. There was wine for the adults and grape juice for Jody.

Wally hadn't been sure until the last minute if everyone would be able to come to dinner. Debbie was swamped with work at the law firm, in part due to her long vacation earlier in the summer. She was paying for it now, as was Elliot, down at the prosecutor's office. They barely had time to have dinner together, let alone with the whole family.

Rachel, with her long, dark hair flowing over her shoulders, took a moment after dinner—but before dessert—to nurse Charlie. Debbie pushed her own blond hair behind her ears and stood up to help her mother clear the table. With the help of the rest of the group, they were soon set up for the next course.

As Wally served the orange chiffon cake and tea, Debbie asked, "How is Paige doing?"

"It sounds like she and Mike are okay."

Rachel, always the most empathetic of Wally's children, was still concerned. "I know her new job will be a good one," Rachel said, "and I know it is a beautiful place to live, but don't you worry that she'll be lonely?"

"I did. But she started meeting nice people right away. In fact, this is kind of funny. It looks like she has two very good-looking men interested in her." She filled her daughters in on Noah, Quin, and Jolene. "They seem to be very generous people up there in the north."

"Sounds good," said Debbie. But Wally could tell that Rachel was still worried. Only time would tell.

Chapter Four

Paige wasn't sure which of them was more nervous on the first day of school. Mike was worried about starting fourth grade and she was about to assume her first post as principal. After dressing carefully in a sedate navy suit and white blouse, Paige drove them to the school. She had spent a day there the previous week, getting familiar with the K-12 school, but this was the real thing. It hit home as she parked in the space designated for the principal.

"I'll walk you to the early care center," Paige told her son. "I can introduce you to your teacher."

"You don't have to do that, Mom. I can tell her my name."

"Okay. Then I'll just point you in the right direction."

They went into the elementary entrance and walked down the halls, which seemed to vibrate with the excitement of the coming school year. Paige pointed to a corridor, which led directly to a playground, and told Mike where he could find the room.

He hesitated for a moment. "Can I still call you Mom?"

"Sure, if you want to."

He seemed relieved. "Okay. See you later."

Without looking back, he went down the corridor alone.

"Welcome to your first official day at Tamarack Central School, Dr. Griffin," said Judy, the short, smiling school secretary, when Paige got to the office. She wore a pink blouse and a flowered skirt, and had clunky open-toed shoes on her wide feet.

Judy was probably under forty but looked about fifty, with brown hair peppered with gray, styled into small curls and lacquered at a beauty parlor. Paige, who towered over her at only five feet, six inches thought of the contrast to her own simply styled chestnut, shoulder-length hair. Maybe she should have listened to her New York friends' advice and cut her hair short, but she couldn't bear to do that. She just couldn't make one more change, not now. Wasn't it enough that she'd become a widow and a single parent, lost her home, and moved out of her beloved New York City?

A worried look creased Judy's brow as she shook Paige's hand. "I'm sorry I couldn't meet you when you toured the school and met with the teachers last week," she said. "I was chaperoning the church camp trip," she rushed to add. "Some of those kids need to learn manners, although I don't think they're going to learn them at home. Not with their parents." She took a breath. "I hope moving up here wasn't too hard on you and your little boy. I understand, with the loss of your husband and all— Ted told us you'd make a wonderful principal and we aren't worried a bit. My son is a senior here, captain of the football team, and you'll meet him and all the others. Oh, why am I rambling on so?"

Paige distilled the essence of the woman's words and zeroed in on the one question most important to her at the moment. "Did you see Ted in person?"

Judy blushed. "I'm not on the school board. I hope I didn't

make it sound like I was on the committee that hired you. That would be so awkward." She rushed behind a desk and picked up a folder. "Mr. King, the superintendent, said he'll be here later to greet you. He was fishing last week, out at his cabin, and told me to tell you how sorry he was to be away, since he had planned to take you out to dinner on Saturday night."

"It's just as well," said Paige. "I haven't had time to find a babysitter for my son yet."

"Oh, no problem," said Judy. "My daughter, who is fifteen, could sit any time you need her. She's really great with children and she has many people who would recommend her. Ordinarily she doesn't sit on Saturday nights, since she's so popular and has so many dates, but I'm sure she'd make an exception for you. After all, you are the principal and new to the area and—"

Paige needed a rest from the incessant talking. "I'll let you know."

While her world and Mike's were in flux, Paige had worked on her research project in the city schools in order to complete her doctorate. Those six months had proved to Paige that she could cope with just about anything. She might not be ready for a haircut, but she was ready to greet her students.

In contrast to the schools in Manhattan, here there were no armed guards carrying communication equipment nor were there metal detectors. But the students coming in, from the smallest kindergartner to the young men and women of the high school, were dressed in the usual array of outfits, from preppie to punk and everything in between.

Paige smiled and welcomed the students as they filed into the building. Beyond them she could see several groups of parents, nodding at one another and looking her way. She had met a few at a gathering for her and Mike, held in one of their homes, and some of the faces looked familiar.

She moved into the auditorium where all the children were being directed to sit, in grade order with the smallest ones in the first row. As she passed them on her way to the stage to welcome them, she took a deep breath.

Her job had formally begun.

"Dr. Griffin," said Judy, "there is a parent here to see you. I know it's your first day and all, and maybe I should just tell him to come back another time, when you're more familiar with the place."

Paige turned away from her computer and pulled her chair up to her desk. "Send him in."

"He's a summer resident," Judy whispered, closing the door so no one in the outer office could hear.

Puzzled, Paige asked, "Why would a summer resident have a child enrolled here?"

"That's part of the problem, as far as I can tell. Usually they all leave when the summer is over, and we don't have to worry about them and their big city expectations." Judy made a face showing her distaste and opened the door wider to admit the visitor.

"You may see Dr. Griffin now, Mr. Dillon," Judy said. She stepped aside to let the man pass and then closed the door on her way out of the office—not before making what Paige considered a childish grimace behind Mr. Dillon's back.

He was a tall man, wearing an expensive, well-cut suit, and he walked with a distinguished bearing. His dark hair was silvered at the temples, and he had a precisely trimmed mustache. But what was most striking were his black eyes and their fiery intensity. He sat down in the same chair that Mr. King had vacated and leaned forward.

"How can I help you, Mr.—"

"I put my daughter, Aurora, into this school because I was led to believe she'd be properly treated. Now I come to find out that isn't the case. What is the meaning of this?"

Baffled, Paige didn't know what to say. Instead she rang for Judy to bring in the girl's file. "Why don't you tell me about Auror—" She was cut off by the door opening immediately, as if Judy had been standing by to be summoned. Paige took the file and waited until she was gone.

The file was thin, with only one paper, Aurora's registration, in it. The guidance counselor had placed a note in it saying that a transcript request had been made the Friday before. "It says here that Aurora only started in this school district today. What is the problem?"

"You've got a computer. I assume it's programmed to show you a student's schedule. Why don't you find my daughter's?"

Paige was about to protest that the man should be discussing the schedule with the guidance counselor, but she realized that sooner or later she'd most likely end up dealing with him. It only took a moment to find what she needed.

"According to this, Aurora is scheduled for all the proper junior classes. Why is this a problem?"

"Because," said Mr. Dillon, through gritted teeth, "none of them are honors classes. I was told that Aurora would be able to take honors classes here. That's why I enrolled her in this school."

"Where did she go before?"

Mr. Dillon sighed. "A very exclusive private school in the city." He told Paige the name. It was not the best, but it was a good school. She wondered why Aurora had transferred.

"It wasn't a good academic match for my daughter," Mr. Dillon said. "And she wanted to move up here, for personal reasons. I agreed, but only if she could still get a good education.

But you didn't put her into honors classes. The schools up here can't be as competitive as a private school in the city."

"If I may ask," said Paige, feeling oddly defensive about her adopted school district, "why did you agree to move your daughter from a superior school to one you felt was inferior?"

"Uh, I don't—it isn't as if—"

Paige stood up and went to the door, planning to show Mr. Dillon to the guidance office. "How did you even hear about the schedule? It's my understanding that the students were only given them in homeroom an hour ago."

Mr. Dillon was standing too. "Aurora called me on her cell phone. I told her to call when she had it. I had to turn the car around and come back up here. It's a good thing I wasn't farther down the Northway. And to make matters worse, I have a meeting back in the city this afternoon."

"Couldn't Aurora's mother have come in, since you had to go out of town?"

A harsh laugh followed. "My daughter's mother disappeared. We haven't heard from her in over eight months. That's why Aurora has been so unhappy in the city." He grimaced. "Yvette obviously doesn't give a damn about Aurora or her education." He shook his head. "It wouldn't have mattered if she'd stuck around, probably. I think you should know that Aurora's mother is unbalanced. I've had to institutionalize her more than once. The private investigator I hired thinks that's probably where she is now, some nuthouse somewhere, screaming that people are after her, and we'll hear from her when she's stabilized again."

Paige stared at him.

"I pay year-round taxes here," said Mr. Dillon, standing uncomfortably close to Paige. "And I have the board president's permission, in writing, for Aurora to go to school here. It was too painful for her to stay in the city."

All of Paige's motherly instinct went into her next question. "Whom should the school contact, if necessary, when you're away?"

"What do you mean?" Mr. Dillon looked completely perplexed.

Surely he couldn't be thinking of letting her stay all by herself, Paige hoped. "Who is here, staying with your daughter?"

"I would say that's my business, not yours," said Mr. Dillon, leaning over her.

"It is my business," Paige said. "The welfare of my students is my number one concern. A minor must be properly supervised."

"We have a housekeeper," Mr. Dillon growled. "And I'll be here three weeks out of four. Now what are you going to do about her schedule?"

Paige looked it over. "I see that she just missed getting into the higher-level English class by one point."

"She complained about that to me," said Mr. Dillon. "She said it was unfair that there were a lot of questions about *The Catcher in the Rye*, and she'd never read it."

"Let's go talk to her guidance counselor," said Paige, moving around him and opening the door. She went out into the main office area and found herself face to face with a slight sixteen-year-old girl with long, blond hair half covering her sad face, barely revealing her light-gray eyes.

"This is Aurora Dillon," Judy explained, leaving Paige in awe of her presumptiveness.

"It's nice to meet you," said Paige. "We'll try to take care of this, I promise. Go back to class for now."

She and Mr. Dillon went to talk to Mr. Fabian, the guidance counselor. "The last principal would never interfere," Mr. Fabian mumbled.

Paige decided to let the comment pass and went back to her

office. The last principal had left suddenly due to a severe heart attack. Perhaps the staff was suffering some anxiety about it, as well as from Paige's expedited appointment. She'd have to find a way to win the staff over. Too bad she wasn't off to a very good start.

She realized she was lost in the hallways of her new school when the bell rang. The halls were immediately flooded with children, many larger than her, on the way to their next classes. She asked one where the main office was.

"Just turn down that hall and go back through the elementary hallway, Dr. Griffin," the girl said. "And welcome to our school. We're, like, so happy you could come here, and we're looking forward to having a good time and of course getting a really great education with you as our principal."

Paige thanked her and made the turn, amazed that someone could have so much to say while giving a simple direction. She wondered if her resemblance to Judy was a mere coincidence.

"I have a new friend," said Mike, when Paige picked him up after work. He waved good-bye to the two remaining children and the aftercare teacher, and followed his mother out to the car.

The car had been a source of some amusement for a few of the students. "We never had a principal who drove a Lexus before," one said. "Those are some hot wheels." That student had swung himself up into the cab of a raised pickup, with several kids on the seats next to and behind him. The contrast of the children here and the ones in New York, whose mode of transportation was either their feet, or a bus, or subway was startling. And for Paige, who'd always expected to stay in New York and have Mike be one of those kids on the subway, it was also sad. They'd been wrenched away from their expectations as well as their friends.

That's why she was so pleased that Mike had already made a friend. "He left right after school," Mike explained. "But he was in the before-school session with me. You have to meet him tomorrow morning."

He chatted on about his new friend, who was also in fourth grade and who also had grandparents in Arizona. "But his other grandparents live right in the next town," he added, "and his grandpa is going to take us both fishing."

It got quiet in the car and Paige looked in her rearview mirror to see if Mike had fallen asleep. But he was sitting there, eyes open, with that same, sad look on his face she'd seen so often during the past year. "Luke doesn't have a daddy either," he said. "But his didn't die, he just went away. And he might come back soon, Luke said."

Paige marveled at how children could disclose such things to each other. Luke was lucky he had grandparents nearby, especially the grandfather. Too bad Mike wasn't so fortunate.

"I'll come into the early care center tomorrow morning," Paige promised, "and say hello to Luke."

Mike smiled a real, wide grin in the back seat. "Great."

Paige's meeting with Luke the next morning went a lot smoother once Mike told him he didn't have to be afraid of his mother just because she was the principal. "When we're at home, she is just Mom."

Luke looked at Paige for confirmation. She nodded. "Yes, it's true. I am just Mike's mom at home."

She left them in early care and went to her office. It seemed as if things were falling into place. The only thing she needed was a babysitter for the following evening, so that she could take the superintendent up on his invitation to dinner. She didn't want to ask Judy's daughter, but she'd called several of the other recommended teenagers on her list and they were all busy with someone's sweet 16 party or had other plans. Her instincts told her to ask Aurora, who was a person who knew New York, could relate to Mike, and might not have been invited to the party since she didn't yet know most of the kids in the school. She'd left a note with the girl's homeroom teacher, requesting her to stop in after school.

"You wanted to see me?" asked Aurora, after school had been let out for the day. Her gray eyes had lost their worried look since Paige first met her, and her expression was more open. She wore her long blond hair pulled back behind her ears, not covering her face at all.

"Yes. I wanted to find out how you were adjusting to the school."

Aurora smiled. "I think I like it a lot. The kids are nice, not pushy, and they don't seem to be trying to figure out how they are better than me."

"That's good. I heard you read *Catcher in the Rye* in one night and answered all the questions correctly. Have you been to your new English class yet?"

"Yes. And it's great. The teacher is really, um, how can I put it? Exciting. She makes it so interesting. Is that all?"

"I don't mean to keep you," said Paige. "But I was wondering if you would like to babysit for my son. He's nine."

"I don't know. When would you need me?"

"Tomorrow night."

Aurora bit her lip. "Yeah," she said. "I can sit."

Something seemed strange in her response. "Is something wrong?"

"No," Aurora said, although her brow was furrowed. "Not really, at least nothing I didn't expect. My dad had promised to let me go to New York this weekend, to be with him, but he called last night and told me he has to go out to the Hamptons on business. So I'll be around." She turned to go. "I'd be happy to sit." She wrote down her address and outlined a route Paige could take easily.

"Thanks, I'll pick you up at six-thirty," said Paige. "I'm sorry your dad had to leave town." As the girl left her office, Paige realized the teenager had something else in common with Mike— a dad whose promises were made to be broken. Then again, Aurora's father still had opportunities to make it up to his child. And Mike's mother would never abandon him in a million years.

Superintendent King and his wife, Edna, were due to pick Paige up at 7:00. But first she had to pick up Aurora, whom she introduced to Mike as the girl got into the front seat.

Aurora turned around and reached over to shake Mike's hand. Then she turned back to Paige. "So, where are you going tonight?"

"The Moose Head Inn in Elizabethtown."

"That's a snooze," Aurora said. "Too bad you aren't going to Lake Placid. It's the closest thing around here to a place with night life."

"Maybe another day. If I ever find my way there."

"It's pretty easy," Aurora said. "Maybe one day we could all go together."

Paige, who had been backing carefully down the driveway, didn't have to look at the girl to know she was lonely. She wondered if it would be appropriate to spend some time with her, considering that she was the principal of the school Aurora attended. She promised herself that she would make time for Aurora, if she needed it. And if the babysitting thing worked as well as she hoped it would, she'd have ample opportunity to see how Aurora, who was a sweet, charming girl, was getting along.

It turned out she was also accurate. The inn was a snooze.

Mike and Paige fell into a comfortable routine. Her confidence levels rose in her job as did her ability to navigate the country roads. She found time on weekends to renew her passion for painting, and Mike sometimes set up his own little easel right beside hers, when he wasn't at Luke's or playing with him along the shore of the lake or up in the huge playroom on the third floor of the house. Paige joined a chamber music group, and Aurora began to sit for Mike on a weekly basis. As the weeks of September passed and October started and the leaves changed from green to yellow and crimson to off the trees, Paige realized that the rhythms of their life felt a lot less new.

Paige's voice on the phone sounded better and better to Wally. She was losing her tentativeness about her job, her new life, and Mike's adjustment to living so far from Manhattan.

"Happy Columbus Day to you too," Paige said, in response to Wally's greeting. "How are things going?"

Wally filled her in on the grandchildren. "School, though, has been rough this year." Since Paige was also an educator, Wally wasn't afraid of boring her.

"What's wrong?" Paige asked.

"I have a little girl in my class who has been having problems. She's getting very possessive about her friends and it's disruptive." Wally explained that the girl's father had left the family.

"That's a shame," said Paige. "Have you talked to the parents?"

"I spoke to Kallie's mother. She's got her hands full." That was an understatement. Play dates that had turned into disasters, endless tears, and acting-out behavior had only made the separation harder on Kallie's mother.

"I've never heard you sound so worried," Paige said.

Wally bit her lip. The last thing she wanted to do was give Paige something to worry about. "I'm sorry. I'm sure it'll resolve itself. In the meantime, give Mike a hug for me."

"I will," Paige promised. "And please give my regards to Nate."

Chapter Five

It had been a much more exciting Halloween than either Mike or Paige had expected. In contrast to the relatively boring march through the halls of their apartment building in New York City, ringing doorbells hoping for candy, the celebration in Tamarack was town-wide. There were hay rides around the town green, a costume parade, apples in barrels, and lots of food, besides the traditional candy. Mike went trick-or-treating with his friend Luke, while Paige and Katie, the petite, bubbly woman who was Luke's mother, stood by, drinking hot cider to try to keep warm. Both Griffins arrived home exhausted but happy.

"Mike," Paige called, after sorting out the last of his candy, "isn't your bath ready yet?" The water was still running upstairs.

Mike didn't answer her, so she went upstairs to check on him. As she passed his room, Paige saw that he was curled up on the bed, fast asleep. Puzzled, she continued on to the bathroom.

Water surged over the sides of the tub and ran along the sloped floor toward the door, where it was now flooding the hall and soaking Paige's feet. She hurried to turn it off and opened the drain.

"Mike!" she yelled. "Wake up. Bring me some towels. Hurry!"

Mike came in groggy and disheveled. "What's wrong?" His eyes widened as he saw all the water. "What happened?"

"The tub overflowed," Paige explained, rushing to grab whatever she had on hand to sop up the water. "I need more towels."

Mike ran to the linen closet and came back with a load of towels. Paige silently thanked the former owners of the house for leaving so many items behind. The fully stocked linen closet was coming in handy.

"I'm sorry," Mike whispered. "I didn't mean to fall asleep."

Paige threw the towels down and as quickly as she could, picked each up to wring it out in the sink. "I know, honey," she assured him. "It'll be okay. But I need your help."

When they got the worst of the water up, they started giggling as they skidded on the wet floor. Paige loaded the towels into a laundry basket and ventured downstairs to see what damage had been done to the kitchen. There was no water on the floor near the kitchen sink, which was under the bathtub, but she remembered that the water upstairs had flowed away from the outer wall of the house toward the hall, so she looked over to the coat closet. There was no water there either, inside or out. She let out a sigh of relief.

Mike had come down by this time, his clothes soaked through from the wet towels he held. Paige took them from him and assured him there was no damage to the kitchen. "Go up and change into pajamas," she told him. "I'll be right up." She went down to the basement with her heavy load of laundry. Amazingly, the floor there was dry too.

When she went back upstairs, she brought Mike some hot chocolate and snuggled with him.

"I'm sorry, Mom," he said.

"It's okay, sweetheart," she said, daring to use a forbidden term of endearment. "No harm done."

Mike smiled and reached up for a hug. Afterward, Paige tucked the warm quilt under his chin and kissed him goodnight. She went to change her own clothes, smiling to herself. All was well.

Somehow they had escaped a disaster. Ted would never have to know about the water overflow.

The crash came at 2:36 A.M. Paige jumped out of bed and was joined by Balto, who was barking to wake the dead. She checked on Mike, sent Balto back to his place at Mike's feet, and ran downstairs to see what was wrong. She was met at the entrance to the kitchen by a flood. She was afraid to turn on the light, in case the electricity would connect to the water, so she couldn't see exactly what happened.

There was a flashlight in the drawer of the table near the front door, she remembered, and she ran to get it. She had to find whatever pipe had burst so she could turn off the water.

She turned on the flashlight and tried to see what had happened. The kitchen-side wall of the coat closet had burst. Black plastic protruded from inside, possibly from some kind of insulation. Paige couldn't get close enough to see what other damage had been done because the plasterboard had disintegrated into a soggy mess. She was sure, though, that there were no pipes in there.

Now she knew where all that water had gone.

She didn't have a clue how she could fix it. But it was too early to call for help. As best she could, she determined that there was no more water coming out. She sopped up the floors with another armload of towels, and went upstairs to change out of her wet nightgown. Maybe, she thought, she could get a few hours' sleep.

But that was impossible. Paige realized she'd have to stay home and wait for someone to come fix the mess, which meant she'd have to call the dispatcher's office early and have the school bus stop at their house. Since she ordinarily took Mike to early care, he didn't ride the school bus. He was sure to be thrilled. She'd also have to call the school and tell them she'd be late. She set her alarm clock for five, the time when the school office opened so they could be ready to call substitutes if necessary. Then she lay down to try to sleep, trying to forget that it was already a quarter to five.

The biggest question, though, was who to call about the closet? Should it be a plumber? There were no pipes in there. It had been an open doorway at one time. So maybe it should be a carpenter. She settled on calling a carpenter just as the alarm went off.

It took several tries to get through to the school office and once that was done she had to call a different number for the bus dispatcher. Finally she got Mike scheduled to be picked up, but it would be at 7:15. She woke him up and had him dress and feed both himself and an oddly nervous and skittish Balto while she made lunch for Mike. Then she loaded them both into the car and took Balto over to the vet's. Noah had told her he fed the animals by 6:30 every morning, so she hoped she'd find him there.

He was. She briefly told him what was happening. "Balto seemed very upset by the mess." He'd whined and avoided the area so much that Mike had fed him in the room off the kitchen, and Paige was hoping that Noah could take him.

Noah agreed to take Balto and invited the three of them in for some hot chocolate. Paige had to decline. She wished she could just stay there, since Mike wanted to help with the animals, and she certainly wasn't looking forward to dealing with the mess in her kitchen, but she had to get back to make her calls and wait for the bus.

The carpenter had other ideas, though, when she called at 7:00. "If there's water involved, Miss," he said, "you've got to get a plumber. When it's dried out, I'll come take a look."

The plumber, Fletcher, came at 7:20, just after Mike's bus left with Mike grinning ear to ear with delight at finally getting to ride on it. "Let's see what we've got," he said, taking off his jacket and revealing neat green coveralls.

Paige leaned against the kitchen sink, which was as close as she could get, and sipped her coffee. If the plumber didn't take too long, she could be at school by 9:00. She was all ready to go.

Fletcher moved some of the plasterboard out of the way, heaving it out the back door. He got a high-powered flashlight and pulled at the black plastic. "There was probably some damage a while back, and this plastic is covering it. Let's see what we have here." He tugged harder and jumped back as something fell toward him. "What's th—oh, shoot!" He let go and ran to the sink, pushing her aside. He was gagging and squeezing his eyes so hard that tears escaped.

"What is it?" Paige asked, wiping up the coffee she'd spilled. She took a step toward the closet.

"No!" said Fletcher, holding up his hand even as he bent over the sink. "Don't go near it."

Paige stopped, suddenly very frightened.

Fletcher scrubbed his hands with water that was so hot Paige could see the steam rising. "There's a body in there."

Fear gripped Paige. She thought of her uncle, and suddenly wondered if the reason she hadn't heard from him was because . . . "Ohmigod." She moved closer, praying it wasn't true.

Fletcher dried his hands and ran them through his black hair. "Stay back, lady. You don't want to see that."

"Just tell me," said Paige. She was near tears. "Is it my uncle?"

"Lady," said the plumber. He himself was standing back. "That ain't nobody's uncle. Not unless he wore skirts."

Relief washed over Paige. It seemed absurd, especially since this person was dead, but at least it wasn't her uncle.

"I'm not a child," she said, holding her breath and edging closer to the corpse. She saw long blond hair surrounding a grotesquely desiccated face. The woman wore a long, black skirt with a black turtleneck. Rope bound her wrists and three of the fingers on her left hand were missing.

"I think you'd better call someone," said the plumber. Paige picked up the phone. In the back of her mind she knew the man had meant the police, but the first number she dialed was that of Wally Morris.

Wally suggested calling the police. But by then Paige was falling to the floor. Everything went black.

Early morning phone calls were never a good thing and this one only proved it. Wally hung up the receiver and looked over at Nate, whose sad, expectant face showed that he understood the gravity of the situation and was waiting for the details.

"Who died?"

"We don't know."

Surprise replaced Nate's somber look. "I beg your pardon?"

Wally sat on the bed next to her husband and explained about

Paige's phone call. Nate listened carefully and then got a pen and a notepad.

"What are you doing?" Wally asked.

Nate looked knowingly at Wally. "You are planning to go up to Tamarack, aren't you?"

"I think I should, don't you? Her mother is too far away."

Not responding to that question, Nate said, "If you're going, I'm going with you. We have to plan. You have to get a sub, I have to postpone clients, we need someone to take care of Sammy—"

Wally jumped up and headed for the kitchen. "You plan. I have to cook."

Chapter Six

Paige had the sense that she was at a cocktail party, except the voices were somber. There were many voices, mostly male, all mumbling.

Additional voices, some female, filtered through Paige's fog, which gradually lifted. When she opened her eyes, she found herself on the couch in the parlor with Noah Oliver's warm, brown eyes staring into hers.

"They called for a doctor," he explained, a grim smile on what she could see of his face behind the red beard as he checked her pulse. "I was the closest one available."

Paige turned her dizzy head to look around. "They called a vet for me?"

"I'm also an EMT," he said. "Fletcher thought you needed some help."

"Fletcher?"

"Your plumber. Don't you remember what happened?"

Suddenly, she did. "Someone is dead in the closet." She tried to swallow, but her mouth was so dry she barely succeeded in moving her tongue. "Not Uncle Ted. Who is it?"

Noah furrowed his brows and started to check her blood pressure, pushing up her sleeve and wrapping the cuff around her arm. Paige felt the pressure build and the cold of Noah's stethoscope as he listened.

"Why would you think it was Ted?" he said, when he finished.

"I haven't been able to reach him and I've been worried. Now there's a body. Who could it be?"

"I haven't had a chance to go look," Noah said. "I was more concerned with you. Did you hit your head when you fell?"

Paige touched it with her fingers. "I don't think so." She tried to sit up.

Noah lightly touched her shoulders, indicating she shouldn't get up. "You should wait here a bit longer and keep your feet up."

Looking at her feet she realized someone had placed them on several pillows. She could feel her skirt hiked up beneath her and was grateful for the blanket over her.

"You won't be able to get near the kitchen anyway," Noah said, "since it's full of police. The sheriff's department is here in force. Besides," he added, "you don't want to see it, do you?"

"Not again. But I don't understand. Why would there be a body in my kitchen?"

The solicitous smile faded from Noah's face. "If you promise to stay here, and I mean it, I'll go see what I can find out."

He stood up and went out of the room. Paige took the damp washcloth he'd held to her head and covered her eyes. She could still hear people going in and out and up and down the steps. And she couldn't blot out the image of the woman. That dried-up face swam before her eyes.

"Paige? I was going past your driveway and saw all the police cars. What happened?"

She pulled the damp washcloth off her eyes and looked up at Quin. His clean-shaven aquiline face was full of concern. "Somebody," she croaked, "uh, there's a dead person—in the kitchen."

"I'll be right back," Quin said.

A uniformed sheriff came to talk to Paige just after she sat up. He was medium height, slightly pudgy, in his late forties with graying hair, a weathered face, and squint lines around his brown eyes. His voice was apologetic when he said, "I'm Sheriff Dover. I know you've had a shock but I have to ask you a few questions, ma'am, if you're up to it."

Before Paige could speak, Noah came back, holding a glass of water. His normally ruddy complexion was pale, and he looked sad. He handed the water to Paige and sat down.

"If you don't mind, Noah," said the sheriff. "I'd like to talk to Dr. Griffin alone."

"I understand," said Noah. His voice was tight, Paige noticed. "Are you okay?" he asked her.

"I guess so."

He looked at Dover. "You know where to reach me."

The sheriff waited until Noah went out the front door. "I understand this house belongs to Theodore Verrill. How long have you lived here?"

"Since the end of August. My son and I moved here to my uncle's house from New York City because of my new job. I'm the principal of the school."

"So you weren't here last winter?"

"No."

"Was your uncle here?"

"I don't know. I'd thought he was, at least part of the time, but now I don't think so."

The sheriff frowned. "Where is he?"

"I don't know." Paige's lip trembled before she blurted it all out. "I think the last time anyone really heard from him was February. Or maybe bef—" She broke off when she heard a commotion in the kitchen. Someone was shouting.

She turned toward the noise and saw Quin, who seemed limp, being held up by two deputies, taking him out the front door. "Those police tapes were up there for a reason," someone behind Paige said. "He had no business going past them."

One of the deputies with Quin said, "Try not to think about it." But Quin's blond head lolled, and as he turned toward Paige, she saw the anguished look on his face.

"Did you ever hear of Ilke Hedstrom?" Dover asked Paige after Quin was gone.

"Quin's fiancee? I heard she left him last winter. Was that who . . ."

"Yes, ma'am, that's what it looks like. I understand she worked here in the house as an assistant for your uncle."

Paige wracked her brain, trying to remember what she knew of Quin's fiancée. She'd left town, Paige thought, but she didn't know exactly when. "How long has she been, um, here?"

He didn't answer right away. One of the deputies who had helped Quin out of the house came over to the sheriff and leaned close to his head, whispering. Dover nodded and said, "Have someone drive him home and stay with him until I can get there. Don't question him, just ask if he needs anything. And call a doctor, if necessary." He turned back to answer Paige's question. "We're going to have to wait for the coroner's report. But I would say it's been a while. Probably since around the time she supposedly left Mr. Wyatt. Poor guy." He cleared his throat. "He's all broken up. Apparently he thinks he's somehow responsible for this. He told one of my deputies that he should have looked for her, not just assumed she'd left him."

"But who would have killed her?" Paige asked. "And why?"

"That's what we're trying to find out. That's why I'm asking about your uncle."

"You can't possibly think that he had something to do with this?"

"It's his house," said Dover simply. "Who else would have had access to it to hide the body?"

Paige bit her lip.

Dover frowned. "Look," he said. "It could have been a robber. I understand she worked here in the house at one time. Maybe she came in and found someone who didn't belong here while your uncle was away and he killed her. We won't know anything until we investigate."

Standing, Dover handed her a card. "Call me at this number if you think of anything, and I'll check back with you tomorrow." He went back to the kitchen.

Paige watched, fighting a wave of nausea, as a gurney carrying a black body bag was wheeled out the front door. She got to her feet unsteadily, grasping the back of the couch until the dizziness passed. With an effort, she made her way to the kitchen.

A team of photographers, crime scene investigators, and various deputies were busy with the mess in the middle of the kitchen. It extended all the way from the former closet to the sink, and soggy building material was being ground into the glossy wooden floor by the many feet walking through it.

Sheriff Dover, who was squatting near the remnants of the closet, looked up when he saw her enter the room. He scowled. "You shouldn't be in here."

Paige motioned vaguely toward the door to the hall. "I saw the, uh, gurney leave. I thought maybe I could help."

"All right. Maybe you can help us figure some things out." He turned toward the closet. "You know, it's strange. There hasn't been any crime reported in the county, with the exception of a few break-ins of summer homes, in a long time. Other than that"—he paused—"a lumber yard–hardware store was burgled in January or February. Our medical examiner thinks it may have been about the time Ms. Hedstrom was killed."

"This closet . . . ?"

"Had a double back wall." Dover turned back to her. "It was built a while ago. But part of it may have been newer."

Paige shook her head. "It wasn't here the last time I came, but that was years ago. There used to be a doorway here, and I didn't notice the closet until I banged into the back of it the first night we were up here." The thought of the bruise she suffered reminded her of what the closet looked like when she first discovered it. "There were raincoats and umbrellas."

"There are some jackets and things in that mess," Dover said, pointing with a pencil, "but we haven't gotten down to them yet."

"The red jackets, the blazer, and the trench coat belong to us," Paige told him. What she could see of them meant she would need to replace them. She would also need to do something about the kitchen. The prospect was daunting.

Dover stood up and came over to her. "We'll be here for hours," he said. His tone clearly said she should get out of the way.

Right then, Paige wanted to be out of the house more than anything. "I would like to go to work," she said, looking up at him. "Are you sure you don't need me here?"

"Yes, Ma'am. We'll finish up, and if you want, get someone in to clean up for you. There are services that do that." He cleared his throat.

"It wouldn't be something I'd want my child to come home

to," muttered a female deputy working with a brush and powder. Her ID said her first name was Wendy.

Paige agreed. She asked Dover to arrange for the cleaning service, but it didn't help her dilemma with Mike. "What am I going to tell him?"

The woman looked back at the floor. "He didn't see this?"

"No, I sent him to school before Mr. Fletcher got here. He felt bad enough about overflowing the tub."

Wendy shook her head. "He's going to hear about this. I think you'll have to tell him the truth."

"But what is the truth? Who did this?" Paige looked at Sheriff Dover, hoping for some kind of answer.

Dover frowned. "We don't have that information yet." He put up a hand. "I'm sorry. The best thing you could do right now is let us do our jobs. I know you're worried and upset, but we can't answer any of your questions yet."

Paige went out to her car, fully aware that she was shaking. Somehow she got the key in the ignition and drove away. A glance in the rearview mirror gave her chills, as it showed a house which had suddenly become sinister.

The news preceded Paige's arrival at school. "How are you holding up, Dr. Griffin?" Judy bustled around, helping her off with her bulky sweater, the only thing she could find to wear over her suit jacket, since her trench coat and parka were under the wet wallboard.

"It's such a horror story," Judy continued, although Paige sensed she relished talking about it. "The phone has been ringing all morning, parents wanting to know what happened. This is the first time anything like this has happened up here." She barely paused to take a breath. "The newspaper office even called. They want an interview. You know," she added, "nobody ever got murdered here before." She stopped talking finally but added a meaningful look at Paige.

Paige had passed the car with the press plates parked outside the school. "I am not going to give an interview. But I'll issue a statement in about an hour, in front of the school. Please ask the guidance counselor to come to my office." She turned and went into her office before Judy could say anything else. Judy was right behind her, but a ringing phone saved Paige from having to listen to her secretary anymore. Paige picked it up on the first ring.

It was Jolene. "I heard you had a problem. Do you and Mike want to stay with me until you get it cleared up?"

Paige recalled the image of the dead woman's body and swallowed hard. The thought of Mike being exposed to anything related to that horrified her. "I think that would be a good idea," she told Jolene. "Thanks."

"It's no problem. When you go home after work, get Mike and yourself some changes of clothes and bring them here. I can pick him up as soon as school is out. That way he won't have to go home at all."

Paige wished she didn't have to either. She still had to write the statement for the guidance counselor to read outside the school though, so she didn't have time to dwell on the prospect. She thanked Jolene and got to work.

She had nearly finished the statement when Judy buzzed her again. "That poor man is on the phone," Judy said, sniffling. "And all this time he thought she'd left him," Judy added, marveling. "I'm sure you want to talk to him."

Paige had no idea what she would say to Quin and wished she had a moment to gather her thoughts. But she couldn't keep him waiting.

"I'm so sorry," she said, when she took the call. She felt guilty just because of where Ilke's body had been found. "Is there anything I can do?"

"I don't know. The police are going to talk to me soon, but I was hoping you could come here later, to go over what you know. I have to try to understand what happened to her."

Paige hadn't a clue, but how could she turn him down? "I'll stop by as soon as I can. But it might not be until tomorrow."

"I hope Mike wasn't too frightened," said Quin, after he gave her directions.

"I haven't told him yet."

There was an uncomfortable silence. "I'll see you soon," Paige promised, putting an end to the call. She wondered how she could find the strength to get through the afternoon.

When Paige left school she was exhausted. She'd fielded calls from the board president, wondering what he was supposed to tell the board, and Mike's teacher, wondering what to tell him. She told the teacher to keep the news from him, but to be alert in case he heard it somehow. It wasn't likely, but some of the children did go home for lunch and many of the teachers left the building during the day. She told the board president that she would get back to him but would not let it affect the running of the school. Instead of going home, though, she went to talk to Mikc.

As soon as she arrived at Jolene's shop, Mike ran to her, brimming with questions. She distilled them down and gave him the answer to his most pressing ones. "We'll be staying with Jolene for a few days," she said. "But I have to go to the house for a while. I want you to be a good guest while I'm gone."

"I promise. But what happened?"

Paige looked at Jolene, wondering what she could possibly

say. Jolene nodded, saying, "It'll be all over the school by tomorrow."

"A lady," Paige began, wishing the words didn't have to be said, "who died, was—" How could she tell her son about the body found in their closet?

She had to try again. "Something happened at home." She paused, trying to find the right words. "You know that a wall was destroyed when the closet flooded, right?"

In a very small voice, he said, "I'm sorry I overflowed the tub and made a flood."

"I know. No one is blaming you." She tried again. "But when the people came to fix it, they found there was something very bad about the closet," she explained. "They found the body of a lady."

"A dead body?" Mike's voice was practically a whisper.

"Yes."

His eyes were wide. "Is she still there?"

Paige knelt down in front of him and gave him a hug. "No, Mike, she isn't. The police took her away."

"Did we know her?"

"No." She didn't mention that someone he knew had been engaged to the woman. "I have to go now, but I'll see you later at Jolene's house."

He nodded his understanding, and mumbled, "Okay." He went into a booth at the back of the cafe to start his homework.

Jolene came over carrying two cups of hot cider. "You looked like a person who could use a pick-me-up," she said.

"I can't thank you enough," said Paige, her frazzled nerves making her frustrated. It didn't make sense. People in Tamarack were so nice. But one of them had committed murder.

Chapter Seven

A car stood in front of her house when she got there. Paige wondered briefly if it was from the sheriff's department and if they were still checking the house. But it looked familiar. She suddenly felt relieved. Although she hadn't realized it, she dreaded going into the house alone.

It wasn't a police car, it was Noah Oliver's. He came down the steps of the porch and greeted her. "I was getting worried about where you were," he said. "Are you all right?"

"I went to see Mike to tell him what was going on. He's with Jolene. He's kind of freaked out."

Noah frowned and stroked his red beard. "I would imagine he is. But I was worried about you. I wanted to be sure you weren't afraid to go into the house."

"That's very nice of you," Paige said, shivering more from what she was about to see in her kitchen than the cold air. "I'm scared to death."

They went up the steps and Paige opened the door. This time Paige noticed there were no more muddy footprints in the foyer. The service the police had promised seemed to have done the job.

"The police said they'd have someone clean it up," she told Noah, "but I didn't know if there would be time. That's why we were planning to stay at Jolene's. And you know where Balto is."

"He's fine, by the way. You did the right thing bringing him in this morning. Your house was no place for a playful dog."

Paige gulped. "I didn't know about that when I brought Balto in—I just thought he'd be better off out of the house when the plumber came."

They got to the kitchen and Paige reached for the light switch. She held her breath.

As the light flooded the area, Paige saw with relief that it was also cleared up. The remains of the closet were enclosed by numerous yellow police tape bands. The floor around it, though, was clean, and even the sink, which had been full of coffee cups and glasses, was empty.

There was still a lot of work ahead of her, but the worst, scariest mess was gone. She exhaled.

Noah nodded approval. "It looks like the service did a good job."

"It's wonderful. I wonder who I should thank?"

"They'll send you a bill." He looked at her. "Are you sure you're all right?"

"I'll be okay. I just have a lot to think about." She opened the refrigerator. "Can I get you anything?"

"I'll take a cup of coffee, if you don't mind."

"Sure. Have a seat. I could use the company. And I wanted to ask you a few questions." She took the nonflavored coffee beans out of the freezer and poured some into the grinder.

Noah took off his barn jacket, pushed up the sleeves of his

rag sweater, and sat down. "I don't know if I have all the answers."

Paige put water into the coffeemaker and hit the switch. Almost immediately the aroma of brewing coffee filled the kitchen, replacing the damp musty smell left from the flooded closet. "Ilke was a research assistant. Could she have been involved in something else, something dangerous?"

Noah's face grew deep red. "No. She was a good woman. Quin didn't deserve her."

Paige had been taking mugs out of the cabinet but she paused when he said that. "Were you in love with her?"

Shaking his head, Noah sighed. "We were friends. It was never more than that. But Quin decided it was a competition, swooped in and made Ilke his. He's been doing that since we were kids. And Ilke got hurt."

Paige could see how Quin, with his money and sophistication, would have an advantage. He looked like a model for those underwear ads Paige's friends loved to look at, while Noah was more likely to be found in an L. L. Bean catalogue standing next to a Labrador retriever with a fish in its mouth. Ilke had obviously preferred Quin.

Paige brought the coffee to the table with a small pitcher of milk and a package of Mike's favorite cookies. "Quin was really distraught this morning," she said. "Seeing her like that"—the image jumped into Paige's mind causing her to shudder—"must have been a horrible shock."

"It was awful," Noah agreed. "Everyone thought she'd left town—gone home." He reached out for a cookie.

"Do you remember when?"

"Quin said she left one weekend in January. I remember he called me around the middle of the month, asking if I'd seen her. I hung up on him."

"Why did he think you'd know where she was?"

"I don't know. I asked him if maybe she was helping Ted get ready for the dig, but he said Ted had left already. He also said all of her clothes were gone, which would have been far too much to take on a trip. Anyway, I told him I hadn't seen her in more than a week, and that was only at the store one night." He took the last sip of his coffee. "I guess he asked Ted where she was, but I don't know what he said."

"Uncle Ted was back here then?"

"I think so. I didn't see him. But Quin told me he thought Ted was in town a few days after he was supposed to leave because he'd forgotten something, but that he left right after that."

A chill went through Paige. "Do you think anyone will suspect my uncle of killing Ilke?"

Noah's red eyebrows went up. "Ted would never do a thing like that. It's ludicrous. Can you imagine he'd kill her and put her body in his own house when he was arranging to have you come live here?"

"Of course not. I'm just worried that some people might wonder about the connection."

"Don't worry."

The sheriffs had left a note tacked to one of the broken boards on the closet. The note said that Paige was free to do whatever she wanted with the remains. Noah stood up and went over to it, inspecting it from several angles. "There is a lot of salvageable material here," he pointed out. "Some of this molding can get pricy." He squatted down and moved a piece of it aside, showing where it was still partially nailed to the floor. "Let me clean some of this up for you."

Paige looked at her watch. "There isn't time," said Paige. "I have to go to Jolene's house and first I have to pack us up."

He scowled. "This is dangerous."

"I'll be careful."

"I used this same molding in my cabin," Noah said, as Paige walked him to the door. "If you want, I can come and fix the closet for you sometime this week. I'm pretty good with a hammer and saw."

Paige gazed into his eyes. He was a thoughtful man. "Thanks. But if it's all the same to you, I'd like it put back as a doorway to the hall. Mike and I can hang the new coats we get in the front closet."

"I understand," he said, leaning close to her and looking into her eyes. "Are you sure you'll be okay?"

She felt reassured by his calm presence and wondered how she'd feel after he left. But she would only have to be in the house alone for a few minutes. And when she and Mike moved back in, she'd have to get used to living in that house again, no matter how creepy. She had no choice. "I'll be okay."

"I'll get started on the closet as soon as I can," Noah said. "And I'll let Mike help, so he can see there's nothing to be afraid of." He opened the door. "Will you be coming to get Balto tomorrow morning?"

"If it's okay with you, I'll get him in the afternoon after work."

Noah smiled. "It's fine. I'll tell him you miss him in the meantime."

When he left, Paige was all alone. She had never before felt so unable to handle things. While she packed, she started to wish for someone, anyone, to come and take the burden off her.

It was getting late, and Paige realized she hadn't eaten anything all day. But she had to finish getting ready to go to Jolene's.

The ringing of the phone stopped her. She ran to get it, hoping for a lifeline to anywhere but where she was. And she got it.

"Paige?" said Wally. "I didn't want to frighten you by knocking on the door."

Paige began to wonder just when she had fallen asleep. This was quite a dream she was having, that Wally, who was 300 miles away, was talking about knocking on her door. Maybe the rest of it was all a dream and she'd wake up to find out there had been no dead body in her kitchen closet.

"Paige? Is the phone working?"

"Wally?"

"Open the door, honey. We're right outside."

Paige went to the door, carrying the portable phone. "Who?" She had her answer once she opened it. Wally and Nate Morris were standing outside, and if Paige's nose was accurate, they had brought more than themselves—they had brought dinner.

"What are you doing here?" Paige asked, after embracing each of them as if they were life preservers. Wally had to catch her breath after that hug.

"You had a problem," Nate said. "We're here to help. Where's Mike? I haven't seen my buddy in months."

"He's at my friend Jolene's house. I didn't want him to have to go through this."

"It'll all work out, I'm sure," said Wally. She picked up two of the packages. "I hope you're hungry. Or should I put this stuff in the refrigerator?"

Paige grabbed Wally's arm. "Don't go into the kitchen!"

"It's, uh, the body, isn't still in there, is it?" Wally asked.

"No," said Paige. "But the closet is all broken apart and it's dangerous. You'll have to be very careful."

Wally followed Paige and Nate into the kitchen. She was appalled by the destruction, and with her mother's sense of protectiveness, she hated the exposed nails and sharp pieces of wood that were visible.

"I'm not much of a carpenter," Nate said, which was not exactly news to Wally, "but I can hang some old curtains around to cover it up, if you have any. Then you can bring Mike home."

Wally nodded. "It would be easier for both of you."

Paige seemed uncertain. "He's probably sleeping by now. I'll call Jolene and find out."

Wally set out some of the food she and Nate had brought and got it ready to be reheated.

They had made preparations for the trip the moment Paige called. Wally went into high gear, cooking the brisket and noodles as quickly as she could. The meat had taken hours, even with a pressure cooker, but they had used that time to clear their schedules and for Wally to get a substitute for her nursery school class. Then they packed a suitcase for a few days, in case Paige needed them to stay for a while, and booked a motel near her house.

Paige came back into the kitchen. "Jolene thought I should let Mike stay there for the night, but he wasn't sleeping yet and I realized I needed him here with me. I told her we were coming to get him." She went over to a kitchen chair where a heavy sweater hung.

Wally picked up her own jacket. "You've had enough for today. I'll go get him. You stay here with Nate and relax. Dinner will be ready by the time we get back."

"It's dark out," said Nate. "Maybe I should go."

"You wouldn't know where to go," Wally pointed out. "But thanks for the offer. I can handle it. Jolene lives just outside of town. See you soon."

Once outside, she had to admit she was a little unsure of where she was going. She, Paige, and Mike had gone past there one day when the café was closed, and they had seen Jolene out in her yard. But that was during daylight, with leaves on the trees, which now looked stark and sinister in the moonlight. Wally was grateful that there was a three-quarter moon to help light the way. Out here in the country there was no light pollution, or even very many lights, to soften the blackness on the sides of the road.

There were lights on in Jolene's house. Wally parked the car and went to the front door.

"I told Paige she didn't have to come get Mike tonight," Jolene said, as she led the way inside. "He's really no trouble and we've been having a lovely time."

"I'll bet," said Wally. "And he probably had a wonderful dinner."

Jolene smiled. "Baked chicken and home fries. Baking powder biscuits. And he ate all his vegetables."

A doorway off the front hall led directly into Jolene's living room. It was warm and cozy, with colorful crocheted throws and needle-pointed pillows all around. Mike sat on the couch with a plate of delicious-looking cookies next to him and a mug of hot cocoa, based on the yummy aroma emanating from it. When he saw Wally, he put down his mug and ran over to give her a hug. "I didn't know you were coming, Aunt Wally." His smile faded quickly. "Something bad happened."

"We're going to make it better," Wally assured him. "Are you ready to go home?"

Mike's face brightened. "I can? Let's go." He turned to Jolene. "Oh, thanks for dinner, Ms. Valley," he said politely. He moved toward the door.

"You're welcome, Mike. But I think you should pack up your stuff."

"I almost forgot. Okay." He darted toward what Wally supposed was a second bedroom.

"You really should have left him here," said Jolene, when Mike was out of earshot. "He'd be better off not seeing the place where the body was found."

"My husband is going to cover it up with some curtains or sheets. Mike won't be able to see anything. And we'll see to it that the damage is repaired as soon as possible."

"It's good that you could come up here to be with Paige and Mike," Jolene said. "But don't you think you should let her learn how to get by on her own two feet? You can't be here every minute to protect her, and there are a lot of people in Tamarack who would be happy to."

Wally mulled that over. "I suppose you have a point—not that we should ignore Paige's needs but that there are other people who can fill them. But don't you think she'd have to realize that for herself and get comfortable with it in order to be able to ask for help?"

"Why should she when she relies on you?"

"I wouldn't say she relies only on us. She asked you to help with Mike today, didn't she? Besides, she didn't ask us to come, we volunteered. That's what we do when someone has a big problem."

Jolene was still frowning disapproval in the upstairs window as Wally helped Mike get into the car. "Some people," Wally muttered, as she got into the car herself.

Wally's eyes misted at the sight of the reunion between Paige and her son in the front hall. It confirmed that Wally had done the right thing in bringing him home.

"How are you doing, big guy?" Nate asked.

Mike pulled away from Paige in surprise. "You're here too?"

Nate stooped down. "Yes. Give me a high-five."

Mike gave him a big one. "I know you know about what happened here, but I don't want you to be scared," Nate told Mike. "We are going to fix everything up."

"That's what Aunt Wally said. But you can't fix that poor lady."

"No, we can't do that. But we are going to make sure everything gets put back together just the way it was. Until then, I've covered it all up. Do you want to see?"

Nate had covered the debris of the closet with a combination of Paige's old shower curtain from her apartment, some brightly colored sheets that looked as if they were manufactured in the early seventies, and a large bath towel. He'd weighted the bottoms with old shoes and boots he had found in one of the closets in an unused bedroom. It looked somewhat comical and Mike's frown softened.

While he was doing that, Paige set the table in the dining room and dinner was reheated and ready to go. Since it was getting late and Mike, who had already eaten, needed to go to bed, they ate quickly.

When he was ready for bed, Mike asked where Wally and Nate's suitcases were. "In the car," Nate said. "We are going to a motel just down the road."

"You don't need to do that," said Paige. "We have plenty of room here. Please stay."

One look at her face was all it took for Wally to call the motel and cancel.

Chapter Eight

"Elliot, can't you find out anything?" Wally asked. "How can I help Paige if I don't know what's going on?"

"The case isn't even in this state," said her son-in-law, Elliot Levine, assistant prosecutor for Essex County, New Jersey. "Why do you think the Tamarack, New York, sheriff department would tell me anything?"

"You have a reputation for solving cases."

"Actually," said Elliot, "you're the one with the reputation."

"Can't you introduce yourself to the local police and tell them that?"

"You don't mean you want me to drive up there, do you?"

"Well, if you think it would help," Wally started. She had made the call to Elliot as soon as Paige left for school with Mike. Nate was out trying to find a hardware store so he could change the locks and she had the house all to herself. She was wracking her brain trying to figure out how she could help when she realized she might have a way to get into the local sheriff's confidence.

Knowing that asking Elliot to drive up there was unreasonable, something she had long ago vowed never to be, along with a meddling mother-in-law, Wally backed off. "Maybe just a phone call. Just to tell him that Nate and I are here to help, and any information he can share will be handled discreetly."

A long pause on Elliot's end of the conversation had Wally wondering if she'd gone overboard again. She didn't mean to sound heavy-handed, but she really wanted to help. She needed the answers to a few basic questions or she'd never be able to stop worrying. She wanted to know how, if she wasn't murdered there, which seemed to be the going opinion, Ilke's body had come to be in Paige's house. And why was there no sign of the body for so many months?

There was another question—who had built the hidden panel in the closet? For that matter, who had built the closet in the first place?

"I'll give them a call," Elliot said, finally. "But I'm not going to strong-arm them with my official capacity, so don't expect anything. And try to stay out of trouble."

"Yes, sir."

Wally gave Elliot a little time to make the call before trying the sheriff's office herself. She expected to leave a message, but the sheriff came to the phone.

"How can I help you?" Sheriff Dover said.

"I'm worried about Paige," Wally said, glancing warily at the remains of the closet. "I thought I'd call and see if there was anything I could do to help make sure that she and Mike are safe. Do you have any leads?"

"I wish I could say we did, but we know very little right now. They promised to rush the autopsy, but I wouldn't expect to hear anything for a while. Meanwhile we're checking leads and verifying what people told us."

"I see."

"But I can tell you," Dover said, "since your friend called and told me about your past successes with this type of thing, that Ilke was killed last winter, and she may have been subjected to freezing temperatures prior to her death."

Wally wondered exactly what Elliot had told Dover but knew he had no other way to persuade the sheriff to confide in her. As the impact of Dover's words sank in, she felt the hairs of her neck raise up. "How long was she in the wall of the closet?"

"We're not sure. The data is not all in, and there are some strange inconsistencies. I was led to believe it could have been as long as eight months."

"Then why didn't Paige . . ." Wally began, but she couldn't finish.

"Why didn't she smell something?" the sheriff said. "The coroner said it looked as if she'd been mummified, not like in Egypt, but with some kind of desiccant."

"How?"

"We're not sure. Look, I know you want to know what's going on, and I don't mind telling you what I can if it won't compromise the investigation, but we just don't know anything else."

"Do you know where Paige's uncle, Ted Verrill, is?"

Dover didn't answer her question. Instead he asked another. "Do you think he knows something about all this?"

"I don't know," said Wally, aware that her worry would transfer to this sheriff, possibly raising suspicion about a totally innocent man. She gathered her thoughts. "He is the owner of the house and from what I understand he knew the victim. Paige hasn't heard from him, as far as I know, and you would think he'd call when word of this situation got out." *That is,* Wally thought, *unless he was out in the middle of nowhere, out of the reach of newspapers and even satellite phones.* She tried to explain that to Dover. "He's been out of touch for so long, I'm afraid something may have happened to him." She didn't add that she was also upset that Quin had said Ted might have been in town around the time Ilke disappeared.

"We are trying to find him, Mrs. Morris," the sheriff said. "He may know something about what happened in his house. We really want to question him."

Dover's tone only made Wally worry more. Ted had done his Ph.D. dissertation on mummification.

At 10:30, Judy's voice came on Paige's intercom. "There is a student here to see you. I told her you have too much to do to deal with her problems anymore, but she insisted I ask you."

"Who is it?"

"That girl from New York City. Aurora Dillon."

"Send her in," Paige said. She was not only exhausted from two sleepless nights, she was tired of the school secretary's judgmental attitude. Judy sat at the high counter in the main office like a judge on a bench, never ruling in favor of any request not on her own agenda. Often she didn't even pass on requests to Paige if they didn't suit her.

Most recently, Judy had been annoyed with Paige that she wouldn't talk about the murder, but Paige wouldn't give her the satisfaction of even mentioning it. This did nothing to temper Judy's mean streak, and the tension between her and Paige was escalating.

Aurora came in carrying her book bag and her jacket, a brightly colored patchwork ski parka. It looked very expensive, not like the jackets the kids in the school generally wore. But in contrast to its vibrant hues, Aurora looked extremely pale and she had dark circles under her eyes. She took the seat Paige indicated and slumped into it.

Paige offered her a piece of the muffin she'd been working on all morning. Jolene's muffins had become a habit and Paige often cut them into small pieces to make them last longer.

Aurora declined. "It's from Jolene's, right?" she asked. "They are so good. I bought one this morning." She picked at her nails. "But I lost my appetite. I don't think I'll ever be hungry again."

Having failed in her attempt to sidetrack the girl, Paige asked, "What's wrong?"

"I just heard about the woman," the girl said, then started to weep.

Paige felt like weeping herself. "It's awful. For someone to die and be . . ."

"It isn't just that. I knew her."

"Really? How?"

Aurora didn't speak for a few seconds because she could barely catch her breath. "She was," she sobbed, "a friend of my father's. I think she's the reason my mom went away."

Paige was puzzled. Mr. Dillon had seemed to think his wife went away because of her emotional illness. Aurora seemed to be implying it was because of her father's philandering. Paige had a sudden, horrible thought. What if Aurora's mother hadn't really left of her own choice? What if someone had killed her too? She pushed those thoughts aside but couldn't stop herself from asking, "Why do you say that?"

"Why else would she go away?" There were tears in Aurora's eyes, the tears of an abandoned child. "She found Dad with Ilke one day a few summers ago. I know it hurt her."

That was before Ilke and Quin got together, Paige thought. And a long time ago. But Aurora didn't seem to think so.

"When did your mom leave?"

"In February. I was really upset when she went away like that." She lowered her eyes and added softly, "She didn't even say goodbye. I think that's why I had so much trouble in school."

Paige thought about what the girl's teachers had said the last time they met. She was turning out to be an excellent student, really opening up now, but she hadn't really connected with any of the local kids. But that other darker thought wouldn't get out of Paige's mind. Had Aurora's mother left at the same time as Ilke disappeared? Could there be a connection? "Did your mom leave from here or New York?" Paige asked, not sure which answer would be better.

Aurora furrowed her brows in puzzlement. "New York. We were home then."

"But Ilke lived up here and the aff—" Paige cleared her throat, "it had happened long before."

"My dad could have taken the train up to see her any time he wanted. He did come here a lot, even after he said it was over. That has to be why Mom left."

Pinning her mother's departure on a possible relationship between her father and Ilke Hedstrom had obviously frightened Aurora, especially in light of recent events.

She was still speaking, struggling to get the words out. "Dad kept a car here and sometimes brought clients up to fish or hunt." More quietly she added, "I think he also brought a few women up, even before Mom left us."

Paige couldn't help wondering why Mrs. Dillon didn't stay and ask Aurora's dad to leave the home. Why would a mother leave her child? But she tried to focus on what was troubling Aurora right now. "Are you afraid your dad had something to do with Ilke's death?"

The girl shook her head, her eyes wide in her ashen face. "I know he didn't do it. He would never hurt anyone, but some people might think he did. I mean if he could do that to my mother and all."

"I'm sure you don't have anything to worry about. Did you talk to him?"

"He's in New York this week. I couldn't talk about that over the phone."

"And your housekeeper? What did she say?"

"I didn't talk to her about it. How could I?"

Paige told Aurora to call if she needed to talk and then scurried to get ready to leave. She felt it was important to be with Mike and let the stuff on her desk just wait until she could get to it.

"How come you came so early today?" Mike asked when she met him at the school doors.

"I rescheduled my meeting for tomorrow. Let's go." She pulled out of the school parking lot and turned onto the road that led to the center of Tamarack.

"Do we have to go home?" Mike said, in a small voice.

"We aren't going home right away, we're going to Dr. Oliver's to pick up Balto. I'll bet he really missed us."

"Hurry, Mom!"

Paige drove over to the vet's office. She didn't see his truck, but she got out and went inside.

His assistant frowned when Paige came in. "Dr. Oliver had to go out on an emergency. He thought you'd be here later, and he said Balto seemed lonely, so he took him along for the ride."

"Can we go to where they are?" Mike's voice behind her told Paige he hadn't listened when she said to stay in the car.

"Sure," the assistant answered, without waiting for Paige's input. "I'll just write down directions." She handed Paige a map with a route highlighted in red. "You'll see the turnoff right after the pond. On your right."

"Let's go, M—" Mike's voice was cut off by the door closing behind him.

They drove north along the main road, then turned west to get to the next village. Right after the center of town, and a pond full of Canada geese, they turned onto a dirt road and followed its winding path to a farmhouse. The barn was right behind it.

Mike jumped out of the car and ran into the barn. Paige was right behind him, just in time to see Noah, shirtless, with soft-looking red hair covering his well-muscled chest and arms, giving directions to the worried-looking man beside him. Right outside the stall, which had a cow laboring in it, Balto sat wagging the tip of his tail in greeting but not moving another muscle.

Mike climbed onto a hay bale next to Balto to see over the side of the stall, and Paige went to stand beside him. They both watched, transfixed, as the cow Noah stood next to struggled to bring her calf into the world.

A half hour later Paige pulled Mike away from looking at the new family long enough to let Noah know they were there to pick up Balto. He turned to them and smiled, introducing both to the dairy man.

"Your dog was a fine companion," Noah told Mike. "He would make a great ride along friend on lonely evenings when I'm called out to a farm."

Mike smiled proudly. "Can we take him home now? Or do you still need him?"

Noah looked at Paige and grinned. "I guess I can spare him now. Let me walk you to your car." He turned back to the cow's owner and signaled he would be right back.

Mike had several questions about the birth on the way to the car, and Paige had to hurry to keep up with him and Noah, so she could hear what they said. She suspected she'd have to field a few more of his questions on the way home. That would take her mind off facing her house again, at least for a few minutes.

"Aunt Wally?" Mike whispered, as he and Paige walked into the kitchen for their after-school snacks. He peered in before stepping over the sill and took a small, tentative step.

When he and Paige had first come into the house, they were both bubbling with excitement about the birth of the calf. They told Wally all about how Noah helped it along. Wally wished she could have seen that. But now that they were getting back to the present, Mike was voicing his fears. "Why did the lady die here?"

"I don't know." Wally didn't explain that it didn't appear she had died in the house. It might bring up too many questions for which she had no answers.

"Will we die here too?"

Wally looked at Mike, seeing the fear in the boy's eyes. "No. You and your mom are safe here." Nate had called about having a security system installed and scheduled an appointment. Neither he nor Wally would consider leaving until after the work was done. "The police came and took away everything to do with the lady." A glance to check on the impact of her words only showed that Mike was unable to take his eyes off the remnants of the closet. He certainly wouldn't step near it.

"You can take your snack inside and start your spelling homework," Paige said, handing him a glass of milk. Mike took two cookies from a plateful that Wally had baked earlier and went into the den.

While Mike was busy copying his words, Wally turned her

attention to Paige. Now that she had taken off her business suit, Paige looked much younger and quite pale. "You had a few calls today," Wally told her. "Some reporters. And there was also a message about Saturday's soccer game and a reminder that you are responsible for refreshments for the next chamber music meeting." Wally hoped she'd make some friends while she was playing her viola. "That person seemed surprised when I answered."

"I'm glad you were here," said Paige. "Not to act as my answering service, but to let people know we aren't all alone here."

"I'm here as long as you need me. But I know you can handle this, or at least you'll be able to."

Wally went down to the basement to unload the dryer. She had spent a good part of the day running the wet towels through the washer and dryer—the towels Paige and Mike had used to wipe up the floor. It amazed her that there was no water damage in the basement. There was new wallboard, taped but not painted, under where the closet had been. It was unblemished.

After dinner everyone seemed to feel a little less on edge. Mike had eaten with gusto and Paige, while not exactly shoveling it in, had eaten a good amount. When Balto returned from outside, Mike spent several minutes petting the dog, trying to make him stop acting so timid. Yet it was as if Balto could see the body. Nothing could make him go near the demolished closet. He just stood staring at it, whining. Mike stood by helplessly.

The sight of the two of them renewed Wally's desire to get to the bottom of what happened to Ilke, even if she had to investigate from New Jersey. That was the only way the little family would have peace of mind. And if she had to do it long distance, so be it.

Chapter Nine

Paige and Mike were at school and Nate had gone into town to find a fax machine when Wally decided to have a look at Ilke's office. The police had finished with their investigation, so Wally thought it would be okay to do a little sleuthing on her own.

The office was next to Ted's bedroom and was itself a bedroom. Wally reasoned that when Ilke first came to town she would have needed a place to stay. Ted's house was certainly big enough. Perhaps she'd stayed there until she had found a place to rent. The police would have taken anything that might have given a clue to Ilke's murderer and Wally had little hope of finding something, but she looked anyway, starting with the desk.

The top drawer held pencils, pens and erasers, and a bag of hard candies. Wally had never seen the brand before and looked at it closely. It was written in another language, including accent marks and strange symbols not used in English. Ilke had come from Sweden, according to Quin, and Wally guessed the candy wrapper was written in Swedish.

She wondered if Ilke's body would be shipped to her home-town for burial, after being released from the medical examiner's office, since there had been no mention of services in town. *How had Ilke's family taken the news of her death?* Wally wondered. Quin had mentioned an aunt as the only relative she had. How had she felt when she saw off her niece to go work for an American professor? Or when she'd become engaged to someone here? And how was she doing since she heard that Ilke's body had been found in the walls of the professor's home? Hadn't the aunt wondered where she was all that time and why she hadn't heard from her? Wally wished she knew.

The next drawer held file folders. Some may have been re-moved, Wally remembered, since Paige had signed a receipt for several things after the house was searched. But Wally went through the ones that were left, confirming that none of them were from during Ilke's time. She knew there had been several assistants before Ilke, and she began to wonder if any of them might know something. The question was how would she find out their names and how to reach them?

Riffling through the papers, Wally took notes on every name she could find, and if possible, she tried to get a sense of where they had gone to school, where they were from—whatever she could find. She planned to try to find them on the Internet.

There were only three. Wally thought back and realized that Ted had lived in this house for eleven or twelve years. It still amazed her that he had been able to purchase such a beautiful house, not to mention the rest of the estate. The popularity of his books reached far beyond academia, though, and that might explain it.

When she finished with the desk, she went to the dresser. There were no clothes in it. Wally even checked behind the drawers in case something fell, some valuable clue, like the kind people find in books. Nada.

The closet was the same, which made sense. Ilke hadn't disappeared from this house, she'd lived at Quin's. There were no secret panels, no hidden caches, no notes taped to the bottoms of drawers. Wally even checked the bed, looking between the mattress and box spring.

It seemed unlikely that during the day, when Ilke was working, she would have used the same bathroom as Ted, since his bedroom had its own. So Wally went to look in the bathrooms, including Mike's. She opened all the drawers that were built in along the walls of the long bathroom. Nothing. It seemed so unreasonable that nothing at all would have been left behind. Or had whoever cleaned out Quin's house and built the closet, removed all trace of Ilke from this house too? Had he been in this bathroom that Mike now used? Chills washed over her.

So far she hadn't turned up anything useful, and nothing that would answer some of her other questions, particularly about the closet in which Ilke's body had been found. Someone had put it in between the time Paige visited when Mike was a baby and when Ilke was entombed there. The police had been fairly certain that whoever hid Ilke's body was not of the caliber, carpentrywise, of the original builder of the closet. Wally hoped to find the original carpenter to see if she could get some useful information. She hoped Paige would be able to find a bill or receipt somewhere in Ted's office. She would have to ask her to look as soon as possible.

Wally heard a car drive up. Paige and Mike were home. Wally would fill her in on what she'd been doing once Mike went to bed. For now it was time to go downstairs and see how their days had been.

Mike seemed to be getting back to his old self, judging by the way he dug into the cookies Wally kept baking. Nate came back just as Mike was going for his third and sat down to see if he could keep up with him. Wally took Paige aside and told her what she'd been doing while everyone was gone.

"I'll look for the carpenter's bill this evening," Paige said. "But right now, I was wondering, if you and Nate wouldn't mind, if I could go see Quin. He was so out of it yesterday I couldn't even comfort him."

Wally could see tension in Paige's sad eyes. She nodded. "Of course we can take care of Mike. But could I go along with you? I'd like to pay my respects. And Nate would be happy to stay with Mike."

Paige let out a sigh, which Wally took to mean she was happy for the company. She grabbed her coat and purse.

They drove south on 9N, past Adirondack Horizon, a summer camp for boys. Wally hadn't been on this part of the road before, and it was nearly dark, making it hard to see signs. After what seemed like miles, Paige found the turnoff and made a right.

The road was long. But then they came into a clearing and Wally saw the house, a beautiful chalet, surrounded by pine trees. There were two cars parked in front of the garage. One was Quin's and the other was a police jeep. She wondered why the police were still there.

They went up the steep staircase to the porch and knocked on the door. After a moment, Quin answered. His eyes were red and he was pale. His usually perfect blond hair stuck up on the left side of his head, but he didn't seem to notice. The playful light was gone from his eyes, leaving only pain.

"Paige," he said. "And, uh, Wally. Thank you for coming. I'm really glad you're here."

Wally looked over at Sheriff Dover, who was sitting in a chair, and back at Quin. "If we're interrupting, we could come back."

"No." Quin put his arm around Paige's shoulder and escorted her inside. "Please don't go. I can answer these questions just as well with you here." He went to a mission-style couch with bright cushions and sat, leaning forward, ready for Dover's questions.

Wally knew the sheriff didn't want them there. "Let me get you a glass of water," she said. "Paige, let's go find the kitchen."

The kitchen was gorgeous, a gourmet's delight. Wally could just make out the lake in the fading light.

But as nicely decorated as the house was, it seemed to be strictly a bachelor's, now that Wally thought about it. There were no feminine touches, although maybe Quin had put them away when Ilke "left."

They didn't hurry to get the water, knowing they'd be in the way in the living room. But there was a passage leading back to the living room and Paige and Wally heard most of the interview. It was awkward, and they glanced at each other guiltily, but there was nothing else they could do. Making small talk to cover the sound just seemed out of the question.

"Mr. Wyatt," said Dover, "please tell me again about the day Ilke left."

Wally heard Quin blow his nose. "I didn't know she was murdered. I've been angry at her for so long for running off on me, and here she's been dead," his voice choked up, "all this time. I feel so guilty."

There was a short silence before Dover asked, "When was the last time you saw her?"

"It was on a Friday last winter. I was getting ready to go to Albany to meet with a supplier and she started yelling at me to cancel, saying that she wanted us to go into Lake Placid. She was all dressed up, wearing a black skirt and sweater, with that vest she loved so much. She wanted to go out to dinner. I told her I had to go there every day and wanted a break, especially since it would be full of tourists coming up for the weekend. She didn't care about that and said she'd be happy to help me pick out her birthday gift first, since she knew I wouldn't remember, and it was coming up soon. I told her I did remember and that I already bought one for her and she made me tell her what it was. When I did, she really let me have it."

"What did you get her?" Dover asked.

"A cookbook. She had no idea how to use a kitchen."

"And she wanted something else?"

"I guess. Probably some jewelry she didn't need. Then she started screaming about how I never paid any attention to her, and she might as well be away on the dig."

"Which dig is that?"

"Ted Verrill's. So I told her to go find Ted and leave with him. Then she got this strange look on her face and she reminded me that he already went without her, since he knew she and I needed time together. As if I needed to be reminded that she was missing out. She complained about it at least five times a day."

Quin paused, calming himself, Wally thought. When he started speaking again his voice was much quieter.

"I saw she was really upset, and I told her I would meet with the supplier and come right back, but that I also had to do some work on my ice shanty. I was just setting it up and I wanted to at least be able to fish the next day. She didn't seem to care that the season is so short. The March fifteenth deadline for taking the shanty off the ice meant nothing to her, but it meant a lot to me. I told her to come along, that I'd only take an hour or so, but of course she wouldn't go. She said she had never set foot in there and never would."

"So you went to Albany?"

"Yes."

"Did you meet your supplier? We'll need his name."

"Uh, no. He stood me up, or at least that's what I thought. I started to call him and noticed I had written a different day for our meeting. When his assistant answered, I didn't even say anything because I was embarrassed. So I called Ilke to tell her I was coming right home, and I'd skip going to the ice shanty, but there was no answer. When I got here, all her stuff was gone."

"She took her car?"

"I guess so. It was gone."

"Did she leave a note?"

"I never saw one, if she did."

"Did you try to find out where she went?" Dover asked. "Did you want to try to get her back?"

Quin cleared his throat. "Not at first. I was so hurt I took off for New York City for a few weeks to clear my head. But I realized that I loved her, so I came back to try to find out what happened. I called all her friends in town, and anyone else I thought might have seen her. I sent so many people letters, looking for her. Paige's uncle was the first. I figured she went back to the dig."

"Back?"

"We had both been there when Ted went to set up."

"When was that?"

"Early December."

"And all three of you came back here?"

"Yes. Ted went back alone, right after—" He stopped.

"After what?"

"Or was it before?" Quin stopped talking for a moment. "I can't remember if it was before or after Ilke left me," he added. "He was in and out of town a few times. I know he had a meeting in Montreal, because Ilke had to type up some notes for him, but I'm not sure when it was."

"You said you wrote to Ted, to see if Ilke was there."

"I e-mailed him."

"Did he respond?" asked Dover.

"No. I figured even if Ilke was with him, she told him not to tell me. But I had to try. I poured out my heart in that letter." Quin's voice quavered. "I know now that she didn't leave me, but what was I supposed to think at the time?"

Wally thought it was time to get that water to Quin. She opened and closed cupboards, seeing sparkling crystal and expensive china, until she found the one with glasses and filled one with water from the sink. The tap continued dripping after she turned the water off, and no amount of wriggling that she or Paige did would make it stop. They finally gave up and went back to the living room. "Can he take a break?" Paige asked, bringing the water to Quin.

Dover stood up. "That would be fine. I'm finished for now. Mr. Wyatt, would you mind coming to my office in the morning? We can have you sign your statement there."

Wally watched the sheriff leave, wondering what they could say to Quin. They'd overheard so much.

"I'm sorry about your sink," Wally said. "I couldn't get the water to stop dripping."

Quin took a sip of the water. "It isn't your fault. It started a few days ago, but I just can't do a damned thing around the house. I'll have to get one of my maintenance men to come fix it."

"I know how to change a washer," said Wally. "And I know a trick. Have you got a wrench?"

He brought one to her. She quickly flipped the washer over and in no time the dripping had stopped.

"It's nothing," she said, after he'd thanked her, "but if it's okay, I wanted to ask you something."

Quin smiled weakly. "Anything. I've got no secrets."

"Was anyone else supposed to be at the house?" He looked puzzled, so she added, "Ted's house."

He seemed to understand. "No. No one else was assisting him. Ilke wasn't even supposed to be over there, not while Ted was away. There wouldn't have been a reason."

Paige expressed her sorrow to Quin. Wally couldn't get over how sad the whole thing was, with both of them having lost their partners to death.

Wally didn't realize that Paige was talking to her for a moment. Then she heard Paige say, "We really should be going. Will you be all right?"

Quin turned his miserable face toward her. "How can I live with myself? All this time I thought she'd left me for someone else. I didn't know someone had killed her." He looked up at Paige. "I should have known. I mean, our relationship wasn't so terrible that I should have jumped to the conclusion that she left me. Maybe if I had gone after her, I could have stopped whoever it was from killing her."

Paige seemed to reconsider her departure and sat down next to him. "But you said you thought she went to the dig. Did you think there was someone there she wanted to see?"

"She didn't go, so I guess that idea was off base."

"Please, Quin," said Wally, "it could be important."

"No, I'm sure it isn't. I was mistaken, that's all." He sat slumped over, staring at the floor.

"Was it Uncle Ted?" Paige asked, her voice rising. "Is that why you won't tell me?" She tried to get him to look at her. "I never heard of him having a relationship with an assistant. Do you think they . . ."

Quin sighed. "I don't know. I know she liked him, even though he's fifteen years older, but then she met me. We were happy." He scrubbed his face with his hands. "I don't know who would want to kill her." He turned reddened eyes toward them.

"Will you be okay?" Wally asked. "Should we call someone?"

"I'll be all right," Quin said. "I just need some time to process."

Paige stood, uncertain, but he waved both of them toward the door.

Wally put her hand on the doorknob and turned it. It was loose too, and she had to fiddle with it to get it to open the door. All it needed was a screwdriver, although apparently Quin couldn't manage that. But right now he needed a lot more than a handyman.

While dinner was cooking Wally and Paige went through the files labeled "house" in Ted's office. There wasn't much—the deed, which Wally thought should probably be in a safer place, and some electric, gas, and oil bills. "My uncle has them all billed to his credit card," Paige said, as if embarrassed. "The bills don't come to me."

Most people would have done well with a deal like that, but Paige had admitted that she was up to her ears in debts left by her husband and his risk taking on the stock market. No one would envy her financial situation.

They found a receipt from a local carpenter. As they looked it over, Wally realized that this was just what they were looking for. Figuring that his number was probably his home number, so it wouldn't matter that it was after hours, Wally asked Paige to call him.

Paige explained who she was and the carpenter remembered building the closet. "How long ago?" Paige asked. She held up five fingers, which Wally took to mean five years.

"Ask him if Ted said why he wanted the doorway closed off," Wally whispered.

Paige asked the question. The answer seemed to be lengthy, but Paige nodded to Wally to say she understood the reasoning.

When she got off the phone, she explained. "My uncle apparently wanted to put in a darkroom in the alcove it formed. I guess he decided against it."

"So many things are digital now," Wally said. "He might have realized he didn't really need it."

Paige frowned. "This doesn't help us figure out who put Ilke into the closet and walled her up, does it?"

"No, I'm afraid not. But it does tell us that the closet was here for a while, and so it's likely that several people, visitors to the house while Ted was here, knew about it." Wally had to wonder who, of the people she'd met in Tamarack, that would include.

There wasn't time to wonder about the other questions buzzing around in Wally's head. It was time for dinner and Nate seemed to be done with his phone calls. He and Mike were down in the dining room setting the table, if Wally's ears were correct as she and Paige came downstairs. It made her both happy and sad—happy that Nate could provide a bit of male influence on Mike and sad that it would only be for a few days.

Wally got Sheriff Dover on the phone early the next morning and told her what they had learned about the closet. "It still doesn't explain about the interior panel that hid Ilke," she concluded.

"I checked around the local lumber yards," said Dover. "Here's what we've put together. The yard that reported a break-in back in the winter, possibly right around the time of Ms. Hedstrom's murder said they might have been missing some wood, maybe some nails, but they really don't keep close track of every single item."

"Was anything else missing?" Wally asked.

"Possibly. They weren't sure. They don't keep the best records. It was either they got shorted from the manufacturer or someone miscounted on a sale or someone pinched some stuff."

"How likely are the first two possibilities?"

"Your guess is as good as mine."

Wally was surprised at Dover's lack of concern, but then he said something that explained it all.

"Working with this information," he said, "we're looking into the possibility that the crime was committed by a vagrant, possibly someone living in the house while Ted was away. Possibly the victim walked in on him, confronted him, and things got out of hand. He may have hidden her body in the house and fled the town or"—he paused, as if considering the likelihood of what he was about to say—"he may have been the drifter whose body turned up in an inlet of the lake in early June."

Wally knew she was grabbing at straws but she let herself believe this possibility. It would explain everything, and it would mean that Paige and Mike were safe. The killer was gone. But it didn't seem likely. Why would a drifter go to so much trouble? Why not just leave town?

"Do you believe that?" Wally asked.

"The timing would be right. He would have still been alive at the time of Ilke's death."

"But if the drifter did it," Wally said, trying to imagine the scenario, "that doesn't explain how Ilke came to get frost bite before she died."

Dover was quiet for a moment. "We're thinking that she may not have been killed right away, although that may be what the killer thought. He may have stashed her body in one of the outbuildings on the property, to keep it cool, while he built the closet."

"Which one?"

"What do you mean?"

"Which building? We looked into all the buildings when Paige first moved here, all but one. It looked like a toolshed."

"That sounds like the one where her blood was found."

Wally had to take a deep breath at the thought of how close they'd come to seeing that. Would things have been different if Noah had known what he was looking at? Maybe some of the nightmare could have been avoided.

"But why go to all that trouble?" she said. "Why not just leave town? And where did he put her car?"

"Those are all good questions, Mrs. Morris," Dover said. "We are looking into all of them. But for right now, we are cautiously optimistic that whoever perpetrated this crime is not a danger to Dr. Griffin or her son. And we'll keep our eyes open. We'll handle the whole thing. You don't need to worry."

Wally got the sense that he was telling her to leave. She knew Nate had to get back to his business and that she couldn't keep asking the school to provide substitutes for her in her absence. She sincerely hoped that Sheriff Dover was right and that she could go home worry free.

Chapter Ten

"I'm going out to lunch," Paige told Judy exactly two weeks after the discovery of a body in her house had become the talk of the town.

The secretary's eyebrows rose. "You make it sound like you are in New York, going to some fancy corner restaurant. What around here could measure up to that?"

While Paige wouldn't say that restaurants in the area were plentiful, there were some quite nice dining rooms in inns nearby. There was also Jolene's shop, which drew a respectable lunch crowd for her delicious homemade soups, breads, and muffins. In fact, it was a wonderful place to go alone, since Jolene kept her company, often joining her while she ate.

It wasn't any of Judy's business where Paige was going, and she did not answer the woman. Her sarcasm and nosiness were often, as now, couched in "innocent" questions.

"I'll be back in an hour," Paige promised.

Paige wished she could replace Judy but had to look at the reality of the situation. If only Judy weren't the PTA president and head band parent, Paige would fire her. Since she was, no one else would take the job, for fear of being faced with Judy's venom on a daily basis. Paige was stuck with the woman.

She went out to her car, noting the bleak landscape she could expect to see for the next six months. The weather had turned very chilly and she pulled the zipper of her new down coat close to her neck.

It amazed her that over two weeks had passed since her house had become the center of a police investigation. Wally and Nate had left soon after the new alarm system was installed, and Wally had promised to stay on top of things from her home. The yellow-taped area still remained in the kitchen, though. Paige had wanted to call a carpenter, but Noah had called asking if she would let him do the work. He claimed he'd run out of renovations to do to his house, and he loved doing them. But so far there hadn't been an opportunity to have him start.

By the time Paige had pulled out of the parking area and had driven past the football field, track, and baseball fields, she was nearly finished with the sandwich she'd packed that morning. There would be no time for lunch today, certainly not a leisurely one like she used to have with her friends, back before her life got turned upside down. In those days, the only thing she had to worry about was collecting data for her dissertation, getting dinner ready for Michael in case he came home on time instead of working late, and picking up Mike from school to take him to his karate class. She had time for lunch with friends, and shows and museums, as long as whatever she did didn't cut into her time with Mike, her work on her thesis, or interfere with whatever Michael might want. Sometimes she missed the person she used to be.

But she had to live with who she was now, a displaced person trying to find a new home and a new balance, while dealing with the problems she'd been left by her husband. The insurance company had claimed that Michael let his premiums lapse, and there were no insurance benefits when Michael died. He'd borrowed against it to play the stock market, lost, and never repaid that debt or the others he'd managed to accumulate on their credit cards. There was so much she hadn't known.

In a few minutes she arrived at the sheriff headquarters. Sheriff Dover was waiting for her in his cubicle.

"Thank you for coming, Dr. Griffin," he said, indicating a chair for her to sit on. "I have a lot of questions for you." He opened his notebook.

Sitting on the edge of the chair, nerves frayed, Paige felt that could wait. She had a more important question. "Have you heard from my uncle?"

Dover shook his head. "No one seems to know where he is. I'm not saying we think he had anything to do with Ilke's death, although we do have an unconfirmed report that he was in town around the time she disappeared."

"Do you think something happened to him? That maybe he was there when . . ." She couldn't finish.

Dover narrowed his eyes and she had a sense that the sheriff was very sharp. "We don't know. Can you tell me about the relationship between him and Ilke?"

"I don't know much about it. She came here as an assistant to my uncle."

"Does he usually have people working for him?"

"When he's writing a book, yes. I don't know if you are aware of this, but he's considered a leading expert in tell technology."

"Tell? I'm sorry, I'm not familiar with that term."

"Tells are just artificial mounds built up over the years. You see, civilizations are quite often built one on top of another,"

Paige explained. "The conditions for establishing a successful community, such as water and good soil, might stay constant for thousands of years, outliving the life of a community. My uncle studies the way the layers are influenced by geological distortions and cultural customs of worshiping the departed."

"I think I understand," said Sheriff Dover. "Does it keep him busy?"

Paige laughed, finally relaxing just a bit. "Sometimes. For the past five years, he's been studying tells on various continents. I thought he was ready to begin the writing process, but then he left again."

Dover leaned back in his chair. "What made you think he was finished collecting data?"

"Ilke. He doesn't hire someone to help him until he's almost done and he knows he won't be flying off somewhere."

"He hired Ilke nearly three years ago," said Dover, after consulting his notes. "And they did do some traveling. Do you think he finished the book already and left to do some new project?"

Paige thought about it. "That's what I thought he was going to do when he left, but I honestly don't know." She looked at her watch. "I have to be getting back soon. I was hoping you could tell me if anything turned up at the autopsy that might be connected to my uncle."

"You are referring to the possibility that the body was mummified in some way?"

"Yes. It has me worried."

Dover shook his head. "The coroner said that it wasn't mummified the way a body is prepared in Egypt. The corpse was complete, no organs had been removed, or anything like that. But it had been dried in some way."

Paige found the subject creepy, but the discussion of the possible mummification might point right at her missing uncle.

She had to try to find out what evidence they had. "It's been a long time, you said, since she died. Why do they think her body dried out in something other than a normal way?"

"Natron. It was found in the bag with the corpse. And several other bags of it were found in the false wall of the closet."

Paige wracked her brain. "Natron. I've heard of it but I can't exactly remember what it is or what it's for."

Dover looked at his notes again. "It's a naturally occurring mixture of salt and baking soda—sodium bicarbonate. It's found along the banks of the Nile. And a solution of it was used to soak bodies for mummification, so they wouldn't decompose."

"Could a person mix that solution here?"

"Yes."

Paige had an image of a mad scientist brewing it up over a Bunsen burner. "Why do you think someone wanted to mummify Ilke's body?"

"I asked the same question. The medical examiner thinks it was for the same reason as in ancient Egypt. So the body wouldn't decompose. That would have brought people with questions."

The earlier image in Paige's mind was replaced by one even more grotesque. "It seems so barbaric. Soaking her body in solution and then sticking her in the wall."

"Oh, I'm sorry," said Dover, "I didn't mean to make you think she was soaked in the solution. It was just found in crystal form, in ten cheesecloth bags in and around the garbage bag she was wrapped in. And unfortunately, there were no finger prints anywhere."

"Why didn't whoever did it just bury her?"

"Your friend Mrs. Morris asked the same questions. I really

should not be discussing this with either of you," said Dover. "But I will tell you that the only theory that fits would be that when she was killed, it was winter and impossible to dig a grave, at least without heavy equipment. Since the killer apparently thought it was necessary to hide her in the closet, she had to be sufficiently unlikely to cause a future problem. The coroner wasn't sure, but he said that the way the body was dried, it might never have been discovered, but for the flood."

Paige shivered violently at the thought of the body being in her house without her knowledge. She thought back to the little she knew of the subject. "I thought that those bodies only stayed mummified, not decomposing, if there was an arid climate. This is definitely not one. Wouldn't something have started to happen, even inside the wall? Even if we didn't overflow the tub?"

"All I can say is it didn't. The coroner was surprised but specific. Until the water came from the bathtub, that body was dry. Although—"

"What?"

"He said there was a possibility that somehow, some moisture had started to make its way in. Not enough to cause a detectable problem, at least not yet. There was some, er, mold. It was as if the extreme dryness had somehow ended. But it was only in the area of the frostbite."

Paige thought back to the body and those missing fingers. "Frostbite?"

"She was apparently exposed to severe cold prior to death."

"That poor woman. How she must have suffered."

Dover nodded. "I only told you this because you live in that house." He put down the pen he'd been holding and leaned back in his chair. "Here's where we are. Discounting the possibility of your uncle being involved," he held up his hand as

Paige opened her mouth to protest. "I'm not saying he is," he continued. "In fact, we're operating on the theory that he is not. We're not even sure he was really in town anytime in the last year."

"Good."

Dover took another deep breath and started again. "As I previously mentioned, it is possible that Ilke went to your uncle's house the day she disappeared. She might have walked in on someone, someone who should not have been there. That person, caught by surprise, might have hit her over the head, rendering her unconscious, and moved her somewhere else, possibly one of the outbuildings on the property. That's probably where she was shot. We're still analyzing data from a few of them, hoping to find some evidence, but I can tell you there was no evidence in your house."

He didn't say it, but Paige knew he meant blood, at the very least.

"Maybe it was too cold to bury her," he went on, "and the person, possibly a squatter, built the closet to hide her body. He could have found out how to keep it from decaying on the Internet. He certainly wouldn't want to live in the house with it."

"Where were the Fosters all this time?" Paige asked. "I thought they were the caretakers for my uncle."

"Yes, but when he travels, he doesn't expect them to come into the house. Mr. Foster doesn't even plow the drive if your uncle is out of town."

"But wouldn't they have noticed tire tracks?"

"Yes, they would. But last winter they went to Florida for two months. They didn't arrange for anyone else to help out because they were told that your uncle would be gone."

A hard lump formed in Paige's stomach. Was he accusing Uncle Ted? She forced her mind to work out other possibilities.

"But where would all her stuff have gone? Quin said it was gone by the time he got home from Albany."

"It was probably plenty of time for the killer to drive over to their house and empty it out. But it means she went to your uncle's house and was attacked almost right after Mr. Wyatt left."

"How would the killer get back to Quin's?"

"Probably took Ilke's car. That way, if he was caught, he could say she sent him."

"But how would he know where she lived? Are you saying he knew her?"

"Not necessarily. He could have found her address on her driver's license. She was a registered New York driver, according to the DMV. And he would have had her keys." He shook his head, and sighed. "I don't know. It's all speculation. But we've had problems with squatters before. And all our digging hasn't turned up anything else."

"And then he just came back to my uncle's house and lived there, building the closet and stuffing her into it?"

"It's possible."

"What made him leave?"

"He probably left in the spring. There would be a lot more activity out by the house and on the lake, and he knew he had to get out of there. He might have even left in Ilke's car."

"So he's out of town?"

"Maybe. Or he could be the dead drifter I told Mrs. Morris about. But if not, I think you should consider that he could come back."

"Surely he wouldn't be so brazen."

"Probably not. But I want you to watch yourself. It may not have been a squatter at all. It could have been someone you see every day."

Paige preferred to think the killer was long gone. She stood up to go. "I'll be fine. I'll keep my eyes open."

Sheriff Dover held the door for her. "Do that. And call me if anything looks even a centimeter out of place."

Chapter Eleven

Mike ran straight to the computer when they got home from school and started one of his games. Life was returning to normal. Paige went into the kitchen to make dinner. But she found herself unable to tear her eyes away from the ruins of the closet. The seepage from the water had dried out, leaving the wood warped. A smell of decaying lumber drifted up from the floor.

The persistent odor nauseated her, reminding her of Ilke's remains. It bothered her so much that after dinner she filled a plastic container with baking soda. She placed it near the torn up ruins, hoping there wasn't just too much there to neutralize.

Mike came in and saw what she was doing. "You don't like being in the kitchen, either," he said.

She had to hand it to him, he was observant. "It's just that it's such a mess. While you work on your math problems, I'm going to start cleaning it up."

"I could help," Mike offered.

"Okay, but only after your homework is done. Deal?"

A smile split his face. "Yes, Mom."

She watched him go. He was such a joy to her that at a time like this she felt as if her heart would swell up and burst from love.

And his father was missing it all. She shuddered. That unwanted thought, as always, brought up strong emotions. Paige's shock at hearing her husband had suffered a heart attack and her grief when he died, had turned into something dark and dismal. He'd been with another woman when it occurred, and Paige thought she would never get over it. She'd known it would be a long time before she'd let a man get close to her again. And maybe even longer before she could learn to trust. But lately she wished she could. A restlessness had taken over her since Ilke's body was found. She wanted to get death and mourning out of her life forever and start to live again.

Shaking herself to get on with it, she carried the plates into the kitchen and loaded them into the dishwasher. After a quick check on Mike, she set to work on the mess.

She quickly filled a large garbage bag as she pried off the smaller smashed pieces of wood. The larger pieces she just threw in a pile out the back door, intending to cover them over with a tarp she'd seen in the carriage house. She had to close the kitchen door to keep Balto from sniffing the wreckage and, in just over a fifteen minutes, had cleaned at least half of it.

"Mom," Mike called. "I'm ready."

Paige went into the den and looked at his homework. "Okay," she said. "Let's get to work. You hold the bag for me and I'll put the wood in."

It went much quicker with Mike helping, but Paige worried that he might get a splinter and sent him to get some work gloves she used for gardening. They were several sizes too big for him, but he put them on anyway.

She bent down to pick up the bag of rubble. It was much heavier than she'd expected and it slipped, causing a rather long piece of wood with a nail in it to hit her. She felt a searing pain in her forehead. "Ow."

"Are you okay, Mom?"

She gritted her teeth. "I'm fine. It's just a scratch." She grabbed a paper towel and after putting some water on it pressed it up against her forehead. "This may take awhile. Why don't you go upstairs and get ready for bed?"

Mike looked pale but didn't argue. "Okay." He left the room, and a minute later, Paige heard him talking. She couldn't make out what he was saying.

"Did you say something, honey?"

"Nothing Mom. I'm going up now."

The blood kept coming so Paige put pressure on it. She tried to see it in the mirror in the powder room. Even though it was small, it kept bleeding profusely. She washed it again, put some ointment on it and held another paper towel on it. After five minutes she thought it had stopped, so she took a broom to sweep up the last bits of wood on the floor.

A small chunk she was sweeping suddenly disappeared. Paige squatted down and looked to see where it might have gone. She found a hole, a little over two inches in diameter, in the floor. It had neat edges, as if it had been cut with a hole saw.

When she stood back up she wished she had done it more slowly because she was momentarily dizzy. Telling herself she'd be able to rest soon, she tried to think of a way to prevent anything else from falling into the hole. She found a well-chewed tennis ball of Balto's and put it into the hole. It was a good fit and didn't roll away the few times she brushed it with the broom while she finished sweeping. But before she wrestled that last bag of debris out the door, she went to find that piece of wood in the basement, so she could put it into the bag.

The laundry room was directly under the kitchen, Paige thought, so she went down there. There was no piece of wood on the basement floor, though, and she couldn't see exactly where the hole was. Maybe the ball blocked any light that might have filtered down from the kitchen through the hole, or maybe not, but she couldn't see it at all.

"Are you down there, Mom?" Mike called.

"Yes. I'm coming up." Halfway up, she said, "Are you ready for bed?" When she stepped into the kitchen, expecting to see Mike in his pajamas, she ran smack into Noah Oliver. "What are you doing here?" she gasped.

"Mike called and said you had a problem."

She looked at Mike for confirmation. "We had his number on speed dial," he said. "You needed help."

Paige put her hand to her head and felt blood. "It's nothing, really. I'm okay."

"You're bleeding, Mom," Mike pointed out. He looked at Noah. "Please help her."

"Let's have a look," Noah said softly.

"You're a veterinarian," Paige argued.

"He's an EMT too," Mike reminded her. "I wanted to be sure you're okay."

Paige looked into Noah's warm brown eyes. "Thank you for coming, but I'm sure it's fine. I figured it would stop bleeding after a while. You know how head wounds are." Mike started to say something, so Paige gave in. "But if you want to take a look."

Tenderly, Noah sat her down on a kitchen chair and leaned her back, letting the light above the table illuminate her cut. He gently pushed back her hair and inspected her head. She was so close to him she could feel the warmth of his body. Whether it was because of how near he was, or her head wound, Paige felt distinctly lightheaded.

"I think it'll be okay," he said. "It isn't deep. A butterfly bandage should be sufficient. When was your last tetanus shot?"

Paige still remembered her sore arm. "Two years ago."

"Okay then." He sat Paige down on one of the kitchen chairs and gently washed the wound again, letting Mike look on.

"I'll need some things from my emergency kit." He stood up to go out.

"Can I get it?" Mike asked.

Noah nodded and Mike went out to his truck. While they waited for him to come back, Noah frowned at Paige. "I told you I'd take care of the closet. I'm surprised both of you don't have more cuts. Or splinters."

"I couldn't stand looking at it or smelling the wood. It was making me sick."

"You should have called me."

"It isn't your responsibility, it's mine."

Mike returned and Noah took the supplies. As he delicately bandaged her head, he estimated how long the wound would take to heal and gave her some instructions. "If you have any concerns, and I can well understand if you do, see a doctor. I can recommend some good ones if you haven't found one yet."

Paige had lined one up for Mike, but hadn't made a doctor for herself a priority. Right now the whole thing seemed like a little problem blown out of proportion and she was feeling a bit sheepish. "Okay."

"Great," said Mike, seeming satisfied. He turned to Paige. "Is it okay if I go to bed now?"

Paige looked at the clock and was surprised to find it was nearly ten. "Oh my," she said, "I'll be up to say goodnight right away."

He ran out and Paige stood up, ready to walk Noah to the door. "I can't thank you enough," she said. She suddenly felt uncomfortable, after having been so close to him for so many minutes. A brief memory of how he'd looked with his shirt off while he delivered that calf went fleetingly through her mind. It didn't seem right to have those thoughts, somehow, not quite like a doctor/patient relationship, especially since she was not his usual species of patient.

But for some reason her body seemed drawn to Noah's, and not just because he was there to help her. Wasn't it too soon after Michael's death to be feeling this attraction to another man?

When he left, she again felt as if her body had a mind of its own and was trying to go out the door with him. She hadn't felt like that in so long. She told herself it was just because he was very nice and she was very tired. It was time to go to bed.

But first she had to turn out the lights. She went through the living room, the dining room, and to the top of the basement steps, flicking switches. When she got into the kitchen and saw the tennis ball in the hole in the floor, she sighed. Something would have to be done about that too. Sooner or later Balto would reclaim the ball, and the hole would be open again.

She cut a piece of stiff cardboard from one of the boxes in the basement that she hadn't yet unpacked. She didn't know why she even bothered bringing the box full of economic textbooks from Michael's office. She should have donated them or thrown them out, but she'd never found the time and, when they moved, moved them right along with the rest of their things. Now the box would be missing part of its top, but it didn't really matter. Next Saturday, she told herself, she'd try to take it all to the recycling center.

She taped the cardboard to the floor, covering the hole, and pulled a kitchen chair over, placing it so it straddled the cardboard as added protection. It didn't look good, that piece of card-board and the duct tape in the middle of an otherwise beautiful oak tongue-and-groove floor, but it didn't matter. It would be fixed.

Halfway up the stairs, the phone rang. She had to race down again and back into the kitchen to get it before it woke Mike up. "Hello?" she said, expecting it to be a wrong number.

"Dr. Griffin? This is Aurora Dillon." Her voice sounded frightened. "You said I could call if I had a problem."

"What's wrong?"

"I heard noises. Down near the cars."

"Are you sure it wasn't an animal?"

"No. It might have been. I just don't know. The flood lights won't work so I got a big flashlight and went out on the front deck. Whatever it was ran away, but I'm really scared. It's so dark and the wind is making strange noises.

Paige thought she could understand how Aurora, a city girl, might be afraid of the long shadows and dark places up in the Adirondacks, when the city was always full of light. Her father should be able to make her feel safe, but it sounded as if he wasn't there. "Will your father be home soon?" Paige asked.

"He had to go to the Caribbean this week."

"The woman who is supposed to be with you isn't there?"

"No. She got a call that her sister was sick and she left."

"Can you call her?"

There was a pause. Paige decided the answer must be no. "Do you want me to come get you? I'd have to wake Mike up, but he could sleep in the car."

"No. I got my license a few days ago. I can drive there if it's okay with you."

"It's so dark out. I'd feel better if you let me get you."

"I'll be okay. Don't wake Mike. That poor kid has been

going through so much. I wouldn't want to put him through any more."

Paige was torn. She worried about Aurora driving so late, and she sounded so frightened, but Aurora was right; it would be better to let Mike sleep. "All right. Make some noise to scare away the animals before you go out. You can stay over tonight and we'll make sure to fix your light tomorrow."

Aurora's house was only ten minutes from Paige's. When Paige was finished setting up a room for Aurora she realized that twenty minutes had passed. There was still no sign of her, so she called the house to see if the girl had changed her mind. There was no answer. But she reasoned Aurora hadn't actually left right away, since she probably had to pack. It was possible she left just a second before Paige tried to call.

She started pacing.

Ten minutes later, Paige was really scared. She'd been staring out the door, willing headlights to appear. Even allowing for Aurora passing the dirt road Paige lived on in the dark, she should have been there by then. With shaking hands, Paige dialed the police.

They called her back fifteen minutes later. "We found the car and the girl," said the officer. "Her car went off the road. It's a good thing you called us. She could have been out there all night."

Paige gripped the receiver. "Was she hurt?"

"We're waiting for the emergency vehicle now. She has to be transported to the hospital."

"The one in E-town?"

"No. Lake Placid. Their orthopedics department can better handle the broken bones."

Perspiration broke out on Paige's forehead. "How serious is it?"

"I can't say for sure. She's unconscious. And very banged up. Do you know where we can reach her folks? They're going to need to sign for the procedures."

"Her mother left the family and her father is away. I don't know how to reach him."

"There may be a number in the house," said the officer. "We'll check it out."

"Wait! She said someone or something was hanging around near the cars tonight. She was frightened. That was why she was coming here."

His voice changed from calming to alert. "We'll look into that too."

Paige's hands shook as she punched in the number for Mrs. Foster down the road. Although she let it ring ten times, there was no answer. Then she thought of calling Jolene.

"I'm so sorry to be calling at this hour," Paige said. "But I have to get to the hospital. Aurora has been in an accident. I have to go to her. She has no one else."

"Bring Mike here. I'll keep the light on for you."

Paige felt so guilty waking and keeping Jolene up. She had to open her shop at 6 A.M. so she had to get up really early to start baking. For that matter, so would Mike. Paige rushed to get his clothes together and woke him up enough to explain briefly and get him into the car. Just as she was leaving, she took the top off Balto's dry food container. He'd have to feed himself.

A half hour later, after copious apologies and minimal explanation, especially about the bandage on her head, Paige was back on the road, headed for Lake Placid.

Chapter Twelve

Paige drove as fast as she dared on the unlit winding roads. A three-quarter moon cast long shadows from the pine trees, and the ski jump looked sinister. It was off the side of the road as she approached the town of Lake Placid. Yet the sight of it was a relief. What had seemed like a long trip during the day seemed endless at night. But finally Paige, following the blue-and-white H signs, saw the lights of the squat hospital.

She ran into the emergency entrance and found that Aurora was in radiology. The admitting nurse wouldn't tell her any more until she answered some questions.

"Were you involved in the accident too?" asked the nurse, eyeing the bandage on Paige's head with her pen poised over a clipboard.

"No."

"We've been unable to contact her parents," said the woman, skipping to the next order of business. "Do you know where they can be reached?"

Paige shook her head. "I told the officer when he called

me that her father was away and her mother doesn't live with the family right now. They don't even know where she is." She stopped to take a breath. "Aurora must have written down the number for her father somewhere. Maybe I should go check her house?"

"That won't be necessary," said a voice behind Paige. She turned and saw Sheriff Dover. "We've sent someone to check. As soon as we get a number, we'll let the hospital know so the doctor can call."

The nurse nodded and walked away. Paige was about to go to the waiting room when Sheriff Dover stopped her. "Were you in the accident too?"

Paige touched the bandage on her head. "No. I got in my own way. It's nothing. Do you know what happened to Aurora?"

"I was hoping you could tell me."

Paige was suddenly weary. "Could we sit down?"

Dover led the way to a small waiting room. "Tell me what you know."

"Aurora called me," Paige said. "She told me there was a noise outside, near the cars, and that she was frightened. I offered to go get her, but she said she could drive and then we wouldn't have to wake Mike. My son," she reminded Dover. "He's nine." Paige sighed, her head dropping back as she looked up hopelessly at the ceiling. "I ended up waking him anyway"—she bit her lip when it started to quiver—"and now Aurora is . . ." She couldn't finish.

"It's okay," said Dover. "I'm going to get some coffee. It will be a long night."

Paige went along with him and they returned to the lounge a few minutes later with two cups. They sat down on the hard plastic chairs opposite each other.

"Have you known Aurora a long time?" Dover asked.

"No," said Paige, realizing she'd only known her since the beginning of school—two-and-a-half months at most. She explained their relationship to the sheriff, including that Aurora was Mike's babysitter, and what she knew of the family situation. Paige's voice shook as she spoke of Aurora's mother.

He took a drink of his coffee, drained the cup, and put it on the table next to him. "I imagine we both see things we wouldn't want our families to experience." He looked back at her just as she wiped away a tear.

His radio went off and he spoke into it. "Good. Give me the number." He wrote it down and stood up. "I'll be right back. I just want to give this phone number to that nurse."

Paige watched him walk away and wondered how long it would take Aurora's father to get there. A doctor walked through the opposite door and seemed to be looking around. He came toward her.

"Are you Aurora's mother?"

"No. Just a friend. Her parents aren't here."

"I'm Dr. Pierre. I wanted to tell them how she is."

"Could you please tell me? I've been so worried."

"Doctor," said Dover, once again behind Paige. "I've given the number where her father can be reached to the nurse. But would you tell us her condition?"

The doctor looked at Dover and nodded. "She will be okay. She has a broken leg and a broken arm. I'll have to repair the arm surgically, inserting both an internal and external rod, because it was essentially smashed in the accident, but I don't believe there was any nerve damage. She also may have a concussion. We're keeping an eye on that. When she wakes up, we'll know more. Now, if you'll excuse me, I'm going to call her father."

Dover's radio went off again as Paige watched the doctor go

toward the desk for the phone number. When she turned back, Dover looked angry. "Her brakes were tampered with," he said. "That's why she went off the road at that curve. It's at the bottom of a ten percent grade, and she couldn't slow down."

"How do you know someone tampered with her brakes?" Paige asked.

"Because they can't drain themselves of fluid. The officer went back to the house and checked the other car. It also had no fluid."

"Why would someone do that?"

"That's what we have to find out."

Paige was finally allowed to go see Aurora at 6:30 in the morning. By then she was full of coffee and exhausted, having only dozed for a half hour around three.

The girl was bandaged around her head and her left eye was swollen shut. Her leg was in a cast and her arm hung suspended in traction. She lay in a pediatric room, with bright colors on the walls and large cartoon characters, but she was pale, almost as white as the sheets.

"How are you feeling?" Paige asked, going close to the bed. When Aurora didn't answer she said, "I'm so sorry. I should have picked you up."

Aurora moaned. "Daddy?"

"He's on his way. I spoke to him a little while ago." He was already at the airport in San Juan, promising to get the first plane he could to New York. Then he'd have to take a commuter flight from there to Burlington and rent a car for the rest of the trip. The best case scenario wouldn't get him there until evening.

A nurse came in and gave Aurora a sedative. "She'll sleep for a long time," she told Paige. "Maybe you could come back later."

"I will." Paige waited until Aurora fell asleep, listening for a moment to her deep, even breathing. Then she raced home to shower and change for school. With difficulty she managed to take off the outer covering of her bandage and hide the butterfly bandage with her hair.

Judy was full of questions when Paige arrived at school. But for once, she didn't sound as if she wanted juicy details, she sounded genuinely concerned. "Will she be okay?" she asked.

"I think so. But it will be a long convalescence."

At 2:00, Paige called Jolene and asked if Mike could stay with her for the afternoon. She'd already talked to Luke's mother, Katie, who was unable to watch Mike but could drop him somewhere. Rather than make several more calls and impose on someone, she took the easy way out. She only hoped Jolene wouldn't mind.

"I have to go back to the hospital," she explained to Jolene. "I want to stay until her father comes. Please tell Mike I'll be there as soon as I can."

"Sure," said Jolene. "Don't worry about it. I'll feed him and get him started on his homework and you can pick him up at my house when you're ready."

Paige went into Aurora's room to check on her every few minutes. Several times she heard her moaning in her sleep, and once she cried out for her mother. Paige thought her heart would break.

When Aurora showed signs of waking up again at 4:30, Paige went into her room and sat down.

"How do you feel now?" Paige asked.

"My head hurts, and my arm—" she broke off, as she looked at it where it hung above her. Steel rods protruded through her skin, which was just about every color of the rainbow, swollen and grotesque, but Aurora couldn't see how bad it was because it was screened with sheets. "What the . . . ?"

"You were pretty badly hurt," said Paige. "But the doctor said you will make a full recovery."

Sweat stood out on Aurora's forehead and she nervously licked her parched lips. Paige poured her some water into a cup and held the bent straw to her lips. The girl could only take a few small sips before she lay back against the pillow. "I was being so careful," she said, staring at her arm in disbelief. "I wasn't going fast, but then I picked up speed. And I couldn't slow down!"

Paige didn't want to tell her that the brakes were to blame. Although it might make her feel better that the accident wasn't her fault, she didn't need the news that someone wanted to hurt her or her father. Smoothing her blanket, Paige said, "Shh. It's all right now. You're safe here."

A nurse came in to check Aurora's vital signs at 7:00 and Paige found herself out in the hall. Sheriff Dover was just turning the corner. "I heard she woke up," he said. "Did she tell you anything?"

"I didn't ask. She's in no condition to talk about what happened."

"We really need to find out what she saw. Whatever spooked her might help us find out who did it."

"Can't you wait?"

Dover frowned. "Assuming this wasn't a prank, she could be in real danger. Even if it was a prank, and whoever did it was unaware of how dangerous it would be, that person should be held accountable."

Paige shivered, not wanting to believe that whoever did it wanted to hurt Aurora. From what she'd seen, the girl was well liked in the high school. Even the cliques of girls who had grown up together seemed to regard her as tolerable. That was high praise in this situation. And few other people in the county were likely to even know of her existence.

Suddenly Paige became aware that Sheriff Dover was still speaking to her. "Will you go in to see her with me? She might feel more comfortable than with a nurse she doesn't know."

"Of course." She followed the sheriff into Aurora's room and introduced him to the teenager.

"I really don't know what happened," she said. "I'm pretty sure it was just an accident. I just got my license last week but I practiced a lot."

"It wasn't your fault," said Sheriff Dover. "You had brake trouble."

Aurora's eyes widened. "Oh. Well, maybe my dad won't kill me when he gets here."

Dover smiled. "Your dad will probably squeeze you nearly to death, not because he's angry, but because he's so happy you are alive. I'm a dad. I know."

An uncertain smile crossed Aurora's lips, but only momentarily. "If you know what happened," she asked, "why are you here?"

Dover cleared his throat. "It looks like someone may have done something to your brakes. And you told Dr. Griffin that you saw someone out near the cars."

Aurora scowled. "I'm not sure what I saw. It could have been an animal." Paige remembered what Aurora had said and knew she didn't believe that.

Dover didn't seem to either. "An animal didn't do this."

"I don't think I can help you. I didn't see anything for sure, I just thought I saw somebody moving in those shadows." Almost to herself she added, "They always scare me. The trees make them, I know, but they look like they are giants. I told my mom, last year."

Paige moved her stool closer to Aurora and took her good hand. She seemed like a little child, in so much pain, scared and needing her mother—who would not be there for her.

"Does your house have floodlights?" asked Dover.

"Yes," Paige said, answering for her. They always popped on when she drove into the driveway to pick up or drop off Aurora.

"Were they on last night?"

Aurora blinked. "No, they didn't go on. Maybe they burned out."

Dover, who sat behind Paige, leaned forward and said quietly, "That's not what my officer said. There were no lights. The bulbs were too loose to make a connection. When he tightened them, they went right on, casting enough light to prevent those shadows."

Paige bit her lip. She was about to speak when the door opened and Aurora's father came in.

"Daddy!" she said, and promptly burst into tears.

Mr. Dillon swept Paige and Sheriff Dover aside on his way to the bed.

Dover's predictions were correct. Mr. Dillon hugged his daughter, gently but firmly. "Don't worry," he said, holding her tight, "Daddy is here."

He stood back from the bed and looked at her carefully. "I was so worried. Your housekeeper should never have left you alone," he growled, anger distorting his face. He had the look of someone haunted by memories. "I shouldn't have left you up here by yourself." He turned away, whispering with heart-wrenching grief, "Oh, God, what have I done?"

"It wasn't your fault, Daddy," Aurora said. "You shouldn't feel guilty. I had a problem with the brakes."

"What do you mean? The brakes on both cars are perfect. I had them serviced when they put the snow tires back on." He stomped around, reminding Paige of so many New Yorkers. "I'm gonna sue those mechanics. You could've been killed."

Aurora began to cry.

"Sir," said Sheriff Dover. He introduced himself. "If I may, I'd like to talk with you outside."

The two men left the room, and Paige was alone with Aurora. Now that her father was back, she'd regained some color and a bit of energy. "I'm going to be out of school for a while, Dr. Griffin," she said.

"I guess so." She was relieved that Aurora had enough strength to worry about her studies. "We'll make arrangements for you to keep up with your school work."

"Thanks so much for staying with me. I really appreciate it. Mike must be so worried. You should go tell him I'm okay."

"I'll do that. You get some rest and I'll visit you soon." She went out, past Aurora's father and the sheriff, who were in serious conversation, into the cold night air.

It took less than forty-five minutes to get to Jolene's. "You look like you could use a hot meal," she said. "Come inside."

Paige gratefully accepted. "Mike," she called. "I'm here."

Mike came running. "How is Aurora?" he asked. "Does she have a cast?" One of the boys in his class had broken his arm and all the other children had signed it at least three times each. Or at least Mike had.

"She certainly does." Paige could only guess what interest that scaffolding on Aurora's arm would generate.

"Oh, neat! Can I see her?"

"Not until she comes home from the hospital," Paige said. "And that might be a while."

Mike frowned. "Is she going to get better?"

"Oh, yes, honey," Paige said, fighting the urge to pick him up and hug him close. He'd made it clear he didn't like that mushy stuff in front of outsiders. "She'll get better soon, you'll see."

"Come and get it," Jolene announced from the kitchen.

Paige found the table set for one, with a steaming plate of

stew and some crusty bread. Jolene had a cup of tea with her while she ate.

When Mike was out of earshot, she asked about Aurora and the accident, and Paige told her what she could.

"I can't thank you enough for the dinner," Paige said, "and for watching Mike."

"My pleasure. I'll get his things." She went out, leaving Paige alone to gather her strength.

"Thank you, Ms. Valley," Mike said, as he went out the door.

"You're welcome anytime," said Jolene. It was almost enough to make Paige lose her composure and give in to tears, but she couldn't do that, not in front of her son.

Wally knew the minute she heard Paige's voice that there was trouble. She braced herself, already thinking of how soon she could get back up to the Adirondacks. "What's wrong?"

"Do you remember Aurora Dillon?"

Catching her breath, Wally said, "Yes." She had encouraged Paige to hire Aurora to sit for Mike, as a way for the two kids from the city to deal with being out of place. She and Paige had hoped it would be helpful for both children. "What happened?"

Paige's explanation of the accident and the cut brake lines did nothing to calm Wally. "I thought Aurora was in the city last winter," she said when Paige was done.

"What are you talking about?" Paige asked. "This just happened."

"I understand that," Wally said. "But I'm wondering if the accident was connected to Ilke, and I was sure the police said she was murdered last winter. I wanted to know if somehow Aurora was there and might have witnessed something, and that's why, now that the murder is out in the open, the murderer wanted to get Aurora out of the way."

"You can't be serious."

"I am. It's possible. And I think you need to get out of there, at least until the criminal is caught."

"I can't do that. I have a job. I'm trying to make a life for myself and I can't just abandon it."

"I'm sorry," said Wally. "I understand. Just promise me you'll be careful."

"I promise."

That did nothing to appease Wally, but she had to let it go. "Tell me how Mike is doing," she said.

"He was shook up about the accident. Thank goodness for Jolene. She took care of him while I went to see Aurora."

Wally's heart went out to the motherless girl. "I'm glad you could be there with her. Will her father be staying around now?"

"It's hard to say. Mr. Dillon really was upset about Aurora, but he does a lot of things regarding her welfare that I wouldn't do, and I know you wouldn't either."

That was something of an understatement. Wally knew she would never, in a million years, have left her children to fend for themselves at Aurora's age.

"Right. How are things going otherwise?" Wally asked.

"Okay. The music group is sounding better and we're talking about having a little concert. But it will be hard to get to rehearsal, since Aurora always sat for us."

That wasn't the question Wally wanted the answer to, but she went along and thought of a solution. "Your house is probably big enough to have rehearsals there."

"Great idea. I'll suggest it."

"How's the job?" Wally asked, which was still not the question she wanted the answer to, but she didn't want to appear to be prying and ask it outright.

"Good."

Wally was hoping to hear about Paige and one of those two eligible men, Noah and Quin, but she'd have to settle for the answers Paige was willing to give. "Have you told your uncle about Ilke?"

"I can't reach him. I've tried every way I could think of."

She didn't sound worried, just sort of annoyed, so Wally didn't push it. It was common for Ted to disappear—he rarely thought about the people who might be wondering where he was. "I'm only asking because I wonder if they finished whatever they were working on before Ilke was killed. It would seem to me that it would have come out sooner if someone was waiting for a manuscript or something."

"I could try to look into it, if you think it's important."

"Good," Wally said. "It might tell us something, who knows?"

After Wally hung up she went to find Nate. She wanted to see if her suspicions about the coincidence of Aurora's car wreck and Ilke's murder seemed as unlikely to him as it did to Paige.

"So do you think I should call Sheriff Dover?" she asked, when she had finished explaining the story.

Nate gave her a long blue-green-eyed stare. "No. But you will do it anyway, so I guess I should be grateful you chose to make it look as if you cared about my opinion."

Wally laughed and held up her thumb and index finger, a half inch apart. "You came this close to getting it to look like I listen to you. All you had to do was say yes." She gave him a hug. "I won't bother him for long, I'll just quickly point out that it's possible they are connected. He can at least look into whether Aurora was up there last winter and whether she might have seen something."

Five minutes later Wally was off the phone again. "What did he say?" asked Nate.

"He said I'm a smart woman, and he'll look into it right away."

"He's right. Now what?"

"Now I will try not to look smug."

Chapter Thirteen

On Saturday morning, Mike went to spend the day with Luke. Katie was happy to watch them both, since this was likely to be one of the last days the boys could be outside before winter. Paige promised to return the favor, as soon as things quieted down.

Mike had made several friends since moving to town and he was no longer so angry about missing his friends in New York. Paige was almost envious, but she knew she shouldn't be. She was lucky to have formed a strong relationship with her new friend, Jolene. Being stuck in upstate New York without a good friend would have been awful, she knew. It took Paige, who was admittedly shy, a while to get close to people. Jolene's exuberant camaraderie made all the difference.

Paige was ready to take some time for herself. But as soon as she'd made the decision, her phone rang. It was Quin. He was sounding much better these days, Paige thought. At the beginning, after the discovery of his fiancée's body, he seemed laden with the guilt of his having assumed Ilke left him. Few people came to call and offer their support. It wasn't clear whether they stayed away because the death had actually been so long before, or because Quin had maintained for so long that Ilke had run away and that he hadn't tried to go after her, even though he had tried to find her for months. But with each successive week, he was opening up more.

"I thought you might like to get out," he said. "Can you meet me at my hotel?"

She'd planned to visit Aurora in the afternoon, which was near the hotel, so she accepted happily. It was good to know that Quin was back to work and trying to put his pain behind him.

When she arrived at Quin's hotel, she was ushered into his office. She barely had time to look at the interior decor of the lobby, but she saw that it was a good combination of cosmopolitan and Adirondack. There were no animal heads on the walls, which pleased Paige.

His office was very similar in style to his house. The rich mahogany of his desk and parquet floor was accented by a leather couch and chairs, and burnished brass lamps. A fire crackled in the fireplace on an adjoining wall.

"Have a seat," Quin said, holding his hand over the receiver of his telephone. "I'll be right with you."

Paige tried not to listen to the conversation but Quin was speaking loudly, and progressively more angrily. "I told her she had to have that report on my desk this morning," he said, barely pausing to listen to the person on the other end.

"I don't care if the computers were down all day yesterday. That isn't my problem. I need the projections right away."

Paige wished she could leave the room. She'd never seen Quin so angry.

"Tell her she's fired," he said a second later. "Tell that witch to pack her desk and leave. I want her escorted out in fifteen minutes." He gripped the phone as he listened to the response.

"Don't argue with me, unless you want to leave too," Quin warned. "I don't want any incompetent, weak people working for me." He slammed the phone down and glowered at the top of his desk.

A moment later, he gave her a warm hello. "I'll give you a tour when we're done talking," he said, "and then we'll go have some lunch. Okay?"

"Sounds good," Paige said, wishing she could change gears so easily. The call and the poor fired woman, unfairly in her opinion, although she didn't have all the facts, weighed on her mind.

Paige carefully brought up a topic that had been on her mind. She hated to do it, but she had to ask about the book Ilke was helping Ted with. She had tried to figure out a way to avoid it, by calling the publisher. But she couldn't get through to the publisher for days, and when she finally did, she found out that Ted hadn't signed with them for his newest book. "He took a big advance from someone else," said the editor. "After all I did for him." He was unwilling to tell Paige anything else.

She took a deep breath and asked Quin about the book.

"I don't know," said Quin. "I thought it was done and that was why Ted was leaving town. But I thought so many things that were wrong."

The ticking of the mantle clock was the only sound in the room for a few moments. Paige glanced at it and saw that it was nearly 12:00.

Quin looked up. "Enough of this depressing subject. It's time for lunch. Let's go somewhere to eat."

Paige said, "Sure. But I'd like to freshen up a bit. Can you point the way?"

Quin showed her where to go, and she told him she'd be back in a minute. But when she went back to his office, his door was closed and she heard angry voices.

"You're way overextended," said a man. "You can't afford the changes you already made, and now you want more. They won't bring in any more income."

"I don't care what you say," said Quin, his own voice as angry as it was earlier. "Marissa put up with you and your penny-pinching. I don't have to."

"If it wasn't for Marissa," the man said, "you'd be out on the street. And if you keep spending money this way, you will be sooner or later. Your grandmother made me promise to keep your spending habits under control. Those last three schemes of yours nearly bankrupted us."

"Me," said Quin. "It's my hotel, not yours."

"Then you have everything to lose."

"I'll think about what you said," said Quin, still sounding angry. "But don't cancel those orders until I tell you to."

The door opened and Paige, who had scurried to a chair in the lobby, smiled at Quin. He motioned her to come back to the office.

He showed no evidence of the altercation, other than a deeper color in his face. "We'll go for a walk first," he said, handing her coat to her and taking his own. "It's a nice day outside, and we'll window-shop and take our time. Then we'll find a restaurant and have a long, leisurely lunch." Quin stopped midway to the door. "Is something wrong?"

"You remember that I introduced you to Aurora Dillon?"

"Yes."

They had been outside a store in Lake Placid on an early October day that was so cold they'd all worn their winter coats. Mike had invited Aurora before consulting Paige. It wasn't as if she minded, she liked the girl, but she worried that people might think it wrong, given her position. There was nothing she could do, though, since Mike had spoken up first, so she decided to enjoy the outing and worry about repercussions later.

Mike's cheeks were red with cold, as were Aurora's, nearly matching the scarlet patches on her bright multicolored ski jacket. Quin had come along walking quickly but he stopped short when he saw them standing on the street. He'd looked stunned and Paige had called his name a few times before he looked at her and said hello.

"Sorry," he apologized, "I was lost in thought." He nodded at Aurora. "Who is your friend?"

"Aurora is a fellow New York City transplant," Paige had explained. "She sits for Mike sometimes and we're exploring the area together."

Quin smiled. "Oh, you haven't lived up here before?"

"Well, yes," Aurora said, shyly. "Every summer. But I haven't gone to school here."

"Winters can be rough," Quin warned.

"I know," Aurora assured him. "I've been up here in the winter on vacations."

Quin frowned. "I'd love to stay and talk, but I'm very busy," he had said that day, before hurrying away.

Now he said, "You're going to visit your babysitter in the hospital?"

Paige didn't tell him she felt a lot closer to Aurora than a simple babysitter/parent relationship. She just nodded, trying to get the painful words out. "She was seriously injured the other day. She's in traction."

"I think I read about that in the paper, but there weren't many details. Is she going to be all right?"

"The doctor thinks so."

Quin frowned. "It was a terrible thing, wasn't it? What exactly happened?"

Paige told him about the accident as they walked down the main street of Lake Placid. "Although," she concluded, "it doesn't appear to have been an accident at all."

"Why do you say that?"

"Someone tampered with her brakes."

Quin stopped walking and stared at her. "How do you know that?"

"The police told me."

"Do they know who did it?"

"Not yet. But they plan to find the person."

"Good." He started walking again, head down and determined. "Let's skip the window-shopping then and go straight to lunch so you can get to the hospital in time for visiting hours."

Quin was greeted several times as they walked to the restaurant by people who obviously knew him. It made sense, Paige realized. His hotel, while not the biggest in town, was one of the nicer ones. She'd learned that when he inherited it, he'd put a lot of thought, time, and money into renovations, taking it from a utilitarian place to crash during ski season to a luxurious place for a getaway any time of year.

"I'm working on my bookings for next year," he said, when he finished his French onion soup. "There isn't much time left. This season has already begun. And I have big plans." He talked about them enthusiastically for the next half hour.

Quin walked her to her car when they had finished lunch. The street was crowded with people from all over, mobbing the stores and sidewalks, all smiling as they enjoyed the day. Quin smiled too, and suddenly put his arm around Paige's shoulders.

He seemed to be looking at someone across the street and Paige looked in that direction.

Noah was standing there, talking to a woman who was loudly telling him about her cat. He'd seen Paige and Quin, Paige was sure, but showed nothing except a polite expression as he listened to the woman.

Paige felt uncomfortable having Quin's arm possessively on her shoulder. She ducked under his elbow to stand opposite him. "I have to go. Visiting hours have started. Thanks so much for lunch." With a wave, she headed for her car.

Aurora had more color in her face when Paige walked into her hospital room. And she was wide awake. "Hi," she said, almost cheerfully. "I was hoping you'd come."

Paige noticed that she was no longer in traction. "How are you feeling?"

"Better. The doctor said I could start trying to walk. The cast on my leg is a walking cast, and as long as I use a cane with my good hand, I should be able to manage. I did a few laps this morning in therapy. It didn't even hurt much. And if I get good at it, I can go home."

"How's the arm feeling?" Paige asked.

The smile turned into a frown. Even though it was no longer attached to pulleys, it was stuck up at an awkward angle and really scary-looking with all that metal sticking out. "It really hurts."

"I'm so sorry. How is your head?"

"Oh, that's okay. They said nothing was fractured, and my bump is even getting smaller. I can't comb my hair anyway, so I don't have to worry about hitting it."

Paige spotted a brush next to the bed and picked it up. "Would you like me to try? I'll be careful."

The smile returned to Aurora's face, accompanied by a shy sparkle in her eyes. "That would be great. There are a few cute doctors here. I can't believe how awful I look." She scooted up higher in bed, taking care to adjust her arm. Leaning on her good arm, she said, "The problem was, when I tried to raise my other hand to brush my hair myself, I fell over."

It was clear to Paige that if Aurora went home she'd need full-time care. She hoped Mr. Dillon would hire a home care worker. It was a poor substitute for a mother's care, but it would have to do.

"I'm going to braid it," Paige told Aurora.

"My mother used to do that for me. She was great. She could do French, and reverse French, and multi with cornrows." Aurora handed her an elastic band to tie the end.

"I'm just doing a plain one down the back," Paige said, feeling somewhat inadequate. But she pushed that thought aside. Paige was the one here with that talented woman's daughter, after all, doing what a mother was supposed to be doing, taking care of the child.

"Sheriff Dover asked me about my mom," Aurora said. "He wanted to know if I knew why she ran away."

"What did you tell him?"

"I told him I didn't know. But that one reason might be that she was afraid my dad would—" She broke off, clearly unable to say the words.

Willing herself to remain silent, Paige just kept braiding Aurora's hair, hoping she'd feel comfortable enough to finish her sentence.

"That he'd put her back in the mental hospital," Aurora said in a whisper. "She told me she couldn't let him see her get upset, or that's what he would do."

"Was she upset about something?"

"I think so," Aurora said. "I told that to the sheriff, but I didn't know what about."

She swallowed. "My mom has a problem. She can't help it. The doctors say she has paranoid delusions. I don't know about that. I do know she's afraid of being taken somewhere against her will. She was once, you know. Dragged away."

Paige didn't know what to say. She certainly didn't know that Mrs. Dillon had once been kidnapped. She made a small sympathetic sound and let it go at that.

"It happened right after my parents got married," Aurora explained. "My dad was out playing poker. If he had been home that evening he might have prevented it." Aurora wiped her eyes. "She was already pregnant with me. Dad had to put her in a hospital for a few months, until she got over it. And she got sick again a few times."

Paige hoped Dover would be able to find out about all of that. She completed the braid and wound the elastic around the end.

"Where is Mike today?" Aurora asked.

"With some other boys. They're building a club of some sort."

"So you're all alone today?"

"Actually," Paige said, "I had lunch with Quin Wyatt."

"Is he still so upset about his fiancée?"

"It'll take him a while to get over it. On top of the loss, he feels guilty that he thought she'd run away."

"I could see why he might think that," said Aurora, but her voice sounded like her thoughts were far away. "She flirted a lot. Men couldn't help looking at her; she was so pretty."

Aurora sounded as if she was trying to convince herself that her father was blameless. Paige certainly hoped he was.

Chapter Fourteen

Wally called Dover as soon as she got home from school. The tensions of her day, caused by Kallie Pepper acting out again, this time making poor little Ruthie cry, had been all the worse because she'd been worried about the situation in Tamarack.

"How is the investigation going?" Wally asked, after apologizing for calling and hoping she wasn't being a bother.

Dover assured her that he understood her concern. "The accident or the murder?"

Wally didn't care, she just wanted answers. "I meant the murder, but did you find something on Aurora's brakes?"

"Not yet. We checked with the repair shop that worked on the cars, and they verified that both cars got new brakes within the last month. They swear the brakes were fine and the fluid reservoirs were full and tight. The cars both showed significant damage around the valves, as if someone with a knowledge of cars, but not the right tools, had loosened them. We also found some fibers, probably from gloves, caught in the underside of the cars."

"Can you trace them?"

Dover paused, causing Wally to worry that she might have overstepped.

"People around here all get their winter accessories from the same catalogues," Dover replied. "It's unlikely we could find who owned the gloves, unless we found the gloves themselves."

"That's too bad. Do you have any other leads?"

"Nothing I can comment on, but I thought you and Dr. Griffin might want to know that I took your suggestion and started a search for Aurora's mother. Mr. Dillon can't tell me anything about where she might have gone, but I'd like to talk to her."

"You're not talking about the accident, now, are you?" Wally asked.

"No," said Dover. "But you pointed out that she left her family around the same time as Ilke was killed. I want to talk to her."

"They were in New York City when she left," Wally said, hoping her comments hadn't sent the sheriff on a wild goose chase. "Or at least that's what Paige told me. She and Aurora had discussed it."

"We found out that Mrs. Dillon was in Tamarack right before that. It may have just been a coincidence, but we want to be sure. Besides," he paused, lowering his voice, "Dr. Griffin pointed out to me that Aurora needs her now. Really needs her. From what Dr. Griffin told me, her father can't be trusted to be there for her, and he can't do all the things a girl needs while she's recovering. I wanted to see if there was some way we could help."

"That's very thoughtful of you."

Dover dodged her compliment. "I'm a dad, I can see these things. But it's getting close to winter. If Mr. Dillon needs to get to New York, he may find himself stuck down there. We've been cut off for a while when the Northway closes."

"Couldn't he take the train then? Aurora mentioned he sometimes does that, comes into town and uses the car here."

"I guess he could."

"Do you have any clue where Aurora's mother is?" Wally asked, suddenly anxious for the woman to come back.

"Not yet," said Dover. "But I'll find her."

Wally was glad. She only hoped there wouldn't be any more hard facts for Aurora to face. "Have you found anything else out about the murder?"

"We got a make on the bullet. It's a nine millimeter. We think it may be from a foreign gun and an older model at that. The markings were sent to Washington and there was a tentative identification with a Walther."

"What's that?"

"A German gun. There were a lot of them during WWII."

"Used by which country?"

"Germany. Sweden had some though, and there were some used in France. The Soviet Union and East Germany used them after the war."

Wally didn't understand. "What was it doing here?"

"Someone may have brought it back from war, as a souvenir, and it fell into the murderer's hands." He paused. "Would you know if Ted Verrill had one?"

"I don't know. Did you ask Paige?"

"She didn't think so. But her uncle travels to some pretty unusual places. He might think he needed protection. It's also more than likely that the gun was picked up out of the country."

Wally worried about those references to Ted. "Are you saying you think Ted did this? You think the gun belonged to him and he used it on Quin's fiancée and built that wall to hide her in?"

"I don't know. Remember, whoever did it was not only murderous but may have been sadistic as well. Ms. Hedstrom didn't actually die from the gun shot. She died of peritonitis, because she was shot in the abdomen and her organs were pierced. It probably took her several days to die, and that's when she was exposed to the cold. And she was bound and gagged the whole time."

"Ted Verrill doesn't seem like the type of person to do that," Wally said. "Did you ever meet him?"

"I'm not doubting you," said Dover. "But I've met a few murderers, and from what I hear you have too. So you know how many people said the same kind things about them."

"But if the gun might have come from Sweden. . . ." Wally hoped somehow it could be traced to Ilke, not Paige's uncle.

"We're considering that," Dover said. But his tone said he didn't seem to believe it.

Paige stopped off at Jolene's for some take-out on the way to get Mike from Luke's house. She figured he could use some warm soup after being outside playing all day. "Do you have time for a cup of tea with me?" Jolene asked. Paige gratefully accepted. It would be pointless to get to Mike early and a cup of tea would hit the spot.

"So what have you been doing all day?" Jolene asked.

She told Jolene about her lunch with Quin and seeing Noah, but feeling uncomfortable about going to talk to him because she was with Quin.

Jolene shook her head sadly. "You know your friends hate each other, don't you."

Paige nodded. "I'm glad you understand they are just friends."

"Why, are some people thinking there's more to it?"

"I have a reputation to maintain," Paige said.

"Don't worry, if anyone asks, I'll set them straight," Jolene promised her. "Just friends. I've got it."

"Good." Paige returned to the subject of the two men's antagonism toward each other. "I get the impression sometimes that Noah feels Quin lost Ilke and didn't seem to notice."

"Some people think she was running around on him," said Jolene. "There were rumors about several people. Quin is such a nice guy, he shouldn't have had to put up with it."

"Was one of those people my uncle?"

Jolene looked at Paige sadly. "Umhm. For a while we thought he'd be the one to marry her. At least that was what Ilke seemed to want."

"My mother never said anything about Ted getting serious. She's given up on her brother ever marrying."

Jolene took a last sip of her tea and put the cup into the sink. "What does she think about everything?"

"You mean about the body being found in the house? She wishes we'd move somewhere else."

With raised eyebrows, Jolene asked, "What did you tell her?"

Paige shrugged. "I said it was out of the question. Where would we go? To a motel? I can't ask Mike to live like that."

"It's so creepy. No offense. I kind of agree with your mother. You could buy another house. It isn't like you can't afford it."

Paige felt her face flush, trying not to think about how much it hurt. Michael's other life, as she now thought of it, that life that she knew nothing about, was full of mystery and reckless, ill-conceived investments. He'd bought on spec, on margin, in swampland, and she was still paying for it. "I'm not ready"—or at all able, she thought—"to make that kind of move."

"Are you saying you aren't committed to living here?"

"I'm committed to my job," Paige said, considering how much she needed it. But she wanted to lighten the mood and get away from the serious talk. "I'm just a little nervous about living through one of these northern winters."

Jolene laughed. "Fair enough."

The thing was, Paige realized while driving over to get Mike, she hadn't committed herself at all to living in Tamarack. She wondered if she should be looking for another job. Maybe she had been wrong to accept this one, but it had been so convenient and included the house. The pay wasn't great, but the expenses were far fewer.

But then again, she had no idea what it would be like for any length of time, living so far from the city. There were too many people who seemed to be on a completely different wavelength from what she had been used to in New York, and that included whoever murdered Ilke. Sometimes she longed for Manhattan, a place where on the surface it seemed dangerous, but where she understood the rhythms of life. This safe haven in the North Country, as some people called it, was just the opposite. Who would tamper with a teenager's brakes? Who would stuff a dead body into the walls of a vacant house and build an innocuous-looking closet around it?

That thought sparked something in Paige's mind. The murderer didn't know the house would be occupied a few months later. He, and Paige was sure it had to be a man, a strong one, considering all the labor and lifting involved, had assumed the house would be empty with Ted out of town.

She called Wally when she got home to exchange information. She had to hurry and finish while Mike was changing out of his wet clothes, so as not to worry him.

"I wonder," said Wally when Paige was done.

"Did you just think of something?"

"I was just wondering how many people knew Ted was going away and for how long?"

Paige thought for a moment before answering. "I guess the post office would have been notified, and *The Valley News,* so they could stop the paper delivery. The utility bills were paid by Ted's accountants, as always. I changed the address back to the house when I moved in."

"Do you have the old bills?" Wally asked.

"Why do you want to know?"

"I was wondering if there was some energy usage surge while that closet was being built. Maybe we should ask Dover if he'll look into it."

"I'll call him, if you think it's important."

"Don't bother," said Wally. "I'll do it. But let me know if you hear anything else. And I'm sorry about Quin. I didn't realize he had such a temper."

"Maybe he was having a bad day," Paige told her. "He's always been pleasant with us."

After once again promising to be careful, Paige got off the phone. She had so much to do and little time or enthusiasm to do it, but she pushed herself to get going. She was, after all, the only one who could take care of Mike.

When she went down to drop the laundry in the basement, she noticed that there were some flakes on the floor. On closer inspection, she saw that they had come off the wall, about four feet from the baseboard. She rubbed her finger along it, and more of the wallboard flaked. If it got any worse, she decided, she would paint it. Maybe they could decorate with some sort of mural, maybe of comic book characters or a big version of the silly fish doodles Mike always did or a baseball stadium or whatever. It would be a fun thing to work on if the weather got really bad over the winter and it would be a lot nicer than the raw wallboard. If Uncle Ted hated it, they could always whitewash it later.

Once the wash was sorted, she let Balto back in and went upstairs for bed. That last burst of energy had left her tired enough, she hoped, to be able to fall asleep. But worries about sinister people living in Tamarack raced through her mind.

"Someone from here has been hacking into the state computer system," Judy told Paige when she arrived the next morning. "The police called."

"Do they know who it is?"

"Not yet. One of the officers talked to the computer teachers. They say it may have been one of the students."

"Any idea who?"

Judy shrugged. But a half hour later two boys, Jimmy Forrester and Walt Kennedy, were brought into Paige's office. With them was Mr. Engles, the upper grade computer teacher, and Sheriff Dover.

"Tell Dr. Griffin what you told us, Jimmy," said Mr. Engles.

"We didn't mean anything," he said, defiantly. But by the look on his face, he wasn't as confident as he sounded. "No one got hurt."

Paige turned to Walt, who stood silently staring at the floor. He looked frightened.

"Walt, is there something else?" she asked.

"No," said Jimmy.

"I was talking to Walt."

"We didn't mess anything up," said Walt. "Honestly."

"But you did something that was against school rules, didn't you?"

"We just wanted to see who—" he didn't finish, because he'd looked up at Jimmy who gave him a warning stare.

"Would you go back to class now, Jimmy?" Paige said. "We'll discuss this with you later."

"Hey, wait a minute. Why doesn't Walt have to go back to class?"

"That isn't your business. Whatever we discuss is private."

"You're gonna confess, aren't you?" said Jimmy, looking accusingly at his friend. "Well, I will first and let you get into trouble." He turned to Paige. "Me and him hacked into the state department of motor vehicles."

"Why?"

"We wanted to check something out."

"That's illegal," said Mr. Engles. "They traced it right back here. Are you trying to lose Internet privileges for the entire school?"

"We really needed to know whose car it was," Jimmy said, sincerely, "So we could tell the police."

Paige didn't point out the obvious—that they could have told the police whatever it was and let them find out for themselves. "What was so important?"

"We saw a car parked over near the driveway of Aurora's house the night she got into that accident. We wondered if maybe that person had something to do with it. So we wanted to find out who owned it."

Paige stood up. "What did you find? And why didn't you tell the police?"

Walt stared at her, terrified. Jimmy, whose face had drained of all color, said, "The DMV said that the license plates were issued to Ilke Wyatt. But a ghost couldn't have ruined Aurora's brakes, could it?"

Midmorning on Sunday, the phone rang. Mike answered it and called upstairs to his mother.

When Paige picked up the phone, Mike whispered that the caller was Quin. "Is Quin going to come over again?" he asked.

Paige nodded and covered the phone while she explained,

"He wants to know if you'd go with him to take a look at a snowmobile he's thinking of buying. Interested?"

Mike nodded.

"That sounds like fun," Paige told Quin, although she didn't seem so sure either. Mike had become tentative about Quin, willing to talk about him, but not anxious to see him.

It would be good for all of them, Paige thought. Mike could become comfortable with Quin again, and it would give Paige a chance to have some time to herself. Maybe she could even find some time to paint, something she used to love to do. The lake was looking especially sharp today. She suddenly felt energized.

Wally had a phone call that same morning from Marion, Paige's mother. She was most distressed about the events in Tamarack. Wally was doubtful that she could change Marion and her husband's minds about wanting Paige to move and she wasn't entirely sure they were wrong.

In order to distract them, and with the hope of finding out something useful, Wally asked Marion if she knew anything about her brother's assistants.

Puzzlement showed in Marion's voice. "Why do you ask?"

"I was hoping to talk to some of them. I have a few questions."

"Well, if you want to know anything personal, you'll have to ask someone else. Ted never dated any of his assistants. He has a strict policy. But I know he had a few flings with some of the summer visitors. He brought one by on his way to a canyon he wanted to see."

"Do you know who it was?"

"Amy something. I don't really remember. That was two summers ago. He's probably dated several women since then, or at least as many as he can fit in between digs. I wish my little brother would grow up already and settle down, but I don't think that's going to happen anytime soon." She sounded frustrated.

"But tell me about your family," Marion said. "How is everyone?"

Wally happily filled her in.

"Are you ready to look at a new snowmobile and trailer?" Quin asked Mike when he arrived at Paige's house. "Something with a big noisy engine?"

Paige looked over at Mike. He had said he wanted to go, but he was just a bit hesitant.

"I sure could use a hand," said Quin.

Motors and engines were a big draw, Paige knew, but Mike was still uncomfortable around this man who had so much sorrow.

Yet her son's face told her he was ready to overcome that. She looked at Quin, as seriously as she could manage. "Are you sure it's really that noisy?"

"It's loud, I tell you." He grinned.

Mike smiled. He looked at Paige as if dying to be deafened. "Can I?"

"Sure. Get your stuff."

"I don't know where I put my gloves," said Mike.

"You need them," Paige told him, expecting further argument. But Mike happily went to get them. "This could take a while," Paige said. "Coffee?"

Quin followed Paige into the kitchen. He frowned when he looked at the cardboard duct-taped to the kitchen floor, but he kept up a light chatter about his research for the best snowmobile on the market. Paige felt uncomfortable not mentioning what the boys in her school had learned about Ilke's license plates, but she knew Dover was right when he said there was no point in discussing it until they knew what it all meant.

As soon as Mike came back, they left. Mike didn't put his hand into Quin's the way Paige had seen him do with Noah. Then again, he hadn't held hands with his father either.

Paige was about to take Wally's advice and go out to the shed where she'd set up her studio when the doorbell rang again. She opened it and found Noah standing on her porch with a carpenter's box. "I thought this would be a good time to fix your kitchen," he said. His eyes fell on her jacket. "Oh, were you going out?"

Thoughts of painting went out the window. Getting the hole fixed was a bigger priority. There still was a somewhat musty odor coming up from underneath and she was anxious to put an end to it. The patch would probably be just the thing.

"It can wait."

Noah smiled. "Are you ready?"

Paige hung her jacket back on the hook and went to help. Balto looked like he wanted to help too. He lay down right next to Noah, with his head up and ears perked.

Noah spread a cloth on the floor and laid his toolbox on top. He wore a carpenter's apron over his jeans and a small satisfied smile on his lips, at least as much as Paige could see of them underneath his red mustache. He measured the hole, which he'd uncovered, but suddenly took off his wire rim glasses, wiping them with his flannel shirttails. By way of explanation, he said, "Balto was kind enough to clean them for me. Is it okay if I ask him to go outside?" At Paige's nod, Balto was sent out to play. A look at the doggie door lock told Paige the dog wouldn't be back until Noah was finished.

"Would you like to listen to some music while you work?" Paige asked.

"Sure."

She turned on the radio. After turning the dial away from pure static, she found a French station, probably from Montreal, with a loud French song. Noah frowned.

"Maybe something else?" Paige said, reaching for the dial. She switched the station. A whiny country music singer was lamenting his loss.

Paige was ready to change it again, but Noah said, "No, leave it." Paige cringed. It was not her type of music at all.

"You know," Noah said, "it's odd. The closet was built on the floor, but not into it, except here, where this two-inch hole is, and where I took out those few remaining brackets. It wasn't built into the ceiling at all, just up to it. And it was barely held in place in the old doorway by these other brackets."

Paige wasn't sure what he meant. It sounded to her as if the closet were a big box basically sitting in place on the floor and attached to the surrounding doorjamb. But it was hard to imagine, since most of it was gone now. It was hard to even tell how far out into the kitchen the closet had protruded. It was as if Ted had a closet built as impermanently as one of the tents he slept in when he was on a dig.

She tried to look at it in relation to the rest of the kitchen. "Where I'm standing would have been right in the middle of the closet, but there wasn't a hole that I was aware of. I didn't see it until we cleaned it up."

"It doesn't matter, does it?" Noah said.

Paige frowned. Maybe not to anyone but the murderer, whoever it was, who was still out there somewhere. And he knew how to get into her house.

She watched Noah steadily work and tried to calm herself. "How are you going to close up the hole?" she asked.

"I'm going to patch in a sub floor, if I can, and then cut a piece of oak plank to cover it, then varnish it. It won't be the same color, at least not for a few years, although I can try giving it a light stain." He pulled a small electric jigsaw out of his toolbox and cut out a square section through just the top surface of the floor. It was only a bit larger than the hole. When he was done, Paige could see a square of the sub floor, with the original round hole in the center.

"I can't use a liner here," Noah told her, "since that would make the patch higher than the subfloor, but I don't think you'll get much of an air leak. I don't feel any draft at all from this hole."

She saw him looking at her, where she stood over him. She thought about how comfortable it was, how homey, and how much she enjoyed his company. It was a shame he and Quin didn't get along. Yet here was Noah, working on her floor, and Quin, spending the day entertaining her son, and she had to wonder what she could do for them. Maybe giving them an opportunity to get along and have a good meal together would be a good idea.

"You don't have to stand there," he said. "I can work alone. If you have someplace to go, you can."

"Are you sure?" That would give her the time she needed to run to the grocery store. She had visions of a big cozy dinner.

"Yes. If I finish before you get back, I'll let myself out."

"Oh, no," Paige said, bringing a startled look to Noah's face. "I mean, would you like to stay for dinner? It's the least I can do."

"Sure. Thanks."

Paige thought about warning him that she was going to ask Quin too but decided against it. Maybe the two men could learn to get along in a civil manner if they were in front of Mike. "So don't leave, even if you're done," Paige said. She picked up her keys and dashed out, intent on being back before Mike and Quin came home. On the way to the store, she thought about getting some reinforcements for herself and as soon as she had parked, she called Jolene. "I know it's last minute and all, but would you come to dinner?" She told Jolene who else would be there, and giggled when Jolene said she hadn't seen a good showdown since her trip to Frontier Town.

"Maybe Mike can show those two so-called adults how to behave," Jolene said, "but I won't hold my breath."

"Thanks," Paige said. "I've got to get going. See you at five."

Chapter Fifteen

Paige had dinner well under way—a nice stew—and the floor that Noah had coated with a quick-dry polyurethane was ready, when Quin and a somewhat grumpy Mike came back. They were followed closely by Jolene. Quin had obviously seen Noah's Jeep out front, judging by the scowl on his face when Paige opened the door, but he grunted a greeting at Noah, whose return salutation was no better. Both were unable to hide their surprise, though, when Jolene walked past them and set a plate of her famous checkerboard minicheesecakes on the counter.

"You haven't been by to see me in such a long time, Quin," Jolene said. "We miss you around the shop."

"I'll come this week," he promised, before turning back to Paige.

She had only the briefest moment to wonder why Mike seemed annoyed, before his face lit up when he saw Noah. Now was not the time to ask, anyway. She offered everyone a drink and she and Jolene set the table in the dining room while the little boy dragged the big boys off to see some really cool stuff, as he put it. Once they were out of the kitchen, the two women had a good laugh.

Jolene went over to the spot on the floor where the hole had been. She looked up at the doorjamb to the hallway, only a few feet in back of it. "I'm trying to picture what the closet looked like," she said in a quiet voice. "It seemed to be so normal when I was here in August, I never really looked at it. But with it gone, that seems normal too, and the kitchen looks so much bigger."

Paige nodded. "Plus I don't have to go all the way around to the other doorway. This is a better traffic flow and makes more sense." Paige showed her the rough dimensions of the closet. "It was all open space when I came here years ago," she said. "And now I understand why—there was no closet at the time. Certainly not one with a body hidden inside."

"You don't think your uncle had anything to do with this, do you?"

"No. My mother said he doesn't know which way to turn a screw," said Paige. "He couldn't have enclosed the body. I guess he's like Quin, in that respect."

"Another thing they have in common," said Jolene, leering a bit.

"You mean Ilke? I asked my mother about her too, anything to get off the topic of us moving out of this house, although I'm not convinced she'll forget about it. But she said that Ted never once mentioned his assistants by name. When he was in high school he talked about his girlfriends by name all the time."

"You know what they say about it always being those quiet ones," said Jolene. "They are the ones doing what everyone is just talking about."

"Did you see him with his assistants?"

Jolene seemed to give the question some thought. "No. Well, yes, but it always seemed to be just business. And believe me, people don't usually put on an act for my benefit. Pretenses, yes, as in 'What do you mean you don't carry that brand of foie gras? It's the only brand worth having.' But hiding relationships? Not really. You wouldn't believe some of the things I've seen happen when people are snuggled up in one of my booths." She looked over at the stove.

"Is something wrong?" Paige asked.

"Uh, no. I just wondered if you put green beans into the stew. Quin doesn't like them at all."

"Thanks for the heads up," Paige said. "I'll put some stew aside for him before I add them."

Thunderous footfalls signaled the arrival of hungry men. Paige just hoped they weren't angry men. She didn't think she could take any more of that.

For a while it seemed as if Quin and Noah were trying to outdo each other in politeness, but Mike kept rolling his eyes and finally the men stopped. A few moments of silence followed, seeming to echo in the large dining room.

"Do you need some more stew, Quin?" Jolene asked. "Paige has more in the kitchen, without green beans in it."

Quin said, "Sure. It's great."

Paige made a move to get it, but Jolene jumped up and said she'd do it and that Paige should relax. Jolene didn't hear Noah say that he'd like some more, though, so Paige ended up taking his plate into the kitchen.

When she got to the kitchen she saw Quin's plate on the counter and Jolene on the floor beside the stove. "Is something wrong?" Paige asked.

Jolene stood up, holding a fork in her hand. "I dropped his fork. I was just picking it up." She brushed herself off and washed the fork in the sink. "There, good as new." After ladling out more stew for Quin, she went back to the dining room.

When Paige got back with Noah's refilled plate, she found him telling a story about a newly weaned puppy who tried to get a sow to be his mother. Quin chimed in with a story of his own about getting stuck on the shore of Long Lake with a very inquisitive city woman who kept asking him questions about movie stars who might be in the area. He kept telling her he had never seen any, but all her talking made it difficult for him to fish.

"Speaking of fishing, it's almost time to do some ice fishing, Mike," he said. "Are you up for it?"

Mike looked at Paige, then at Quin. "Yes."

Was it Paige's imagination or did Mike hesitate before saying yes?

Quin seemed to have noticed, too, because he said, "Oh, don't worry. You won't feel the cold. Wait until you see my ice house."

Paige did her best during dinner to keep the conversation moving. Surprisingly, the quietest one was Noah. He had little to say unless it was to Mike or Paige. He wasn't rude, exactly, but he had Paige wondering about his relationships with the others when they were young.

Shortly after dinner Jolene left, since she had to get up early to start baking for her shop. Paige was exhausted and looked forward to putting Mike to bed and maybe reading a good book, but both Quin and Noah seemed to want to hang around. Or maybe neither of them wanted to be the first to leave, Paige wasn't sure which. Either way, she was beginning to get irritated when Noah's pager went off. Quin looked up in triumph when Noah frowned and grabbed his jacket and tools, but Paige made sure she hustled Quin right out the door behind the vet. Finally, she had some peace.

"Did you have fun with Quin?" Paige asked Mike as he got ready for bed. She'd noticed he had barely said good-bye to the man when he left, and she wondered why.

"It was boring. And dumb."

Warning signals went up in Paige's mind. That usually meant one thing; there had been trouble. "Do you want to tell me about it?"

"No." The way Mike's head was down meant questioning him would not do any good.

"Maybe we'll let Quin pick out his snowmobile on his own," she said, trying to gauge whether that was the problem.

"There wasn't a sign about not sitting on the snowmobiles," Mike mumbled. "And he didn't have to yell at me."

Paige had her answer. Now she had to figure out what to do with it.

Louise Fisch, Wally's best friend, came over to Wally's house on Wednesday afternoon. She was still dressed for her job as a real estate agent, wearing a skirt and soft jacket with her long, red hair pulled into a low chignon. Without asking, she reached for a cookie that was cooling on a rack. It was fine with Wally, as Louise was her best friend. But her reaction after she bit into the cookie was unexpected.

She put the cookie down and looked closely at Wally. "What's wrong?"

"What do you mean?"

"This cookie. It's, um, not up to your usual standards."

"I beg your pardon?"

Louise handed her another cookie from the rack. "See for yourself."

Wally took a bite and instantly knew what was wrong. Unable to keep from making a face, she went over to the microwave where she'd melted the butter earlier for use in the recipe. It was still inside. "Oh."

"Oh?" Louise repeated. "That's all you have to say? You never make mistakes like that. So tell me, what's wrong?"

"I'm worried about Paige and Mike. Strange things are going on up in Tamarack, some of them very scary."

"Like what?"

"You mean aside from a mummified body being found in a closet?" Wally had told Louise all about it. Louise had offered to drive Wally back up there so they could both sleuth around, but then something else caught her interest and she had rescinded her offer. Wally wouldn't have taken her up on it anyway, the police would handle it. "A teenager was nearly killed when she was frightened into leaving her house late at night. She got into her car, which had been tampered with, the brakes, I mean, and she got into a wreck."

"What do you mean she was scared out of her house?"

"Someone made it so the outside lights wouldn't go on and made some noise. I don't know, exactly. But she was on her way to Paige's when the accident happened. And a car with Ilke's plates was seen nearby."

Louise shook her head in disbelief. "What did the police say?"

"I haven't heard the latest. They are looking into it. I'm hoping to hear something soon."

"So who do you think is behind it? The vet? He's kind of a loner, isn't he? Aren't loners the ones who do evil things?"

Wally looked at her friend. "I, uh—"

"Just as I thought." Grabbing her purse, Louise stood up and went to the kitchen door.

"Where are you going?" said Wally. "You just got here."

"You have no cookies for me and a phone call to make to that sheriff. It's time for me to leave."

"Are you telling me you only come here for the cookies?"

"No, and you know it. But what I am telling you is throw those cookies out." She blew Wally a kiss and went out the door.

Wally opened her phone and scrolled down to the sheriff's number. While she waited for the call to go through, she dumped the cookies in the trash. Sammy looked at her in disbelief, but she assured him that even he wouldn't find them good. That was an outright lie, of course, since she knew Labs would eat just about anything. They weren't the healthiest thing for a dog, though. He'd have to settle for a dog biscuit.

Sammy was busy chomping away on the one Wally threw him when Sheriff Dover came on the line.

"As I explained to Dr. Griffin, the car the boys saw was one that had been reported stolen in Lake Placid and was later found abandoned," he told her, "about two days after Aurora's accident."

Wally suddenly felt real fear. "Were the license plates on the car when it was found?"

"No. They've disappeared again. I put a call in to Mr. Wyatt to ask him if he has any idea how that could have happened. He said he'd thought his fiancée took her car with her when she left, and didn't think to worry about it when her body turned up. We still have no idea where Ms. Hedstrom's car is."

"Did you find anything in the abandoned car that would help?"

"That car was a mess when it was found. The owner had it junked a few days ago. I think we'd be lucky to find a usable fiber at this point, but we're taking a close look anyway."

"Sheriff Dover," Wally said, trying to keep the shakiness out of her voice, "why would the person who had Ilke's license plates steal a car and tamper with Aurora's brakes?"

"I have no idea."

But Wally did. She'd been working on a theory and thought now might be the time to try it out. "What if the murderer thought Aurora knew something about what happened to Ilke? It seems likely there is a connection, doesn't it?"

Dover was quiet, hopefully mulling over Wally's idea. "I'll post a guard outside the girl's door."

Wally was glad that her suspicions were being taken seriously, but that didn't make things any better. There was still one big problem with that theory. Aurora hadn't been anywhere near Tamarack at the time of the murder. But there was someone who could have been up there.

"Aurora wasn't in Tamarack at the time of the murder," Wally said. "But her mother was. Do you think it's possible that Mrs. Dillon left because she saw something up here and got scared?"

"I guess it's possible. It doesn't explain why Aurora was attacked, but your theory may have some basis."

Wally thought about Paige's report on Aurora. Her gray eyes still had a haunted look when she spoke of the accident. "If she knew something, she would have told Paige or someone, wouldn't she?"

"Perhaps. But what if she doesn't know that she knows? That's one of the things we are going to find out."

"Have you had any luck finding her mother?"

"Not yet. We got a lead from a Southern California hospital where she was taken after an apparent collapse."

"What was wrong with her?"

"According to their records, she had a mild concussion and possibly some minimal frostbite."

"In California?"

"We thought the same thing," said Dover. "She might have gotten that here, before she left. But we don't know because she was released. We had a lead on where she had been staying, but she left there recently, without a forwarding address. We're still working on it. Since her disappearance isn't a criminal investigation, there are some methods we can't use, but I will stick with it."

None of the conversation made Wally feel any better.

Saturday evening of Thanksgiving weekend, after dinner, Paige got out some of the fuzzy material she'd been working on for Mike's costume for the fourth grade play. It was the exact shade of raw sienna as some of the bare trees outside the window, and she wished she had paint that color. She'd have to look for some so she could do a picture of them when she had a chance.

Luckily, Mike had decided to be Indiana Jones for Halloween. She'd had the clothes in the house to throw something together. This costume was much harder. Paige was doing her best, with her minimal sewing ability, to turn the felt into a suitable bear suit with the help of a sewing machine she'd found in one of the guest bedrooms. Her mind stayed on Ted, though, wondering if Dover had found someone who could communicate with him. The whole time she was pinning the next seam, she imagined someone driving a Jeep to whatever remote dig Ted was working on, trying to deliver him the message that he should call Tamarack. She was so deep in the fantasy, that she didn't at first notice when the sewing machine lights blinked out and the needle stopped.

She checked the plug. It was firmly in the wall and the switch was in the on position, but the machine showed no signs of life.

Slowly, she became aware that the lamp near the table was also off, and it had been on earlier. The lights in the kitchen and hall were still on, though. Mike was upstairs in the third floor playroom. She figured his lights were fine or she would have heard from him.

Relieved that it wasn't the machine, or the whole house, Paige went in search of the circuit breaker board. She went down the basement steps and tried to figure out where the circuits might be.

It took her far longer than she expected and by the time she found it Mike was at the basement door plaintively calling her to see if he could have some ice cream. "I'll be right up," she called, opening the panel.

The inside was a nightmare. Not one single circuit was labeled, and Paige had a hard time deciding which switch was in the off position. She gave up and went upstairs to scoop out ice cream and find a flashlight for a close up view.

Ten minutes later, she was at the circuit breaker again. She finally narrowed the possibilities down to two, concluding that they were both in the off position, at least halfway, and she flipped them both on.

As she went back upstairs to see if the machine was back on, she had a vague sensation of something humming. She dismissed it when she heard the sound of one of Mike's favorite television shows, turned most of the way up to maximum.

After he went to bed, she went back to her sewing machine, which now sat brightly lit up with buttons showing several of the functions it could perform and Paige could not. Her new Jazz CD provided company while she finished the costume.

When she turned off all the lights and went upstairs, she found Mike and Balto asleep in Mike's double bed. She shooed the dog off, covered Mike, and got ready for bed herself. After reading only one page of her book, she, too, fell asleep.

A vague sensation of humming disturbed her dreams. She slept fitfully, dreaming of Aurora, inexplicably waterskiing with her broken leg.

Chapter Sixteen

In the morning, when the steam hissed and the timed coffee maker burbled, Paige groggily came downstairs. She let Balto out while she made Mike breakfast.

The dog's barking made her open the back door. He came in, leaving one dark-brown footprint on the floor every few inches.

"What did you get into?" Paige asked, fearing something unspeakable. On closer inspection, she realized it was just mud. That was odd, though, since it hadn't rained. In fact, she would have expected any left over puddles from the last precipitation to be solid ice, since the thermometer outside read way below freezing.

After a busy morning trying to do all her chores, she and Mike got into the car and headed west to go see a movie in Lake Placid. The bare trees did little to screen the bright sunlight that poured into the car. Paige rummaged about in her glove compartment for her sunglasses. Instead of feeling them, though, she felt the wooden-knobbed plane that Noah had left behind after he fixed her floor, and she had planned to return to him. "Do you feel like going on a detour?" she asked Mike.

"Okay."

She drove over to Noah's. She was in luck, his car was in the driveway. It really wouldn't have mattered to her, since she could just leave the wood plane with a note, but Mike had gotten so excited when he realized where she was going, she would have had to put up with his disappointment if Noah were out.

He must have seen them drive in, because he came out of the house. "Balto hasn't gotten into trouble again, has he?" he asked, while Mike jumped out of the car right behind Paige.

"No. Not this time. I just wanted to stop by and give you this." She held out the plane.

Noah looked at it. "What's that?"

"I found it after you fixed the floor. You must have left it in the mud room when you were carrying out the remnants. I'm afraid Balto saw it first, though," she added, pointing to the large, black, wooden knob used to steady and guide the plane. It was full of teeth marks. "He seems to have chewed it."

"It isn't mine."

Paige looked at him in alarm. She suddenly realized that it may have belonged to the person who changed the closet—the murderer. And she had put her own fingerprints on it, potentially blocking out any incriminating information. She dropped the plane on to the hard packed snow.

Noah turned to Mike. "Do you want to see some of the animals? I have a few pets boarding here and my horse is in the barn." He didn't have to ask twice. Mike shot around the side of the clinic and ran to the kennels, slipping and sliding all the way. Noah ran to keep up with him.

Paige heard them laughing as the barn door creaked open but

it did little to make her feel better as she picked up the suddenly sinister item. "What have I done?" she asked Noah, when he returned.

"You didn't know," he said, bending to inspect the wood plane. "This should have been picked up by the police when they searched your house. Tell me exactly where you found it."

"It was just sitting there, next to his water dish. I hadn't seen it before, not until the morning after you fixed the floor. What if it belonged to the murderer?"

Noah shrugged. "I guess there's no hope of finding fingerprints now."

"Where would Balto get it?"

"I'm afraid we'll never know. He's smart but he can't talk."

"Do you think there may be more tools?"

"I don't know. Are you sure it isn't Ted's?"

"I don't think so. I've never seen carpentry tools in the house. And my mother said Ted only knows how to take things apart. He wouldn't use a plane for that."

Noah frowned. "Do you want me to come help you look for more?"

"I don't—" The sound of Mike coming back made Paige stop. She didn't want him to find out. "Could you just take it? I'll call Sheriff Dover and tell him you have it."

"Don't bother," said Noah. "I'll call him."

Mike was standing next to the car, impatiently waiting to get in. "C'mon, Mom," Mike called. "We have to get to the movie."

Paige assured him they wouldn't be late.

"Can Noah come too?"

She turned to ask. "Would you like to join us?"

"Just let me get my beeper," said Noah, putting the plane on his front step.

Paige and Mike got into the car and waited for Noah. He was back in less than a minute. "Tell me about the movie," he said, when they were on the road.

"You may be sorry you agreed to go," Paige warned. She told him about the movie review she'd read. "It is rated G but sounds like it should have been a D for devoid of any redeeming features."

"I'll take my chances," Noah said. "Right, Mike?"

The movie was even worse than Paige had expected, although, somehow, that hadn't seemed to matter. But it was already dark and quite chilly when they got out of the theater. Frost had appeared on the windshield of her car and she shivered, but she warmed up once they were inside the car. When they dropped Noah off, though, the heat seemed to leave with him.

Mike talked about Noah all the way home. Paige was happy for him and, if she were to be honest, happy for herself. She had made a nice friend.

She was still thinking about him when Jolene called. Paige told her about going to Noah's to return what she thought was his plane and him ending up going to the movie with them, and Jolene seemed delighted. "Your first date with him. Congratulations."

"It wasn't a date," Paige protested but not too forcefully.

"So you say."

"I'll talk to you tomorrow," Paige said, trying to avoid any further speculation.

She had been itching to look around in the house for other tools when they got home, but first she had to feed Mike and Balto. It had been a long day, and after dinner, Mike fell asleep.

As Paige searched, she heard that soft humming again. She spent some time trying to track it down, with no luck.

A huge Dumpster stood outside Louise's house blocking several parking spaces. Wally parked three houses away and walked through a nearly freezing December downpour up to the front door. By the time Louise opened it, Wally was soaked.

Louise welcomed her in and took her coat but frowned when she saw the state of Wally's hair. "Come into the kitchen and let me get you a towel."

Wally took it gratefully and attempted to dry her hair. What it would look like when it dried was anybody's guess. "I can't believe it's raining again."

"It's the fourth day in a row," Louise pointed out. "The forecasters said we can expect two more, since the front is stalled." She poured two cups of coffee. "Here, sit down and get warm."

Wally sat on one of the kitchen chairs and took a sip of the coffee. She was puzzled, though, that they were even able to sit in this room. The container was outside, ready for the demolition, but there were no workmen around. "I expected to see this room all torn up. What happened to the renovations?"

Louise sighed and rested her chin sullenly on her hand. "They can't work because of the rain. I waited two whole years for Norman to agree to redo the kitchen, and the first week of the job is a washout. I should have gone with my original plan."

Wally laughed. She knew Louise's usual way of renovating was to sell her house and move into another, usually one that had just come on the market and featured all the latest upgrades. Although she was a successful real estate agent, Louise occasionally bought what she was supposed to be selling. Norman had put his foot down this time, though, and so they were redoing their kitchen. Since they were building out, Louise explained, they needed a dry day to open up the back wall.

"Don't be impatient," Wally said. "It's going to be beautiful."

"At least I'll have lots more closet space," Louise said. She put her hand up to cover her mouth. "Oops, I didn't mean to remind you."

"Don't worry about it," Wally said. "It's never very far from my mind. I don't know how Paige deals with seeing her kitchen every day, even though the closet is gone. Even the dog is spooked by it, and he never goes near it."

"Did you find out anything from that Sheriff Dover?"

"Not really. He's polite but doesn't exactly seem to like talking to me. I don't think he has any expectation that I might be able to help. To tell the truth, I'm becoming convinced that he's right. So even though I'd really like to talk to him and get an update, I don't dare call."

"Don't worry," Louise said. "You'll think of something."

Wally shook her head. "I'm not so sure. Marion called me yesterday. She's getting worried about her brother, but she doesn't want to mention it to Paige. I didn't want to tell her that the police are really beginning to wonder about Ted, at least according to Paige. She's been trying to get hold of him, sending him e-mails, but no one has heard from him. They're not even sure where he was planning to be now. Ilke was the only one who had his itinerary, and that's probably in her computer, which is missing along with all her other things."

"There isn't anyone else who knows where he was going?"

"I asked Marion," Wally said. "She didn't know. Paige already tried calling his publisher, but he's not with them anymore."

Louise grimaced. "That's bad. What else can you do?"

Wally put down her now empty coffee cup. "I'm not supposed to be doing anything, as Sheriff Dover keeps reminding me. And

I'm fresh out of ideas, anyway. Unless . . ." She took her drenched raincoat off the door Louise had hung it on.

"Where are you going?"

"To the library. I want to find one of Ted's recent books and see who his agent is. This is Grosvenor, New Jersey. We're right across the river from Manhattan, and that's probably where his agent is. If he won't talk to me on the phone, I'll go find him and make him figure out where Ted could be. After all, if Ted doesn't come up with another book on his trip, the agent won't make his fee."

Louise looked at Wally with appreciation. "I knew you'd think of something."

It was a bit easier than Wally thought to find the agent, but he wasn't so ready to talk to her. It didn't really matter, she realized. She knew who to call, someone who could get the information. She placed a call to Sheriff Dover and quickly told him her idea.

The wariness with which he'd started the conversation eased a bit. "That's a good idea," he said. "We'll look into it."

While she had Dover on the phone, Wally asked if he'd found Aurora's mother. Aurora would be released soon, according to Paige, and Wally really hoped her mother would come to take care of her.

"We found out where Mrs. Dillon was living from her former employer, but she moved out in the middle of the night," Dover told Wally. "She didn't go back to work. It almost seems as if she was afraid someone was after her."

"Do you have any leads?" Wally asked.

"Not yet. But I haven't given up."

"Did you have a chance to look at that wood plane Paige found?"

"Wooden plane?"

"No. The kind people use to shave down the bottom or top of a door." Wally explained how Paige, or actually Balto, had found it, but she began to feel uneasy. Why didn't he already know this? "Paige gave it to Noah Oliver thinking it was his," she added. "It wasn't but he said he'd call you about it."

"Maybe he forgot," said the sheriff. "I'll give him a call."

Wally had a creepy feeling when she hung up the phone. How could Noah forget something so important? She wanted to call and ask him because he was getting close to both Mike and Paige. Was he someone to be trusted? Or not?

Chapter Seventeen

Sheriff Dover called right after Wally got home from school at noon the next day to say he'd had no luck tracking down Ted. "His agent has been waiting to hear from him also. I didn't want to tell Dr. Griffin this, but it seems Ted is missing." Wally was sorry to get that confirmation. He promised to keep looking.

"Oh, about that planing tool," he added. "I asked Noah about it. He said when he was ready to come into town the next morning, the plane wasn't on his front porch where he left it. He said he thought Paige had picked it up before they left and that she would call me about it."

A chill ran down Wally's spine since she knew Paige thought Noah had given it to Dover. "Then maybe the murderer took it."

"I've considered that and I've increased surveillance of her house. But we have a small police force and she is well back from the road. I told her she'd better be very careful."

That was the last thing Wally wanted to hear. This did not look good. It was time for a trip to upstate New York.

* * *

Paige signed a requisition for new test materials for the practice college tests. The board had been opposed to putting money into her ideas, but new tests cost less than photocopying, with much better quality. She considered it money better spent than on a new trophy case in the front hall and hoped they would see it her way.

Judy told her she had a call from Sheriff Dover. "Dr. Griffin?" he said. "I'm sorry to have to tell you this, but I've just heard that there was a sighting of a car in the lake. Heavy equipment is being sent out to your house since it offers the best access."

Paige's blood froze. "Someone drove into the lake?"

"No. Nothing like that, at least not today. But there was some emergency work being done on the entrance to the inlet and the engineers reported something unusual in the lake. They sent down a robot and found a car."

"There isn't anyone in it, is there?"

"We don't know."

"I'll be right there."

By the time Paige got home, there was a crowd of people standing along the icy shoreline, watching as a huge crane strained to pull the submerged car out of the water. Paige had noticed the day before on a jaunt with Balto a thick coat of ice forming close to the edge of the lake. But now the shore and the water were churned to mud by the equipment.

Noah greeted her as she approached the crowd. "It's hard to keep something like this quiet in such a small town," he said, indicating all the people gawking nearby.

Paige couldn't be sure but it seemed as if some of them, the ones she didn't know, were looking at her accusingly. She shivered.

"Don't mind them," Noah said, standing close between her and the thickening crowd. He looked at her. "I'm so sorry you keep having all this trouble. You're probably beginning to see this town as evil, but it isn't. I promise."

"I don't," said Paige, although she wasn't sure she sounded convincing, maybe because she wasn't convinced.

"At the very least," said Noah, "you and Mike deserve more peace than you're getting."

When he turned back to the lake, Paige noticed he was wearing his EMT jacket. "You don't think anyone is in there, do you?" she asked.

Noah shook his head. He took off his glasses and cleaned them with a handkerchief. "No one could survive in water that temperature for any length of time. But Dover asked me to come over as an EMT backup for the divers. They had to go down to attach the cables. The water is very cold, and even with their wet suits, there is a danger of hypothermia."

Paige looked into the water. It was partly frozen in places near the shore, on its way to being a huge ice sheet. "I was just here. Why didn't I notice the car?"

"It was probably covered with some of the plants that grow in the water here." He put his glasses on and pointed to the shallows. "It might have gone unnoticed for years if not for the work being done. Probably did already."

A taxi drove up to the front of the house. Paige recognized it as the one usually parked at the train station. The driver unloaded a familiar-looking suitcase and brought it up the steps. When Wally got out of the car and hurried over to her, some of the fear gripping her began to ebb.

* * *

"What's going on, Paige?" Wally said, looking at her friend's pale face and the heavy machines and other equipment. She saw Sheriff Dover, Noah, and several other people, all staring at something in the lake.

Paige pointed. "There's a car . . ."

The crowd quieted as the car was pulled up and out of the lake. Mud and water streamed out. Wally heard Noah catch his breath.

"What is it?" she asked him.

"That car hasn't been in there long. There isn't much mud." He turned his gaze away from the water and looked over at Paige, who was trembling.

The crane they were using pivoted and turned the car so that it was more visible. "Oh, my God," said Noah. "That's Ilke's car."

Wally remembered the license plates from Ilke's car were on the car seen near Aurora's the night of her accident. She could see plainly that there were no tags on the car now. "How did it get here?"

The crowd moved aside as the car was swung around and put on the shore. A tow truck started pulling it onto the flat bed.

"Stand back," Dover ordered, as people reached for the door handles.

Noah moved forward, with Wally right beside him. He and several police officers peered into the windows, while one of them popped the trunk.

"No one inside," Noah said, sounding relieved.

Dover came over to where Paige, Noah, and Wally stood. "I'm glad you're here," he said to the veterinarian, as he shook his hand. "We may need your opinion on a few things." He showed Noah a soaked branch with a few small leaves on it. "Let me know what you think."

He turned to Paige and Wally. "Noah is somewhat of an

expert on the flora around here," he explained. "He once told me he was considering botany if he didn't get into veterinary school. But of course he did. He's a bright guy."

Dover looked over at the car being hoisted out of the lake, then at Paige. "Did you see the car go into the lake?"

"No."

"Have you seen it before?"

"I don't think so."

"Did you notice any tire tracks near the big drop off?" Dover indicated the rise that overlooked the lake. "Our guys said that the car must have gone off there, to get that far into the lake and be in the position where they found it."

"I'm sure I didn't," said Paige. She responded negatively to all his other questions.

Finally he said, "The car would have had to go mighty fast to take off that far into the lake."

Paige said she hadn't seen or heard a thing. Foster, from down the road, came up and said he too had been unaware of the car going past his place. Since so few vehicles ever went down the road, it was likely the car had been brought in at some time when no one was home in either house, which was just about all day every weekday.

"We'll examine the contents at headquarters," said Dover. He waited while one of the wet-suited divers whispered into his ear. "They found the car in drive and a brick tied to the gas pedal. Someone planned this." He turned to go. "I'll call you."

Noah took Paige by the arm and steered her away from the crowd. He motioned for Wally to follow. "Are you okay?" he asked Paige.

"Yes. Sure, why not? A dead woman was found in my uncle's house, I can't reach him, and now a car that belonged to the dead woman, whose license plates were put on the car of the vandal who tampered with Aurora's car and nearly killed her, has turned up in the lake. Why wouldn't I be all right?"

"Come with me," said Noah, not waiting for a refusal. "You too, Wally." He guided them to his truck and put Paige in the passenger seat. She was too weary to question him, and, after Noah helped Wally in beside her, he went around to his door and got in.

"Where are we going?" Paige asked.

"We're getting away." He handed her his cell phone. "Call your office and say you will be out longer. I'm taking you to a nice calming lunch."

Jolene's eyebrows rose when Paige walked into her shop with Noah and Wally. She took their orders without commenting, but Wally knew they'd have some explaining to do.

Noah's cell phone rang and he stepped into a quiet corner to answer it. Jolene didn't waste a moment.

"What's going on?" she asked. "Why are you having lunch with Noah, especially when you should both be at work? And when did Wally come into town?"

Wally stayed quiet while Paige explained about the car, not adding any information, even though Paige hadn't mentioned the weeds caught in the front grill that Dover had pointed out. Jolene was still asking questions when Noah came back to eat. She offered to pick Mike up after school, if Paige needed more time, but Paige declined. Wally would be at the house, after all. That didn't seem to appease Jolene, but she didn't say anything else about it.

They warmed their hands on the cups of soup and ate their lunch in silence. Wally wondered what she could possibly say to make things seem better, but the look of fright on Paige's face and grim determination on Noah's kept her silent.

Paige, who was sitting next to Wally, seemed to relax after a while. But her calm was short-lived.

"There was another finding," Noah said hesitantly, as if he feared Paige would be upset.

She immediately proved him right. "What now?"

"The car turned out to have been in the water for several months. But they also found it had been hidden on your uncle's property. One of the branches that was caught in the front grill was from an imported shrub planted on the far side of the acreage. The police checked and found evidence of it having been parked there."

Wally remembered what Noah had said about Paige's uncle and his experiment with nonnative plants. "Do they know for how long?"

"Not really. They're guessing the car was hidden there around the time Ilke disappeared and moved when the lake thawed, but they really have no idea for sure."

"Did they find anything that would point to the murderer?"

"They didn't tell me, if they did."

The group went silent again. No words of encouragement came to Wally's mind.

"Everything will be okay," Noah said. "You'll see." He sounded confident that what he said was true.

Paige looked at him. "You say that as if you know the person who killed Ilke and caused Aurora's accident is gone. How could you know it will work out?"

"I don't. But I just have this feeling."

"There is no basis for all this comforting, is there?" Paige didn't keep the tears from falling. Wally put her arm around Paige's shoulder.

Noah frowned. "You're right. In the last few months so much has occurred that I would never have expected. I just keep wishing that none of this had ever happened. It was probably all just a mistake that got away from someone." His voice sounded far away, and when Wally looked at him, she saw him staring off into space.

Chills rippled across Wally's skin. She clearly remembered Noah telling her and Paige, when they were dog proofing her uncle's property, to skip looking in the bushes where the foreign plants grew. Had the car been back there then? "Maybe you should go back to work," she said to Paige, as calmly as she could. "I'll walk to the house and I can pick you and Mike up in your car later."

Noah stared at her. But when Paige didn't make another suggestion, he nodded and got his coat.

When he was gone, Wally looked at Paige. She hated to say it, but she couldn't hold herself back. Maybe Louise was right "I think you should distance Mike and yourself from Noah."

Paige bit her lip.

"It's only until we can be sure he had nothing to do with Ilke's death and everything else." Wally shook her head at the sad turn of events. She'd never suspected Noah, but between the missing carpenter's plane and his odd statements at lunch, she knew they couldn't take a chance.

Chapter Eighteen

Wally punched in Dover's number. She'd put off doing it for an hour, while she caught up with her messages and re-arranged her schedule to make up for the meetings she'd missed and make sure she had coverage for her class, but she had difficulty concentrating. She had to find out what the police had learned from the car.

"It was Ilke's car," he confirmed. "And we're fairly sure it went into the lake last spring, which explains why Paige didn't see anything. The tags were removed to make identification more difficult. If Noah hadn't recognized the car, it might have taken a little longer to identify."

"How can you be sure it went into the water in the spring?" Wally asked.

Dover didn't respond immediately and Wally hoped he wasn't losing patience with her endless questions. She held her breath.

"We aren't sure. It makes sense, though. Dr. Griffin has been here since August, and it was a fairly well-known fact that she was coming. If the murderer wanted to get the car out of sight, he'd probably want to do it as soon as possible, after the lake thawed. The good news is killer probably left town right after that"

Wally wasn't so sure about any of that. "Noah said there was some vegetation caught on the car, possibly from Ted's exotic garden. Do you know if it had gone to seed?"

"Seed?"

Wally thought back to one of her favorite lessons in the nursery school—seeds. The children all planted a seed in a little pot and learned to care for it, but first they learned about how seeds traveled in the wild and how new plants got started. "Maybe you couldn't tell," Wally conceded, "but maybe you could get a better date on when the car went into the lake if you figure out what stage that vegetation was in. What I saw on the car didn't seem small like it would in the spring."

"I'd have to get back to you on that."

Could the car have been there the day they were inspecting the property? Wally wondered. But maybe it didn't matter. "Even if you prove the car went into the lake in spring, it doesn't mean that whoever put it there didn't come back."

"What do you mean?" Dover asked.

"I'm talking about Aurora's accident."

"We still have no confirmation they are related."

Wally sensed by the tone of his voice that she shouldn't push it, but she didn't need confirmation. She knew it, deep down inside. And that was what scared her. The killer wasn't long gone, not the way some people seemed to think. "Did you find anything else in Ilke's car?"

"We found some personal effects: a glove under a seat, a few papers, and some bangle beads."

"Bangle beads?"

"As I understand it, they are small decorative beads, used for clothing. Mr. Wyatt said his fiancée had a vest covered in them."

When she hung up, Wally wondered where that vest was now. Quin had mentioned that Ilke was wearing it the day she disappeared.

The road to the house was even more deeply rutted than it had been, after all that heavy equipment. Mike, in the back seat, thought it was great fun to bounce around, but it only served to set Paige's teeth on edge. She'd decided to forgo her afternoon meetings in favor of coming home with Wally.

She told Mike about the car in the lake. He didn't sound scared when he asked her a few questions, but she was frightened herself. The thought of someone sneaking around on the grounds, certainly before and possibly while they were inside the house, made Paige lose her appetite. Fortunately, Mike was chattering on about his day at school and didn't seem to notice how she felt.

Once they were home and Mike was settled into his afternoon routine, she and Wally discussed what had happened. But first she wanted to know what brought Wally to Tamarack.

"It's just for the weekend," she said. "Nate is away, so I sent Sammy to stay with Debbie and Elliot, and I came up here. They've been asking to watch him for a while—I think they are considering expanding their family."

Paige felt a pang of envy. "A baby?"

Wally smiled. "Maybe. I think they are yearning to take care of someone. For this weekend, it'll have to be a dog."

"I'm so happy you're here," said Paige. "I feel much better somehow."

But later, when Mike and Wally were in bed, she roamed around, feeling as if the walls were closing in. That mysterious rumble in the basement didn't help. She'd tried to figure out what it was again, with no luck. She only heard it when the big old furnace was off, which happened less and less as the weather grew colder. Tonight again, just after the thermostat clicked into the night mode, she heard it for a while. But it seemed distant from her bedroom, and she decided it was probably the old refrigerator in the basement. It was filled with soda and beer, as if waiting for Ted to come back and throw a party. Paige wished he would.

Aurora's color was back, thanks to the nurse, Priscilla, one from the old school, who insisted her patient should sit out on the sheltered deck during milder weather. That was where Wally and Paige found her, sitting in the sunshine. Wally had come along as she was eager to see how Aurora was doing.

"You remember Wally Morris," Paige said, when they arrived.

"Hello, Mrs. Morris," Aurora said. "Thank you for the get-well cards and the magazines."

"You're quite welcome." Wally was pleased to see that Aurora had improved so much that she could get around on her own with the aid of a cane. Her leg and arm were still in casts, but they'd been changed to lighter materials. She wore a lot of makeup, reminding Wally of her own teenage years and those of her daughters and all the hours spent applying makeup. It was a good cure for boredom, something Aurora must be suffering from.

"I've been experimenting," Aurora said. "Do you like it?"

"It's a little heavy for daylight," Paige said, smiling. "But it's just right for that special black tie affair."

Aurora laughed. "Like there would ever be that kind of party up here."

"Don't laugh, Aurora," said Priscilla, who looked like she had submitted herself to the teenager for a makeover. She had bright-red lipstick on and cherry-red cheeks, with a daring blend of pink, blue, and lavender eyeshadow. Two stars had been artfully drawn on her temples. To her credit, she acted as if she didn't feel as uncomfortable as she looked. "Long before Ted Verrill bought the house Dr. Griffin lives in, it was the site of parties that would make people in New York City jealous."

"What do you mean?" Aurora asked.

Priscilla turned her knitting and started another row. "It was the summer home of the owners of one of the biggest beer barons in the United States. This whole county was full of rich people who had camps up here."

"Camps? Like summer camps?"

"Yes," said the nurse. "But not in the way you think. That's just what they were called." She took up more of the azure wool from the ball in her lap. "Some of them were small and remote—simple cabins. But around here, many of them were quite large." She paused, as if thinking, and chuckled. "Lavish parties were common and considering that it took people nearly a week to get here from New York City, the houses were full of guests for days on end."

"Wow," said Aurora, but not enthusiastically. She seemed to have lost interest.

But Wally was very interested. She leaned forward. "Did you go to any of the parties?"

"In a manner of speaking," said Priscilla, with a smile. "My grandmother, mother, and her sisters used to help out in the kitchen at the house. Later I helped, too, but by then the parties weren't as elaborate."

"That was before it was remodeled, I imagine," said Paige. Wally wondered where they prepared all the food.

"Oh, the kitchen used to be so busy," the nurse said. "It was in a separate building altogether."

Wally thought she knew which one. It was quite a shambles now, but the stone chimney was intact.

"Once we brought the food into the main house, we each had a station during the set up," Priscilla continued. "My sister was in the butler's pantry and I served."

"Ask her about the closet," Aurora prompted.

"It's gone," said Paige. "And it wasn't there back then." She looked as if she sincerely wished it had never existed.

"I'll go make some tea," said the nurse.

Pushing aside seven or eight teen magazines, Paige sat down on the couch next to Aurora. "How are you getting along with Priscilla?"

"She's nice, I guess. But I feel like I'm living forty years ago. She's always, like, when I was young I did this, you know."

"How is your dad?"

"He's okay. He's getting over his guilt. He'll be back soon, if you want to wait."

"I don't think we can," said Paige. "But tell him we said hello."

A much less flamboyant Priscilla brought them a pot of tea, cups, and a basket of muffins, then went back inside. She had obviously decided to go with a fresh scrubbed look. Aurora didn't seem to mind.

"Those muffins look delicious," Paige said, reaching for one.

"Ms. Valley sent them. She's been sending a basket every few days, to cheer me up. She said she can't let one of her best customers go into withdrawal. Isn't that sweet of her?"

"Very sweet," said Wally, who also took a muffin.

"Your tutor says you're doing very well, that you are all caught up," Paige said.

"She's been great. When I couldn't write because of how I had to sit, she did it for me, but she insisted I had to use my own words. And if I have a visitor, she tells me we'll catch up the next day, instead of making the person wait."

"Have you had a lot of visitors?"

"Some. Not that many kids really got to know me before the accident, but some come over. And I've had other visitors."

"Who?" Wally asked.

"Mr. Wyatt came over. He was so nice, and told me to call him Quin. He brought me some books and a bunch of CDs."

"That was thoughtful of him." Surprising too. Wally would never have guessed he'd be so thoughtful, especially after seeing him with Mike. It set her radar on alert. Could he have had something to do with Aurora's accident and the murder? She'd have to think about that.

"And he didn't just drop them off and leave," Aurora added. "He stayed and talked to me. He told me about his hotel and about the fishing he does when the lake freezes." She looked off into the distance. "People really seem to get into that whole ice fishing thing around here, don't they? That's all they want to talk about. The lake gets so cold, they say, that you can't stand next to it sometimes."

Paige sighed.

Aurora continued. "One person asked me if I remembered that from when I visited before."

"Did you?"

"No. I told her I was never here when it was completely frozen, since I didn't come up for vacation last winter as I had planned. It was when my mom went away."

Wally saw the pain in her eyes.

"The people around here seem to take the really harsh winters for granted," Paige said. "It makes me a little nervous."

Aurora looked at her. "Haven't you ever driven in snow?"

There had already been several snowfalls, but none had

amounted to much. "Yes. But not a lot of it. And that's what I'm told to expect."

"Well," said Aurora, "you'd better learn how, or you could end up like me."

That was not something Wally wanted to imagine.

Chapter Nineteen

J ody's eyes lit up when Wally brought out the menorah for the first night of Hanukah. With little Charlie in his infant seat beside her, she helped Wally light the Shamash, the candle that lit all the others, and the first night's candle. They said the blessings, along with Rachel and Adam, Debbie and Elliot, and Mark, who was on break from his graduate studies in Philadelphia. Nate stood opposite them, taking pictures with his new digital toy.

Wally had barely had time to prepare for the festival since she'd stayed in Tamarack until Paige and Mike were ready to leave for Phoenix. She sincerely hoped the problems up there in the Adirondacks would be resolved by the time their holiday vacation was over.

It was sunset on Friday night, so the Morrises also lit the candles for Shabbat. The room glowed with candlelight and warmth amid the deepening dusk of late December.

"Is it time for dinner, Grandma?" Jody asked afterward.

"I think it's time for Charlie to eat, but not for us. It's only

190

four-thirty." Wally looked at the little girl. "But you can have a snack if you want."

Jody followed Wally into the kitchen, with her mother, Rachel, and her aunt, Debbie, right behind. There were latkes to fry and they would need tasting, for "quality control." Wally could hardly wait for that part.

She got Jody happily set up with a bowl of cut cherry tomatoes, baby carrots, and celery sticks while everyone else got to work. Wally wasn't orthodox about observing the no working—translated, cooking—rule on Shabbat. She did a lot of things on Shabbat that a stricter person would not do. But she felt it was right for her and her family. It was the way she and Nate had been raised.

As the oil heated, Wally took the potato-and-onion mixture that she had ground up, and added salt and pepper, flour, and a beaten egg. Once the pan was ready, Wally spooned silver dollar–sized pancakes into the oil. Debbie had another frying pan going of zucchini latkes.

"How is Paige doing?" Rachel asked while she fed Charlie baby cereal and applesauce.

Debbie turned a pancake over with a spatula as Wally took several pancakes out of the other pan and put them onto paper towels. Oil was important for the holiday, symbolic of the meager amount of oil the Maccabees had that somehow lasted eight days. It was why latkes were traditional, but she didn't want her latkes to be dripping with it. "The investigation is not going well."

"I sometimes wonder how she stands it," Rachel said. She looked troubled.

Debbie broke off half of one of the cooling zucchini latkes and gave it to Rachel before eating the other half.

"Yum," said Rachel. "That was good."

Wally broke two of her latkes in half and shared them with her daughters and granddaughter. They were as good as ever, and for a brief moment she thought of her own mother and grandmother. No matter how happy she was now or what had gone on before, she still missed those other women in her life.

Debbie took a few more latkes out of the pan and put in more batter. "Are the two men still coming around? That sounds so romantic."

"I think so," Wally said. She put some of the cooled potato latkes on a cookie sheet to keep warm in the oven. "But I'm not sure Paige is looking at it that way at all."

"These are all done," said Debbie. She turned to Rachel. "Why don't I finish feeding Charlie?"

After handing her the spoon, Rachel exchanged a look with Wally. Wally smiled and shrugged. Maybe she'd have another grandchild sooner than she thought.

Jody was in her pajamas by the time dessert was served. She and Charlie had already been bathed when Wally brought out the jelly doughnuts. They, too, were traditional because they were fried in oil. But unlike most of the other baked goods in Wally's house, which she made herself, these were from the bakery. Some things were better left to the professionals.

Rachel's family was staying overnight, but Debbie and Elliot left at nine and Mark went out for the evening at 10:00. Adam and Nate were talking business, as usual, and Rachel and Wally decided to have a second cup of tea and a nice chat.

They avoided speculation about Debbie and Elliot's possible family expansion. Wally only briefly mentioned that the young couple had offered to babysit for Sammy if necessary. "It did come in handy when I went up to Tamarack," Wally admitted.

As she explained, Wally felt increasing uneasiness. She realized she was happy that Paige had gone to see her parents in Arizona for three weeks. "At least I won't have to worry about her for a little while," Wally concluded.

"Do you really suspect the vet?" Rachel asked

Wally sighed. "I like him. Or at least I did. But the carpenter's plane that got lost while in his custody and his ability to build things, such as the enclosure that Ilke was in, and his comments the last time I saw him have me worried."

"Isn't it always the husband or boyfriend who is the chief suspect?"

"Quin couldn't hammer a nail into the side of a barn," Wally said. She'd been considering whether he could be involved ever since her visit to Aurora, but by the time she was ready to leave Tamarack, she was reasonably sure Quin was not the likely suspect. "He couldn't have put that extra wall into the closet."

"What about the police theory that it was a vagrant?"

Wally shook her head. "I just don't know. It's so unlikely." She sighed. "At least for the next three weeks, Paige and Mike are safe. But once they go back to Tamarack, I'll be worried all over again."

When Paige and Mike came back to Tamarack from sunny Arizona they were met with blankets of snow covering everything in sight. The driver of the taxi that took them from the train to their house seemed to take it all in stride.

After calling her parents to tell them they had arrived safely, Paige called Wally. She got the sense that Wally had tensed up once she knew that Paige and Mike were back in Tamarack. "We'll be fine," Paige assured her, wishing she believed it was one hundred percent true.

The drive to school on the first day back proved easier and more exciting than she expected. The fields were crisscrossed with snowmobile tracks even this early in the morning, and the sun glaring off the bright-white mounds that softened the landscape made her wish she had brought her sunglasses. The roads, though, were relatively empty. Paige soon realized that all the crazy people who didn't know how to drive in snow were in the city. Out here, with the traffic so much lighter, and the roads plowed so much better, there was less danger of colliding with another car.

But after one particularly long spin, while Mike applauded and cheered, Paige was left panting. Her heart was beating wildly and her hands, gripping the steering wheel for dear life, felt sweaty inside her gloves. Even when she'd calmed down, she still thought about it and was reminded of Aurora's accident and how she must have felt going out of control.

It was business as usual when Paige got to school. She marveled at how people took the inclement weather in stride. When someone remarked that those thirty-nine inches of snow were nothing, she sighed. She'd already had enough.

Judy gave Paige an update on what had been going on around town since she and Mike left. Taking much of the editorial slant that Judy put into her news report with a grain of salt, Paige distilled it down to a few key issues. People were still talking about Ilke's murder and Aurora's accident, and eyebrows were being raised about Paige and her goings on. Her movie attendance with Noah, along with her lunch with Quin, hadn't escaped notice. People seemed to be waiting for more news.

"Where did anyone even hear about it?" Paige asked, hoping the answer wasn't Judy herself. Then again, she'd never discussed any of that with Judy, who seemed somewhat miffed about it.

"At Jolene's café."

Probably from Jolene herself, Paige thought. She'd have to think twice about confiding in her, if she wanted any privacy at all.

Meetings and conferences kept her until nearly 6:00. The snow had completely stopped by the time she left work, but she knew Mike had been able to play in it at Luke's house for a while before it got dark.

She drove to pick up Mike under the light of a full moon, feeling renewed. This was how she'd expected life to be when she agreed to take the job and move to Ted's house. The fields surrounding the road were still covered in soft white mounds, but the road was clear. Everything seemed nearly perfect, as long as she didn't think about all the bad things that had happened.

"Do you want to see the snowman we made?" Mike asked when Paige came into Katie's house.

"Sure."

Both boys bundled up again to come out and show Paige the snowman they'd built. The snow had been the packing type and their creation was truly impressive. She congratulated them, wishing she had a camera to take a picture of the two kids with the huge snowman between them.

Katie spoke from behind her. "I took a bunch of pictures, and I'll get doubles when I process them."

"You think of everything, don't you?"

"Yes." She grinned. "For example, I thought that you should bring Mike over early in the afternoon on Saturday, so the boys could play and be out of your hair while you get ready for your date."

Paige was grateful that she had a place for Mike on Saturday night, but she regretted even mentioning the date to Katie, almost as much as she regretted accepting a dinner invitation from Quin. He'd caught her off guard when she came back from Arizona, and now there wasn't a way to get out of it. She hoped it wouldn't soon be on the gossip circuit. Besides, it really wasn't a date. She opened her mouth to clarify, but Katie was ahead of her.

"I know, going out with Quin isn't a date by your definition. But you can't expect Mike to provide all your male companionship."

That kept Paige's mouth shut. *And,* she thought, driving home, *maybe Katie was right.* Maybe it was time to stop putting off finding someone, using Mike's being orphaned by his father as an excuse. And she couldn't deny that Quin was an attractive man. It didn't mean she was attracted to him. In her heart she knew it was unlikely that anything would develop between them.

Paige was wearing her new off-white cashmere sweater and a long, flowered challis skirt, with knee-high boots. A patterned scarf, which had taken fifteen minutes to knot properly, completed the outfit. She wore small, gold hoop earrings, and for once, her dark hair was down around her shoulders.

Quin picked her up exactly on time. He was wearing an expensive, charcoal-gray suit, which brought out the intense blue of his eyes and made his longish blond hair stand out against his collar. She hadn't seen him much in several weeks, since before Ilke's car was discovered, and she found herself somewhat tongue-tied.

He held her door for her as she got into his SUV. "We're not going to eat at my hotel," he told her. "I want to be alone with you tonight so we're going to the Mirror Lake Inn."

Paige didn't know what to say, so she said nothing. She felt she was there under false pretenses because there was no chemistry between her and Quin, yet she'd agreed to go out with him.

The thousands of tiny white lights of the inn were brilliant against the black sky behind it. They outlined the gables and cupolas of the expansive facade and the windows overlooking the entrance looked warm and inviting. Inside the inn, with the woodwork glowing from the light of several fireplaces, Quin led the way to the dining room. The maitre d' greeted them and led them to a quiet table near another fireplace, secluded and elegant. The crystal gleamed from the firelight as Paige picked up her white linen napkin.

They were each handed a menu and the maitre d' asked Quin if he'd like to order wine. Quin's knowledge of the wine list must have been extensive since he ordered a bottle without even consulting the menu.

"This is a beautiful inn," Paige said, "and the company is very nice." She hoped her face didn't show that, unfortunately, she didn't have the same feelings for Quin as he seemed to have for her.

"I was hoping you'd feel that way." He was quiet while the sommelier opened the wine and poured a bit into his glass. He tasted it and nodded, and the wine was poured into Paige's glass before Quin's was filled.

He held up his glass to toast. "To our new friendship," he said. "May it grow." Leaning close to her, he clicked his glass with hers and stared into her eyes.

She could see the reflection of the fire that burned in the fireplace along the wall opposite him, but she could also see a deeper fire.

Quin seemed to be waiting for her to say something. But she didn't trust her voice at this moment. She didn't want to be the object of his desire. Not when she didn't feel attracted to him and the subject of his fiancée could still stop a conversation dead in its tracks. She made sure to stick to neutral topics.

"I'm sorry you got involved again," he said when he'd finished his smoked rainbow trout appetizer.

Paige put down the fork she'd been using to eat her duck ravioli. It seemed Quin was thinking the same thing. To be sure, she asked, "What do you mean?"

"With Ilke. Her car. It must have been upsetting when they found it and found it had been on Ted's property."

"I'm more sorry for you," Paige admitted. "You don't get a chance to get over it before you get another painful reminder."

Quin took her hand. "You're helping me more than you know."

Paige fought the urge to take her hand back but he didn't seem to notice how she felt. It wasn't until their entrees were delivered that he let go of her hand.

Since her ravioli had been filling, she picked at her Shrimp and Scallops Marcy, named, she presumed, after Mount Marcy, the highest in the area, as well as the state. Quin attacked his Roast Loin of Venison Hurricane with gusto. As the wine in his glass diminished, he became more animated, telling her about many things, from his youthful pranks in prep school to problems he'd had with his last boat.

"We had gone to lunch in Vermont. When we got back to the boat we realized we had zebra mussels stuck to every surface of the hull and they were clogging the intake valves," he said, waving a piece of potato on his fork. "I had to hire someone to put on gear and go scrape them off or we'd still be sitting on the dock." He took a sip of wine. "Ilke got tired of it after a while and rented a car to drive back home. She didn't want to leave Ted hanging, in case he needed her."

Quin looked Paige straight in the eye. "He'd call at nine o'clock at night to have Ilke come and look up a reference for him." His bitterness chilled Paige.

"Ilke would ask if it could wait until morning, but he'd say no, because the librarian he wanted her to check with was on the other side of the world. He didn't want a simple e-mail, he wanted a conversation, but he didn't want to do it himself. Ilke always said she didn't mind and off she'd go, leaving me." He stopped suddenly, as if embarrassed to show his feelings of loneliness.

Paige had to change the subject, quickly. "Tell me about your grandmother."

Quin's smile was full of love. "She was a wonderful lady. A real character. Here she was operating this rundown motel when Lake Placid was designated as the site of the next Olympics. She called on every favor she could and expanded the motel enough to make a killing when the Olympics were held. A lot of people didn't do that, and while they had small windfalls, Marissa's was really big. She reinvested, reasoning that now that the area was well-known with all new winter facilities, she could continue her good fortune. And she did."

"That must have been an exciting time," Paige said.

"It was. My parents helped out of course. Everyone did." He looked at Paige. "Marissa was really special. She was so good to me, and I don't think she ever once said no to me." He took a sip of his wine. "She told my mother not to be so strict with me, but my mom had her own ideas. Marissa would say, "He's just a young teenager, leave him alone," but Mom wouldn't listen. She sent me away to prep school. But as it turned out, Marissa was the one who ended up raising me, after my parents' accident."

It struck Paige that Quin had suffered so much, between the loss of his parents and Ilke. She didn't know what she could possibly say to make him feel better.

"I fought with my parents like crazy," Quin said, with more than a touch of regret.

Paige was dreading letting Quin down, so she grabbed at the

chance to talk about something else. "All children fight with their parents about something. Why did you fight with yours?"

"Oh, the usual, I guess. They didn't like the way I was dressing, or the people I was hanging out with. I wish . . ."

It was time for another conversation change. "Mike loved the snow the other day," Paige said. "He's looking forward to a lot more."

"He'll probably get it."

"That doesn't bother you?"

"Not at all. There will be lots of skiers in my hotel and I'll get a nice long fishing season that way."

"I still don't understand that. Isn't it easier to fish in the summer?"

"Maybe, but it's a lot more fun in the winter, in the ice shanty. I have all the comforts of home, which you don't get in a boat on the lake."

"But isn't it cold?"

"Not at all. I have a good heater. I don't sit directly on the ice, you know."

Paige had trouble imagining it.

"You don't believe me?" Quin's eyes were happy again and held a challenge. "Just wait. I'll take you out as soon as I get set up."

The waiter came to take their dessert orders. Paige declined, since she was full, but Quin ordered a slice of pumpkin pie.

He took her hand again after the coffee was served. "I can't tell you how happy I am that we're here together. I've thought about it since the first time I saw you."

It seemed like such a long time ago. But she didn't feel the same way Quin did and she had a hard time understanding how he could feel that way so soon after he learned of Ilke's death.

Given time she might to be able to warm to him, but somehow, she just couldn't see it. It wasn't just too soon after Michael's death. It was that Quin held no attraction for her, not like—

"Paige?" Quin interrupted her thoughts. He had a sad look on his face as if he suddenly understood . . .

She smiled at him. "Thanks for dinner. It was lovely. I'm glad you are a friend."

The Martin Luther King, Jr., holiday brought Wally up to Tamarack for the first time in the New Year. Paige seemed delighted to see her but expressed some guilt that Wally wasn't spending it with her own family.

"Oh, don't worry about that," Wally assured her, unloading some home-baked goodies onto the kitchen counter. "It's business as usual for us—Nate is away at a seminar; Rachel is tied up with her husband's family for the weekend, which is about the longest she can tolerate them, don't ask; and Debbie and Elliot are doing their own thing. Luckily for me, their own thing includes letting Sammy stay with them. And, Mark is in the Caribbean taking a vacation until school starts up again."

"I wish I was looking at pink sand and a blue ocean," Paige said, looking out the window. Wally followed her gaze and saw water, lots of it, in Lake Champlain, but it was all frozen. Little huts had started springing up near the shore where it was shallow and the ice had fully formed.

"I wouldn't mind that either," Wally said. "But the ice against the blue sky is pretty too."

Paige smiled. "I suppose you're right. What's wrong with your scarf?"

Wally was holding it up because it was sopping wet. "I somehow managed to get this caught in the taxi door. Do you mind if I run it through the wash?"

"Go right ahead."

Wally frowned. "I hate to waste the water on just one thing."

Paige had a solution. "There's plenty down there to put in with it. I'm a bit behind on the laundry." She moved to take Wally's scarf.

Wally was eager to hear how the people she knew in Tamarack were doing, so she followed Paige downstairs.

"I haven't seen too many of them since I got back," Paige admitted. She selected a load of towels to wash with the scarf and put them in. "I haven't seen Noah at all and I only saw Quin once, when we went to dinner."

"Wasn't that two weeks ago? He hasn't called you since then?"

Paige shook her head. "I don't know what to make of that. I had hoped we could stay friendly."

"Maybe he just needs time. How is Jolene?" Wally asked.

"I haven't really seen her."

That was a surprise. Wally had thought Paige and Jolene were good friends. "Have you given up on your daily muffin and coffee fix?"

"Never. I am convinced I couldn't get through a day without them. But although I saw Jolene every morning that first week after I came back from Arizona, I haven't seen her since." She turned on the machine. "There are so many tourists in town now she must be totally swamped with work."

When Wally went down to move the load of towels and the scarf into the dryer, she heard a hum start up. It reminded her of the dehumidifier in her house, but she couldn't see one anywhere, even though it sounded as if it were close by.

She looked at the wall next to her, the one that looked like new wallboard. There were several flakes on the floor below it and it seemed to have a bulge near the bottom. Wally ran her hand along the wall, trying to figure out what was causing the protrusion. A heavy dusting of white powder sifted to the floor near the bulge.

She stood back to look at the wallboard. When she did, she gasped. There, in the gray underlayer, where the top layer of white paper had come off, was the distinct outline of a gun.

Chapter Twenty

Wally waited anxiously while Paige called Sheriff Dover. He cautioned that she and Wally were not to touch anything, and he came to the house immediately. After examining the wall, he shook his head. "It's going to have to come down."

While they waited for the team of identification experts, Dover asked about the partition. "When did your uncle remodel the basement?"

"I don't know. This was here when I moved in, but before that it was all empty on this side of the basement."

Wally shook her head. "Why would anyone enclose an empty space?"

Dover shrugged.

"We can check with the local contractors, although it wouldn't have taken much to build it. But based on that outline," he gestured at the wall, where the gun-shaped water damage flaked a bit more, "I don't think we're going to find it empty."

Wally pulled over two boxes of books that Paige still hadn't unpacked and she and Paige sat down on them. "You don't think that outline is really a gun, do you?"

Dover's face was grim. "Yes, actually. I do."

"Why do you think we can see it?" Wally asked.

"It's probably due to the water. The gun must have been pushed up against the wall when the closet got flooded, and it eroded the wallboard in that shape."

"Mom?" Mike's voice at the top of the stairs sounded scared.

Paige went over to the steps. Looking up at his frightened face, she smiled encouragement she clearly didn't feel.

"Are the police going to dig up another dead body?" he asked.

Paige seemed to have no answers for her child. She took a deep breath, looking over at the boxes they'd sat on to view the search. Wally knew immediately what was on her mind. It was wrong to sit there gawking, leaving Mike alone upstairs.

"Let's hope not," Paige said to Mike. "We'll come upstairs until the police tell us it's okay to look."

Wally and Paige got up to the kitchen just as the doorbell rang. After Paige let in a dozen investigators, she and Mike went into the living room and watched an old movie. He cuddled up next to her and she put her arm protectively around him. When they were settled Wally went back to the kitchen and heated a bag of popcorn and brought it and some drinks in for them. They munched in silence for a while. Below them they could hear drilling and voices calling to one another.

"Luke's dad is nice," Mike said, during one of the commercials. "He came over and bought Luke a new sled and they're going sledding today. They'll be up there all day, and then they're going to a movie."

"That sounds wonderful," said Paige. "Maybe later, after the police leave, we can go see a movie."

"No, thanks," said Mike.

Mike dozed off after a while, probably because he'd been up all night at Luke's on another sleepover. Paige took the opportunity to talk to Wally about what was on her mind. "I know Mike needs a man to look up to, someone who could play the rough-and-tumble games he craves."

His father had never been any good at it, Wally remembered. Not only had Michael never had that kind of warmth with his son, he had distanced himself from the child, claiming he was too busy or too tired. Wally suspected the truth was he wasn't interested enough. But she knew Paige couldn't explain that to her son any more than she could make up for it.

"What about Quin?" Wally asked. "He seems to like making time for him."

"I don't know. Mike's been quiet about Quin for weeks, ever since the snowmobile purchase expedition. He likes Noah better, but I haven't been pushing it, not while things are up in the air. And even if things had been like they were before, an adult male friend couldn't fill the space Mike's father left."

Sheriff Dover coughed from the doorway. "If you'd like to come see what we found, it would be okay." He extended his arm to Mike, who was awakened by the noise, and put it around his shoulders as they walked to the basement steps.

The basement was full of people wearing latex gloves, examining the area and taking multiple pictures. The wall had been removed, and Wally saw it leaning against another wall. A black gun was on the floor next to a pile of wet, mildewed clothing. The female deputy, whose name Wally knew was Wendy, bent over the section of wallboard, holding white powder and a small brush, and a man carefully put the gun into an evidence bag.

Dover motioned toward it. "One of our crime scene investigators is also a gun buff. He says it looks like a Walther P38, possibly like one used during the Second World War. We'll be checking to see if it belonged to the deceased woman."

Wally turned questioningly to the deputy. "Ilke?"

"We believe those are hers."

He gestured to the clothing inside of the walled area. Now that it was open, Wally could see that it was an alcove built out of the natural corner of the basement, and it was filled with clothing and personal items. A man stood photographing the interior.

Dover put his hand on Mike's shoulder. "It's just clothes, toiletries, a hair dryer, a briefcase, and some jewelry." He gestured toward the woman who had been dusting the wall section. She nodded back at him.

"There are some other personal items too. At least that's what we can see so far," Dover was saying. He looked at Mike. "But there is nothing in there to be afraid of."

Mike stepped closer to the wall. He avoided the photographer, who was backing up, and peered at the gun. "Is it loaded?"

"Yes," said Dover. "But there is one bullet missing. We found the shell with the clothing."

Mike stood wide-eyed, as if trying to decide if this was really a neat thing or something to be frightened about. Paige seemed to be in no frame of mind to help him choose.

Wendy brought something over for Dover to see. He looked at it and showed it to Wally and Paige. It was a tiny colored bead.

"Is that like the bangle beads you found in Ilke's car?" Wally asked.

"Yes. We've been trying to find out where they were made, and the information we received indicates Sweden."

"I think I see where they came from." Wendy was holding up a worn garment. She seemed unwilling to say anything else.

"Mike?" asked Dover. "Would you please get me a glass of water, buddy? I'm really thirsty."

"Sure." Wally and Paige watched Mike go upstairs and turned back to listen to the female deputy.

"This vest seems to have a few of the same beads, it appears to be unraveling," she said. "There is a bullet hole in it and quite a bit of blood."

Wally looked at an obviously handmade garment and wondered sadly how the person who had made it, if she made it specifically for Ilke, felt about the young woman's death. That sent her thoughts back to Quin. When had he last seen her wearing it? And did he know how it came to unravel? She hated the thought that he would soon have to identify all of Ilke's things. Hadn't he been through enough?

Another investigator pulled a laptop computer out from the pile of clothes. He opened it and shook his head. It was probably ruined. The thought that this might have held the information on Ted's whereabouts went through Wally's mind, and with it, a sense of utter disappointment. The situation only seemed to get worse.

Wally put her arm around Paige until she stopped shaking. "We'll get through this."

Mike came back with the water, and Dover thanked him. He had just drained the glass when something else commanded his attention.

"Sheriff?" said a young man, who was half inside the walled-in space, handing the contents out to be bagged and labeled. "You have to see this."

Dover went over to where the man pointed and looked in. "That's odd. Trace it."

Wally wondered what he meant. "What's in there?"

"A dehumidifier. Have you heard it working?"

Paige nodded and swallowed hard.

Wally nodded too. "That's why I was examining the wall. I heard humming, but it didn't make sense, since there wasn't a dehumidifier anywhere." She stared at Dover. "What is it doing in there? It can't dry out any air in a sealed closet. That isn't how those things work."

Dover took a flashlight and shined it up at the ceiling. "It looks like there is some new wood up there." He turned to another policeman. "Let me see those chunks of wood you found. And would someone please get me a tape measure?"

After he examined the pieces of wood, which Wally realized were probably bits that had fallen through the hole in the floor when they were cleaning up the remnants of the closet, Dover measured the distance from the east wall to the new wood, then went upstairs and repeated it in the kitchen. Wally, who had followed him, along with Paige, saw him stoop down at the new patch that Noah had put in to close the hole in the floor. "The dehumidifier may not have been put there just to dry the air in that closet," he said, frowning. "It may have been to keep moisture out of Ilke's tomb."

His phrasing caught Paige by surprise and she gasped.

"Did you think of something?"

"No. It's just that . . ."

"What?"

"It reminded me of Uncle Ted and his work. He's gone into tombs and seen mummies, but it always sounded so distant, like the dead person had been gone for centuries. This was too recent."

"And well planned," said Wally. She looked at Dover. "Whoever did it must have had an understanding of what it would take to preserve a body so that it wouldn't decompose and generate suspicion, don't you think?"

Dover nodded.

"Who would know that?" Wally asked.

"You mean," said Paige, her voice shaking, "would my uncle? I'm sure he would. He did a lot of research in the field."

Dover put up his hand. "No one is saying it points to Dr. Verrill. Any person with a background in biology or medicine would have known the same thing. And it isn't as if you can't find out just about anything on the internet."

Paige shook her head impatiently. "Who would build the closet enclosure and set up the dehumidifier? And why didn't I hear it before a few weeks ago?"

Dover signaled to one of the investigators. "Have you figured out how the dehumidifier was set up?"

"We found the water outlet on the side of the house."

Paige sucked in her breath.

"What is it?" asked Wally.

"I just remembered Balto getting muddy on a dry day," said Paige, "and I wondered if that was the spot."

"And," the investigator continued, not paying attention to the conversation, "we traced it the other way, back to the circuit breaker."

"Thank you." Dover turned to Paige. "Are you sure you didn't hear it before?"

"Yes. And I would have before the furnace started coming on all the time. Unless . . ."

"Did you think of something?"

"I tripped a circuit several weeks ago, and I wasn't sure which one was out. There were two that were sort of halfway over, so I made them both go on. The noise started right afterward."

Dover called the man back over and instructed him to dust

the box for fingerprints other than Paige's. "Someone must have turned the circuit breaker off at some point. Possibly right before you moved in."

It was Wally's turn to suck in her breath. "Who?"

"That's what we have to find out. And we will."

Just after the last police car and truck pulled out of Paige's driveway, Noah Oliver showed up. Mike ran out to his pickup to greet him, taking Noah's hand to pull him out of the truck. Paige realized he'd done it before, quite comfortably.

"Mike, you don't have a coat on," Paige called from the porch. "Come back into the house."

"Can Noah come too?" Mike asked. Without waiting for an answer, Mike ran behind Noah and pushed him up the steps. Bounding through the door, he told Noah all about the hidden area in the basement and what the police found.

"I guess he isn't upset by all this," said Noah, wiping the fog off his glasses while Mike ran to find Balto. "I was afraid it would frighten him." He looked into Paige's eyes. "And you. That's why I came over."

She shivered. Noah came forward and put his arms around her. She went into them without thinking and found a feeling of safety and comfort she hadn't expected.

"Hello, Noah," said Wally from behind Paige.

Paige pulled away from Noah and looked at Wally. She knew her friend did not think it wise to be seeing Noah, not while he was under suspicion, at least in Wally's mind. Paige didn't believe Wally was right about Noah, and she fervently hoped she was wrong—seeing him only reinforced that hope. But she couldn't help wondering why every discovery was accompanied by a visit from Noah. It almost seemed as if he wanted to find out what the police had learned as soon as possible. The next thing she knew, he'd offer to remove the remnants of the hiding place, just as he had removed the debris from the closet.

"Wally?" said Noah. "I didn't realize you were in town. When did you arrive?"

While Wally filled Noah in on the timetable, right up to when she discovered the shape of the gun in the wallboard, Paige looked at him, standing there in his down jacket. She did not offer to have him stay. She suddenly felt afraid of this muscular man, whose strong arms and ability with carpentry reminded her of all Ilke's remains had been through.

"I'm so sorry you have to go through this," Noah said, turning to Paige. "As if you didn't have enough trouble already."

"Thank you for your concern," she heard herself say. Why was he apologizing? Was it because he was the reason for all the trouble? It couldn't be true; she felt that in her heart. Yet she had to protect herself and Mike, so she had no choice but to say, "I'm sorry you can't stay. But Mike, Wally, and I need to get some things done, and we don't have time for company right now."

Noah looked unhappy but he didn't argue. "I wish you'd . . ." He cleared his throat. "I just wanted to see if you were okay. I can see that you are and I won't keep you." He reached for the doorknob.

"Where are you going?" Mike asked. He stood with Balto at his side. "You just got here."

"I can't stay," said Noah, opening the door. "I'll see you soon." He was gone before Mike could protest.

"I wish he could have stayed," said Mike. "I wanted to show him the new trick I taught Balto."

Paige had her own wishes, but she wouldn't allow them to fully form in her mind. With a sigh, she booted them out and said, "Show Wally and me. I'd be happy to see it."

Mike hung his head. "Nah. It wouldn't be the same." He walked across the hallway and went upstairs.

Paige held herself in check. Her first thought was to follow Mike, to go up and talk him out of his doldrums. But what could she say? That she was beginning to be suspicious of Noah Oliver? That she thought he knew a little too much and was a little too interested in the circumstances surrounding Ilke's murder? That this man they liked so much, and whom Mike seemed to trust, was possibly a murderer?

After a cup of tea and some of the cookies Wally had brought, Paige voiced her doubts about Noah's involvement in all the trouble.

Wally listened carefully. "I have no real theory about Noah," Wally admitted. "From all I know about him I'd trust him completely. But there have been so many coincidences. Let's hope the police find the real murderer, then you can go back to being friends with him."

It surprised Paige how much she looked forward to that day.

Wally and Paige were working on dinner when the doorbell rang. Wally went to open it and found Quin. She wondered if he was as surprised to find her there as she was to see him, standing there with a bakery box from Jolene's.

"How nice of you," Wally said.

"I heard about the discovery of Ilke's belongings," he said. "I thought Paige could use this. Something sweet to replace the bad memories."

Wally's heart went out to him and she invited him inside to see Paige. The poor man didn't seem able to get away from the horror of his fiancée's murder. It was as if it would never end because every time it looked like there wasn't any more to it, there was another discovery. And every time it was at Paige's door.

"I was worried about you," Quin said to Paige when he got into the kitchen. "Your life is in a constant state of upheaval."

"We're okay." Paige said. She sounded so sad. Wally thought about Mike upstairs sulking and Paige's feelings for Noah. Even their dog liked Noah. They couldn't all be wrong, could they? Wally hoped not.

"Something sure smells delicious," Quin said.

"It's nothing, really," Wally said.

"Don't be so modest," Paige said. "This is your famous chili."

"It's probably better than the frozen dinner I'll have," Quin lamented.

He looked so hopeful that Wally wasn't surprised when Paige asked him to stay for dinner. Wally set another place at the table.

Paige called Mike to come downstairs. But he was obviously still annoyed with her, because he didn't hurry.

"We have a dinner guest," Paige said, when they heard his slippered feet scuffed along the floor of the hallway. His steps quickened, and he ran into the kitchen smiling. But, most unexpectedly to Wally, when Mike saw Quin, his smiled faded.

"Oh, hi," he said. Balto, right behind him, bounded in but backed up when he got close to Quin, sniffed, and walked away. It was somewhat awkward that not only Paige's son but also her dog made their preferences for Noah so clear.

"I'm sorry I'm not up to your standards," Quin said to the dog.

"Don't take it personally," Paige said. She turned to her son. "Will you feed Balto? Then we can all eat at the same time."

"He'll be done before we are," Mike said, pulling the huge tub of dog kibble open and scooping out the food. Nanoseconds later, Balto tore into the kitchen and gulped down his food.

"Twenty-nine seconds," Quin said, staring at his watch. "It must be a record."

Wally smiled. She'd put her own dog up against Balto in a food eating race, any day.

Mike giggled but stopped when he looked at Quin.

"I don't know if any of you have noticed, but the lake already has dozens of ice shanties on it," Quin said.

"That was fast," said Paige. "I only saw a few two days ago."

Quinn nodded. "People don't want to waste time. They can only be on the ice until March fifteenth."

"Can you drive on the lake yet?" Mike asked.

"Soon," Quin assured him.

Mike was so caught up in the conversation that he spilled the glass of juice he was holding.

Wally jumped up to get some paper towels. Quin stared at Mike with disbelief while Paige sopped up the mess.

"You haven't been around children much, have you?" asked Paige.

"No. I was an only child, like Mike. It was great."

"Noah said he has three brothers and two sisters," Mike said. "I think that sounds like fun."

The mention of Noah's name had the same effect on Quin as always. Wally could see him grinding his teeth.

He didn't stay after dinner. Paige seemed uncomfortable with Quin, nearly as much so as Mike and Balto. Later, when she was in bed but unable to sleep, Wally put that into her data banks and tried to come up with a scenario that would explain it. Could Quin actually be the person responsible for everything that had gone on? Yes, he was the bereaved, but it so often was the boyfriend or husband who was responsible for a woman's murder. Who else would have as much emotional stake? Paige had said that Quin had met Aurora. Could something about her have been threatening to him? Was suspecting the fiancé just too obvious? Or for that matter, was something about Aurora threatening to Noah? How could that be?

They were at a dead end, Wally thought. Without new leads, they were unlikely to get any new evidence. Paige might have to live with this hanging over her head for a lot longer. It was a terrible possibility.

Chapter Twenty-one

Dover called at 11:00 the next morning. "I have some news," he said, in his usual unemotional manner.

Paige was almost afraid to ask. "What is it?" she whispered.

"It's about the gun. We got a positive ballistics match. We were able to trace the serial number." He paused, as if to let Paige digest the information.

"And?"

"The gun was registered to your grandfather. Apparently he was given permission to bring it home as a souvenir of World War II. I received a faxed copy of the certificate a little while ago. Do you want me to read it to you?"

Paige's stomach knotted when Dover told her the gun belonged to Grandpa. She vaguely remembered hearing about it. But how did it get into the wall? And was it the weapon used to kill Ilke? "Y-yes."

"It's dated September 19, 1945. It says, 'Certificate on items of captured enemy equipment in the possession of Stanley Verrill,' and that the bearer is officially authorized by the 'Theater

Commander,' his name, 'Section VI,' of the such and such, 'to retain,' and so on. In other words, your grandfather owned this gun."

"Until he died," said Paige.

"Can I assume your uncle took it?"

"I'm sure my grandfather said he could."

"I don't doubt that. And it wouldn't have been a problem if it hadn't been the gun that was used to kill Ilke."

"Someone must have stolen it," Paige insisted. She gestured to Wally to come listen in to the call and held out the receiver to make it possible.

"I suppose that's a possibility," said Dover.

"Are you saying you think Uncle Ted used it to kill Ilke?"

"I'm not saying anything. Yet. But we'll be looking into it."

"My uncle wasn't even in town when Ilke was killed," Paige said.

"That isn't necessarily true. The forensic exam showed that Ms. Hedstrom had been tied up and left in a cold place for several days after she was shot. By the time of her demise, she had nearly frozen to death already."

Wally's eyes got wide as Paige fought the revulsion and fear she felt. "So?"

"It makes the actual date of death even harder to determine, and it's impossible to say when she was shot. Your uncle might have been here, or might have returned unnoticed. He'd been in town for one night only a week earlier and wasn't scheduled to fly out of the country for several days afterward. We don't know where he might have been for that whole week, although we're checking. And that's why Mr. Wyatt thought that his fiancée had gone with your uncle."

"And what do you think?" She knew her voice sounded shrill when she said that, but she couldn't help it.

"I'm sorry, Dr. Griffin," said Dover. "I know this is hard for you."

"It's not your fault."

"There isn't much to go on," Dover admitted. "I know. But as of now, your uncle is our number one suspect."

Tears sprang to Paige's eyes. "He can't be. He couldn't have done all those things in the one day he might have been here. You said yourself that the closet wall and the enclosure in the basement were projects that would have taken quite a long time to complete."

"He could have done that ahead of time."

"No," Paige said, fighting to keep her voice steady. "He's not a cold-blooded murderer."

"Maybe that's why he's hasn't been heard from. He might not have meant to kill her."

"You think the person who killed her and built the closet and the hiding place did it accidentally?"

"We can't rule it out."

"Oh, so he built an enclosure for a body and then accidentally shot her, froze her nearly to death, let her die of infection. Then he installed a dehumidifier and hid her car." The mention of the car reminded Paige of Aurora's accident, stretching Paige's nerves to the breaking point. "Do you also think he snuck back into town to move the car, again to turn off the circuit breaker for the dehumidifier before I moved in and possibly came again to tamper with Aurora's brakes using the license plates from Ilke's car on one he stole, and no one saw him any of those times? And all this while he was arranging for me to come and live in his house?"

"We don't have all the pieces yet," Dover said, in what Paige took to be an attempt at a soothing voice, but which only made her angrier. "I'll be the first to admit that," he added. "But we have several big ones pointing at Ted. I'm sorry."

"Do what you have to," Paige said, slamming down the phone. She had to take several deep breaths to keep from screaming.

"He can't be serious," said Paige after a while. "My uncle can't have had anything to do with this mess."

Wally knew Ted even less than the two men who were her main suspects. She couldn't offer any words of encouragement.

While Paige went to wash her face, Wally called Nate with the news. "Anything you can do," she said, hoping it would be something. She also asked him to check out Noah's background. She hated to do it, and Nate seemed surprised.

"I've always had a good feeling about that guy," Nate said.

"Me too. But there are just too many weird coincidences."

Nate agreed to do what he could. He had a few old acquaintances who might be able to find Ted. Not for the first time did Wally disagree with Dover's insistence that they could handle this case without outside help. The New York State Police Bureau of Criminal Investigation was there for a reason. Wally thought they should be used for more than just lab tests.

"Let's get out of here for a while," Wally suggested to Paige a half hour later. "I'm sure Mike could use some fresh air."

They walked over to Jolene's for lunch. Afterward, when Mike was at the bakery counter selecting a cookie, a woman who had been eating lunch at the next table stood up and walked over to them. "How's Aurora?" she asked Paige.

Paige smiled at Dyna, the owner of the stationery and gift store. "Much better. She's still pretty much stuck at home, but some of the kids visit and her dad is around most of the time. I heard your daughter has been a regular."

"She likes Aurora and feels sorry for her," said Dyna. "That poor kid. So much has happened to her. First her mother runs away, then this."

"Did you ever meet her mom?" Wally asked.

"Sure. She was a frequent flyer at my shop." Dyna looked over at Paige. "If she showed up tomorrow, you'd recognize her in a minute."

"I never met her," Paige said.

"You'd know her, trust me. She looks exactly like Aurora. Same face, height, hair, everything." Dyna opened her purse and took out some money. "She was here, you know. I saw her the morning she left. If I had known she was leaving forever, leaving her daughter, I would have tried to talk her out of it."

Paige was confused. "I thought she left from New York. Aurora wasn't up here then, was she?"

"No. I thought she was Aurora for a minute, though, because she was wearing her jacket."

"How do you know that?"

"It was really nice, with some great colors, and I complimented her on it. And Yvette, Aurora's mom, said it wasn't hers, it was Aurora's. She said her daughter was in school in the city and that she always left the jacket here since she never needed one like that in Manhattan."

Wally knew the multicolored jacket she was describing. "If it wasn't black, I can understand that," she said, thinking about how so many kids dressed in New York. "Did Mrs. Dillon seem upset that morning?"

"Not really, although I wouldn't say she was in a happy mood. She said she was going out to the lake with her camera. She was pretty good. I've seen some of her pictures. When she left, she said she'd see me the next day, for her *New York Times*."

"Mrs. Dillon didn't say she was leaving town?"

"No," Dyna said. "She told me Aurora would be coming up in a few days on her winter break. It would be the first time she was ever here for more than a weekend in the winter. Her mother said she'd come up ahead to make sure the house was ready, although as I told you, I kind of thought she was making sure it wasn't occupied with her husband and his latest friend. But maybe she didn't even know about that."

"So he had a reputation for cheating on his wife," Wally said. She wondered if everyone but the wife knew about such things. A glance at Paige gave Wally a pang—she was obviously thinking the same thing—but from a more personal viewpoint.

"Everyone around here knew," Dyna said. She started to move away but turned back. "By the way, everyone is so happy to hear you are dating Quin Wyatt. He deserves some happiness."

Paige's face suffused with color as she sputtered to find a response. She was saved from having to do so by Jolene coming out of the kitchen. But it was not the respite Wally hoped it might be because Jolene had obviously heard the comment and had questions of her own.

"Yes," said Jolene. "Tell us all about it."

Paige stood up, smiling awkwardly, clearly uncomfortable about talking about the date. "Oh, hi, Jolene. I was afraid I wouldn't see you. You've been very busy, haven't you?"

Paige's obvious attempt to change the subject was successful. Jolene excused herself to go back into the kitchen. "Sorry I can't talk now," she said. "You understand, don't you?"

"Of course," said Paige. "I think we'll ask for Mike's dessert to be put in a bag. He can eat it on the way home."

"What are you thinking?" Wally asked Paige when they were nearly back at the house. Paige had been silently brooding the whole way, leaving Wally to make conversation with Mike as the three of them trudged through the frozen landscape. Although Jolene's Café was visible from the shoreline near Paige's house, the walk around on the roadway was well over a mile.

Paige turned to Wally and there were tears in her eyes. "I was thinking that no matter what happened in my life, I wouldn't have left my child behind the way Aurora's mother did."

"Ugh," said Paige just as they got home. "I'm running out of clothing and I can't stand the thought of going down to the basement."

"Didn't the police take everything out of there yet?" Wally asked. "I thought it was all evidence."

"Yes and no. They took it all, but there are still walls. And nails and splinters."

Wally considered the problem. As much as she wanted to follow her head, she let her feelings take over. "Didn't Noah offer to take care of that?"

"Yes. But I thought . . ."

"I'm here. If you are going to let him in, it may as well be now."

Paige seemed glad to put aside her fears and she called him. Wally started a pot of soup, cutting in a lot of vegetables that she would pull out and puree after they cooked, and then put back into the soup. Mike would never know he was eating them. While that bubbled on the stove, she mixed up some baking powder biscuits. It was the perfect thing for this freezing day.

Nate called Wally's cell phone when the biscuits were ready, and she had to juggle to get them out and maintain the conversation.

"I haven't learned Ted's whereabouts," Nate said. "But about Noah Oliver—"

Wally caught her breath. "What about him?"

"His name came up on a list of people the government has tracked. I'm looking into it. Okay?"

Her heart sank. "Okay."

Noah was at work on the last of the basement closet when Wally came downstairs. She seemed surprised when Paige told her that Noah was making it into useful space. Mike, who was wearing the pared-down tool belt that Noah brought him, watched raptly as he worked. Paige watched too, as he measured the door and the related doorway and put his goggles on to drill.

He assumed a position and aimed the drill at the door. Bits of sawdust flew off, coating his rag style sweater. He turned around.

"That looks right, doesn't it, Mike?"

Mike put his hammer back into his tool belt and came over to inspect the hole. "Yes, sir. It's a good hole." He and Noah high-fived and looked at Paige and Wally for approval.

Paige went over to the door. "It's good," she said, then looked over at Noah.

He had removed the goggles and looked expectantly back at her. There was a sliver of wood in his beard and Paige reached over to remove it. The beard was surprisingly soft and Paige suddenly had an urge to stroke it.

"Let's put this on," said Mike, bringing some hardware over to Noah. It was a knob for the door he'd just installed.

Noah looked down at the boy and smiled. Paige stepped back and let them get to work. She hoped he hadn't noticed the flush she now felt spreading from her hair down to her throat. She went upstairs, leaving Wally to oversee the project.

As soon as they were done, Mike and Noah cleaned up and came upstairs for lunch. Wally, looking thoughtful, followed.

Mike seemed so happy, chattering on and on with Noah. Balto snuggled up to him, too, rolling onto his back for a belly rub.

"This soup is wonderful," said Noah. "And the biscuits are great."

"Wally is a really good cook," said Mike. "And so is my mom. You should come over more often."

Noah wiped his mouth and mustache on his napkin. "I'd like that. And not just because of the food. The company here is very nice."

"We're not company," Mike argued, "we live here."

"It's an expression," Paige explained, "for which we cheerfully say thank you."

"You're welcome," said Noah. "Are there any other chores you need to have done around here?"

"Not really, no."

"I can't understand how all that building got done, under everyone's noses," Noah said.

Wally shook her head. "It wasn't exactly, was it? The way I understand it is that anyone could have gotten into the house. That's why Nate bought those new locks."

"Why would you think anyone could get in?"

"As far as I know, Paige has one of the only keys. Mr. Foster down the road has one, and Ted has one. So how did the—" she broke off, not wanting to say murderer in front of Mike.

"I don't know," said Noah. "But how would someone get in without a key?"

Any school kid could have done it, Wally knew. Her own town of Grosvenor, New Jersey, was not immune to break-ins, although the burglars usually left a lot more traces of themselves behind. "With a credit card or something. At least that's what I thought."

"Let's try it. Then we'll know." With Noah leading the way,

all four of them went to the back door. Paige tried her credit card, which was still in her pocket after the morning's purchases. But no matter how she wriggled it, she couldn't get it to open the door. There was a piece of molding in the way.

It was the same with the front door. "This molding doesn't look new," she said.

Noah inspected it. "I don't think it is."

"Then a credit card wouldn't work."

"I guess not."

Wally shook her head. "And Nate didn't need to put in those dead bolts."

"I think you did need them, as well as the window locks," Noah said. "For your peace of mind."

He didn't add that there was a murderer out there who obviously knew how to get into the house, but she could see it in the way he scowled.

Noah picked up his tool box with one of his strong arms and with his other he grabbed Mike and tossed him up on his shoulder like a sack full of potatoes. "I'm done here," he joked. "I'll just be going now."

Mike twisted in Noah's grip to look at him. "Can I really go with you?"

The big man pretended to be surprised to find Mike under his arm. "How did you get here?" he asked.

"You picked me up." Mike giggled so hard he had to hold his sides.

Paige laughed, but inside she was in knots. It was painfully obvious that Noah would have had no trouble at all carrying Ilke or her belongings around, as well as building the enclosures to hide them. Maybe Wally's instincts had been right. "Please put him down," she said. "Mike," she said, "could you please make sure Noah didn't leave any of his tools behind?"

Mike looked as if he'd been given the most important job in the world and ran down to the basement. Paige looked at Noah. "I want to trust you," she said, laying it all right out. "But there are some things that worry me." She looked over at Wally, who nodded agreement.

Noah took up her challenge. "Such as?"

"Have you ever been in trouble with the law?"

"Yes, I have."

Paige, who had expected a denial, was brought up short.

"I was charged with theft of valuable property," Noah admitted, a wide grin on his face.

Had she been right to be suspicious? Paige wondered. But why was he telling her this as if he was proud?

"I stole two dozen rabbits that were being used to test cosmetics," Noah explained. "And when I was arrested and ordered to produce the goods, I didn't. I had found them all good homes and I wasn't about to ask those kind people to return the rabbits so they could have mascara put into their eyes."

Noah looked deep into her eyes. "I have a record. Can you live with that?"

Paige didn't know whether to laugh or cry. "I can."

"Do you trust me now?"

That was a harder question. "I'm working on it."

He looked over at Wally. "Mrs. Morris," he said, going back to what he'd originally called her. "I know that you have some reservations and I know that Paige trusts your judgment. I wish I could get you to believe in me."

Her look was noncommittal. But she was smiling.

The hopeful look in his eyes faded, but only for a moment. Mike came back and gave the all clear. "Maybe I should wait until you both do," Noah said, looking from Wally to Paige. He picked up his jacket, said good-bye to Mike and Balto, and nodded crisply at Paige. Then he was gone.

Balto ran to the kitchen and Paige heard the dog door slam. A second later she saw him following after Noah's truck until he gave up and sat staring at it. *The poor dog's heart was broken,* she thought. A look at Mike told her he felt the same way. And if she were to be honest with herself, she'd admit she felt very sad too.

Chapter Twenty-two

"**A**re you up for an outing?" Paige asked Wally the next morning.

"Always," she said. "Where to?"

"We're going to see Quin's ice shanty," Paige said. Judging by the look on her face, Wally wasn't all that sure that Paige was looking forward to it.

"Okay. What does one wear to an ice shanty?"

"Something warm, I'm guessing. I sent Mike to put on his ski pants and jacket. I can lend you something if you don't have enough clothes."

"I'll see what I have. But before I go up to swaddle myself, I have a question. Didn't you decide not to let things progress with Quin? Aren't you afraid of leading him on?"

"Yes and no. I think we came to an understanding. Besides, he didn't ask me, he asked Mike. I couldn't say no after that."

Wally nodded. "It should be interesting, at least."

They trudged through the snow to the lakeshore with Balto running around them. Not far away sat Quin's ice shanty. The roof was peaked, different from most of the huts in the distance, which were smaller and looked more like square outhouses with windows. Quin's, Wally knew from what he'd told them, was larger than most, because it was custom-made. It was very neat and tidy, except for a plastic crate and a coil of rope right outside the door.

Wally gazed north along the shoreline at the other ice shanties, which had sprung up this second to last week of January, once the lake was deemed fully frozen. They stood in a group on the ice, looking like a shantytown. She'd seen pictures in magazines of literal towns with street signs and roads on some of the frozen lakes of Michigan, Minnesota, and Wisconsin. The Lake Champlain ones were not quite as formally set up as that, but there was a certain hominess about them. People walked from one to the other, and children and dogs ran between and around them.

For some reason, though, Balto would not set a paw on the windswept ice. He whined and ran along the shore but refused to go any farther. Mike tried to get him to go but finally told the dog he'd see him later.

It felt so strange to be walking on the lake. Even though Wally had ice-skated before, it was a little scary to think there were many feet of water just inches beneath her. She could understand Balto's innate reluctance to walk on it. Many of the features on the shore were softened by drifts of snow, but Wally was able to make out the inlets and where the docks were in the summer. Paige's house towered above them on the bluff.

They knocked on the door and Quin ushered them inside. The warm interior surprised Wally, and she guessed Paige and Mike as well, based on their exclamations. It was like a miniature cabin with a stereo system; a cushion-covered bench with more cushions on the wall, forming a couch; and a pull-down table, which Quin reached over and pushed up into the wall, revealing a magazine rack that had served as the table leg. It also had a tiny television and small curtained area she assumed was a commode.

She hadn't realized how much carpentry and planning went into such a place. She gritted her teeth at the realization. Could Quin have been the murderer all along?

"That'll give us some more room," Quin explained when he'd snapped the table leg into place between the magazines.

"You know, I'm amazed at this place. It's like a tiny cabin in the woods." Wally tried to sound impressed.

Quin laughed. "Without the woods."

"I guess. I just never expected it."

"What did you expect?"

"A milk crate."

"What?"

"A milk crate next to a hole in the ice, with a really big doghouse over it. That's all I thought it would be."

Quin laughed again but seemed pensive. "Is that what you thought? Well, maybe that's why Ilke never came out here. Maybe she thought the same thing."

His casual mention of his dead fiancée's name did nothing to quell Wally's concerns.

There was an awkward silence and Wally came up with something to fill it. "This couch can stay out here and not get ruined?"

"Yes. It's the kind of fabric that people leave outside in the summer. And I don't even have to worry about mold, since it never gets warm enough. The heat is only on when I'm staying for a while."

Mike was looking at the floor. "Where is the hole, anyway?"

Quin pulled open a three foot hatch and Wally saw the black water underneath.

"It looks so cold," Paige said.

"Believe me, it is."

All that week, after Wally went back to New Jersey, after much protest even though there was a wedding she and Nate had to attend the following weekend, Paige tried her best to reconcile her feelings about Noah. She missed him. Maybe it was sooner than she would have expected for her to have these emotions, but she couldn't use Wally's imaginary suspicions to keep herself away from him. Hadn't he come clean about his arrest? Didn't that mean he was telling the truth?

She and Wally had talked it over before she left, and it was a condition of Wally's getting on the train. Wally wanted Paige to stay away from Noah. Following a long discussion, Paige had agreed.

It was true that Noah hadn't seemed to even wonder what had happened to the wood that fell through the hole, as if he knew it would have fallen into the closet the murderer had built, and he knew carpentry and he was very strong. He had discouraged them from looking in Ted's experimental plants grove when they were dog-proofing the property, and that was where Ilke's car had been hidden. He had also prevented them from looking in the outbuilding where she had been hidden—where the police determined she had ultimately died. He could have done all the things that happened. Yet he seemed to be a good man and Paige sensed he would not hurt her or Mike. Considering how she felt when she was with him, especially when he was close to her, she hated being suspicious of him.

She couldn't understand it. Noah was unlike anyone she'd have expected to want to be close to. He was practically a backwoodsman, the complete opposite of the cosmopolitan men Paige knew. He listened to country music, something she'd never done, and no opera, no classical music at all, not even much rock. And he couldn't tell a Rembrandt from a Picasso from a Jackson Pollack. Or could he? Occasionally some of the things he said made her think he was teasing her, that he knew just as much as anyone about the things that interested her. And there was no doubt he made her feel deliciously lightheaded some-times, like when he had examined her wounded head, and when she had felt the softness of his beard.

Someone had told Paige not to make a big decision of any kind for a year and a half after Michael died, and here she'd al-ready completely changed hers and Mike's lives, and she was now considering whether or not to fall in love.

She wished she could just go over to Noah's and tell him she trusted him completely, but somehow she couldn't. Whatever was holding her back, it wasn't fear of him. It was fear of letting go, becoming vulnerable again. Wasn't that the part she didn't trust? Yet whenever the phone rang, she hoped it would be him. Hearing his voice would help, but she couldn't call him until she was sure she was ready. It wouldn't be fair. And as time went by, it became clear he would not make the first move. He was wait-ing for her to do it.

On the last Friday in January, to get her mind off her pre-parent conference jitters, Wally tried to work on the other great problem in her life, the incidents in Tamarack.

She thought about the people who were involved and the oth-ers whom Paige knew. There was Quin Wyatt, whose fiancée had been murdered and who seemed to be better at carpentry than she and Paige had thought, based on his beautiful ice shanty. Noah Oliver was strong, handy with tools, and had "lost" sight of the carpenter's plane that might have been evidence. Wally knew a lot about both men because Jolene Valley was a repository of information on them when they were young. Paige had remarked that Jolene seemed distant lately, so that source of information was likely a dead end. Wally would have to find another source of information, hopefully someone who had a clue to who really killed Ilke. If only she had an idea how to go about it.

"I'm here, Wally," said Mr. Pepper. "What's this about Kallie acting out?"

Snapped out of her reverie, Wally focused on her visitor. He seemed to fill Abby's office. It might have been a better idea to meet with him in a classroom, because his presence here was overwhelming.

As if by magic, Abby, the school director, stepped into the doorway. Wally didn't know whether to be happy or annoyed. She'd thought she could handle the meeting on her own, but Mr. Pepper's body language did not say friendly. Maybe he was annoyed about her allegations that his nearly complete absence since the divorce was causing his daughter emotional trauma, or at being called away from work. Abby had obviously seen him coming in the door and was here to run interference.

Whatever her reasoning for coming into the meeting, Abby soon took it over. Wally gave the facts. Kallie, ever since her father moved out, had become very possessive, especially about Ruthie. She hated it when Ruthie played with anyone else, and acted out. Wally stated her worries that Kallie was upset because she loved her dad and missed him, and Abby used her sledge hammer approach to bring the point home. The words *suffering, heartbreak, insecurity, possessiveness* and *jealousy* were used, and the threat of future emotional problems followed. "Her self-esteem is at stake."

Mr. Pepper sat and listened. Then he argued that nothing was wrong; Kallie's behavior was like any other child's. Wally cited examples of the problems. Mr. Pepper refuted them and added that if there were any problems it had to be the school's fault.

That sent Abby over the edge. "Mr. Pepper," she said, "one day you may find that Kallie is in terrible trouble because she has tried to keep someone close to her from forming a relationship with someone else. It may take the form of simple rejection by that person, or it may escalate. That behavior is not something a child develops at nursery school. That behavior stems from damage done in the family. Do you want to be responsible for that?"

Mr. Pepper put his head into his hands. "No. I'll fix it. And if I can't, I'll find someone who can." He stood up, looking shaken. "Thank you. I didn't know about any of this. I guess I will have to work out something with Kallie's mother."

Abby was all smiles, even though Wally was a little stunned by her heavy-handedness. "That's all we ask," Abby said. "Anything we can do to help, just call. And you should thank Wally for her efforts."

An awkward mumbled exchange between Wally and Mr. Pepper ended with him leaving. When enough time had elapsed to let him get into his car and after checking to be sure he was gone, Wally went to her car. She didn't even mind that she might look cowardly by avoiding another confrontation with Kallie's dad.

On the ride home, she wondered if Abby was right. Could Kallie, as she got older, be so possessive of someone, maybe a man she loved, that she would do something drastic to keep him? It was a horrible thought, but not something out of the realm of possibility. Some people blamed people who had betrayed them for their misery, while others blamed the person who had taken the loved one away. People got hurt in situations like that, and not just emotionally.

Wally was driving on autopilot, unable to get focused on

anything other than the murder. Was that why Ilke was dead? Did Quin kill her because she'd found someone else? No one seemed to think she was unfaithful to Quin after they became engaged. Wally shook her head as she pulled into her driveway. Poor guy. He'd already lost so much. First his parents, then his grandmother. Then his fiancée.

She slammed on the brakes nanoseconds before she would have hit the garage. She knew who had killed Ilke.

Chapter Twenty-three

On Saturday morning after breakfast at Jolene's café, a very excited Mike went to Aurora's for a visit. She had called on Tuesday evening to see if he could come and he had happily accepted. They had formed a strong bond before the accident and Mike had been very concerned about her. Paige felt it would be good for him to see how well she was doing. They planned to spend several hours together without Paige's presence inhibiting them and she would pick him up in the afternoon.

He had talked about it for the rest of the week and was chattering about it the whole time they ate. When they got to the house, Paige only stayed long enough to say hello to Aurora and her father, then left them alone together.

When she got home, she began straightening up. She was still uncomfortable about how she'd left things with Quin when he called last night. He seemed to be hoping she would change her mind about them being just friends. She had carefully, but firmly, made it clear that they had no future. She only hoped it wouldn't get all over town. The subject of the principal's love life had no place in local gossip.

She felt restless and in need of answers. Wally had called and asked her some questions, but hadn't given her any information. Those questions raced around in Paige's mind. Wally had seemed happy to hear that Mike would be with Aurora and asked what Paige's plans were for her day alone. "I'm thinking of going shopping at the mall in Plattsburgh," she'd said. But that didn't appeal to her so much now.

She soon found herself in the room Ilke had used. So much time had passed and yet there was still no solid lead on Ilke's killer. It frustrated Paige because, until the person was caught, she could never relax. She hated being startled at ordinary house noises late at night; tiptoeing around Quin; feeling sorry for Aurora, another probable victim of the killer; and most of all, suspecting Noah.

This out-of-sorts feeling could only be put to rights with some positive action. No matter how small, Paige had to do something that would prove to herself she had things under control.

To get her mind off all these useless questions, Paige grabbed a quick lunch and went out to paint the wintry sky where it met the ice on the lake.

Nate kept his eyes on the road but didn't stop questioning Wally. "Why didn't you call Sheriff Dover?"

"I did. I called him three times last night. Finally, this morning, somebody at police headquarters told me that he's away on a fishing trip. Not only that, there isn't any cell service where he went. And to answer your next question, the person who is filling in for him wouldn't give me the time of day. He told me to call back when Dover is back."

"Tell me again why you think you figured out who killed Ilke."

Wally knew Nate was just trying to get her to calm down by letting her talk. She appreciated it. "I was thinking about what Noah had said about the locks. That no one without a key could have broken in and not left a trace. There were no signs of a forced entry in the wood. Only someone with a key would have been able to come in and out of the house. But who?" Wally looked at Nate. "Only the person who had Ilke's key. It wasn't found with her things."

"I remember. Okay, I see your reasoning, although it's a little frightening that I can follow the way your mind works."

Wally feigned insult. "What's that supposed to mean?"

"Forget it. But what I don't understand is why you didn't tell Paige. Shouldn't she protect herself until the police can?"

"She's safe. She went out of town for the day."

"So what's your plan?"

"To get there, make sure they're safe, and wait for the cavalry. I only wish we had more concrete information. All we have is negative information, but in a way I guess it's positive."

Nate, ever the loving husband, seemed to be working on what Wally had said. Eventually, he gave up. "Okay, you lost me."

"You got confirmation from your contact that Ted hasn't been in this country for over a year, since well before Ilke was killed. He couldn't have done it."

"You never thought he did."

"Right. But I'm glad we're sure. It makes our case stronger." She looked at a road sign they were passing. "Can't you go faster?"

Nate pushed the speed up a notch. "Why do you think that today, when you are so close to catching the murderer, it will suddenly be the day for the murderer to make a move? And why do you think it will be against Paige?"

"Because based on my conversation with Paige, I think she has fallen out of favor with the murderer."

Nate gripped the steering wheel tighter. "We'll be there in an hour. Maybe you should try calling the police again."

Wally called again and got the same response. No one had reached Sheriff Dover yet, and no one was willing to do anything without his say-so.

Nate shook his head. "There's one thing that has been bothering me."

"What might that be?" asked Wally, wary of his tone. He sounded a bit like a person who was about to say she didn't have much of a case.

"I was wondering about the little matter of proof."

Wally bit her lip. She wondered about it too. It was there, she was sure.

Closing her eyes, she let her mind go over every minute, every nuance, every gesture. It was all so clear, but something was missing. Unless . . . It suddenly came to Wally. She'd had no pockets.

Wally made one more phone call, then, teeth gritted, waited until Nate got her to Tamarack.

There was a typewritten note taped to Paige's door when she got back to the house. "Meet me at my ice shanty," it said. Although it was unsigned, it was obviously from Quin. Hadn't she made herself clear?

Shaking her head, she decided to go meet him. Maybe he just needed more of an explanation. Maybe he just wanted to be sure they could still be friends. They surely both needed friends, didn't they?

Balto went to the shore with her but refused to step onto the ice. He sat there when Paige set out onto the frozen lake. She walked for several minutes, and Paige marveled at the various views of Vermont on the opposite shore silhouetted against the suddenly clear blue sky.

She knocked at the door and it opened. But instead of Quin, Paige found Jolene staring out at her. "Welcome," she said. "Come right in."

In a daze, Paige went through the doorway, out of the brilliance of the sunshine on the snow, into the dim interior.

"You can take your jacket off," Jolene said a moment later, taking off her own and making herself at home as if she owned the place. She pulled the curtains over the windows closed, making the room even darker. "Can I get you a drink?"

"I don't understand," Paige said. "Where is Quin?"

"Where is he always? At his beloved hotel. But I'm sure he's also planning another fancy date with you."

"I don't think so," Paige said. "I told him I don't feel that way about him."

Jolene stared at her. "Do you think he's going to give up so easily? Not likely. As long as you're around, he's going to keep trying to get you."

How creepy, Paige thought. But then she caught her breath. Was Jolene saying that Quin was a murderer? Or just that he couldn't take no for an answer. Paige had to find out what was going on. "I'll take that drink," she said, tension filling her from head to toe.

Jolene handed her a soda and motioned to the couch. "Sit down. We can't stand here all afternoon."

Paige sat as directed but kept her jacket on. She didn't know what was going on and she was getting a really weird feeling. She put the can of soda down, unopened. She didn't plan to stay long enough to enjoy it.

"Is something wrong with your soda?" Jolene asked, her tone menacing.

"No. I—"

"Drink it." It wasn't a request.

Paige opened the can. Her mouth had gone dry and she took a few sips.

"You can watch me fish." Jolene offered pleasantly, moving to uncover the hole.

Fish? She wanted to fish?

"I didn't know you used Quin's hut," Paige said.

Jolene smiled. "Of course. Everything of his is mine."

Paige tried not to show surprise, although she was very confused. One thing was clear. She wanted to get out of there. It was too weird.

While Jolene's head was turned, Paige searched for the right words to say she was leaving. Jolene kept twisting her way, though, so Paige tried her best to look calm. Inside, her mind was reeling. She was sure that Quin regarded the hut as his private domain and had never said anything about sharing it with anyone, let alone Jolene. She didn't think they were even that friendly.

"This is cozy," Jolene said, while munching on a bag of potato chips she'd opened after her fishing line was set. She offered them to Paige.

Paige's hands were shaking so much that she dropped a chip between the couch cushions. She reached her fingers down to get it and pulled it out. But it wasn't the potato chip. It was one of Ilke's beads, from the same bloody vest the police had found in the basement closet.

A chill swept over Paige. Had Quin lied about Ilke never being in the hut? Could this be the place where she had been shot, before being dragged, wounded and bleeding to the outbuilding on Uncle Ted's property?

Paige looked at her watch. "It's late." She stood up and,

pushing one of the curtains aside, saw that the sun was low in the sky. "I should go get Mike." She reached for her coat.

Jolene jumped up and stopped her. "He'll be fine at Aurora's."

"Yes, but he might want something."

"You're smothering him."

That statement, along with Jolene's know-it-all attitude, made Paige's already frazzled nerves fray even more. She took her coat back from Jolene and moved toward the door. "I am leaving now," she said as firmly as she could.

"You're staying here," Jolene shouted. She reached out and pulled Paige by the hair back toward the couch. "Now sit down." Jolene stood glaring over her. Without moving away, she managed to close the blackout curtain again. The only light was from an electric lantern on the table.

"What's the matter with you? You can't keep me here," Paige said, unable to keep her voice from quivering.

"Shut up. You're getting to be just as bad as she was. Always telling me how things should be. Always arguing. Always scheming, trying to take Quin away from me. But I'm the boss here. Too bad I don't still have that gun."

Suddenly it hit her. Jolene was insane. Paige gasped as the huge, sinister pieces of the puzzle fell into place. "My grandfather's gun?"

"Is that where it came from?" Jolene asked, calmly, as if they were discussing the weather. "I always wondered."

Fighting the fear that was gripping her, Paige tried to keep her own voice calm. "Why did you kill Ilke?"

"She was going to marry Quin. He's mine."

Her cold words sent shivers down Paige's spine. She tried to swallow but could not.

Jolene leaned toward her. "Get up."

Paige did as she was told. "There is no reason to hurt me. I won't tell anyone that you were the one."

"Yeah, right. You'd never keep my secret any longer than the length of time it took you to run to the police. And even if I believed that, Quin only has eyes for you, not for me. But with you out of the picture, and both of us comforting each other over the loss of our dear Paige . . ." She pulled Paige away from the couch. "I don't believe you'd keep my secret at all. So I'm going to keep you from telling."

"I would. I don't have any proof, anyway." said Paige. "I thought we were friends. I know you wouldn't hurt me."

"You don't know anything. Like those new locks your friend installed. They were a waste. No one broke in. I had a key. Ilke's." Jolene chuckled. "And you almost caught me, that first day. I was in the house, turning off the circuit for the dehumidifier and looking over my handiwork when you drove up. I almost got there too late. I guess that's the price I pay for success—my café is always full, but it doesn't give me much free time.

"It's a good thing your mutt was running around, or you might have seen me come out." Jolene turned to her, demanding admiration. "The basement was a good hiding place for her stuff," she declared, proudly. "Only the place I hid her body was better."

"Why did you go to all that trouble?" Paige thought letting Jolene talk would be a good way to keep herself from facing whatever was planned for her.

"The ground was frozen. I couldn't bury her. And if the ice hadn't been so solid, I could've gotten rid of her car immediately, instead of having to wait. That was a real pain in the butt, although I've found several uses for the license plates." She chuckled. "You know about one, but how would you feel if I told you they are now underneath the steps to your friend Noah's front porch? Yours will be too, when I'm done with you. It never hurts to point the finger of suspicion away from oneself, does it?"

She sneered. "Are you wondering what I'm going to do with you?" She went over to the door and reached out for the coil of rope that was just outside. "As we already said, I have no gun. So it'll be harder, and I won't be able to put you in the same place, but I've figured out something even better. When the time is right, your car will go off the road and burst into flames." Jolene started tying Paige up, but paused, adding thoughtfully, "Your friend Wally will be so upset."

"People will be looking for me," Paige said. "My son, the school, and others. No one will believe I went off like that."

"You mean like Noah Oliver? What a pain in my butt he is, Dr. Good Samaritan. He's always watching me."

Jolene cinched the rope on Paige's wrists tight, tearing her skin. She gritted her teeth against the pain. "Did you do something to him?"

"Not to him, no. But one summer when I was up here I had this mangy dog who chewed up my new shoes. I wanted to make him pay. So I tied him up, just the same way I'm tying you up, and put him out in the woods. Noah came at me, screaming that the puppy could have been killed by a wild animal. He never let me see the dog again."

Jolene moved on to tying Paige's feet together. "No gun for a quick ending, but you'll die soon enough once I put you into the water. No one can stay in it for very long." She turned Paige so that she could look at her. "It's a pity, you know. I thought you could be my friend."

"I am your friend. You were my first friend up here. I don't understand—"

"Enough," said Jolene. "If you had only stayed away from

Quin. But I don't want to watch you die. I'm going to leave you now." She stood up, expressionless. "Later, I'll come and move your body. It worked fine with Ilke and I didn't have to worry about a smell, with a frozen corpse. It would've worked with that other one, too, if I could have caught her." Jolene picked up her parka.

"Wait," Paige said. "What are you talking about?"

"That girl with the jacket. It wasn't Aurora, it turns out, just someone wearing the same jacket."

A piece of the puzzle clicked into place, not that it would help Aurora, or Paige. "You must have seen Aurora's mother. What did you do to her?"

"I saw her running away from the lake, when I had to drag Ilke back the second time. Ilke wasn't exactly happy about being with me that day. She thought she was meeting Quin here, that they were going to make up."

"Why did she think that?"

"Because that's what I told her. Quin stopped by the shop on his way to Albany and told me all about the fight he and Ilke had. After he left I called her and said he had changed his mind about the trip but that he was going to do some errands and then go to the ice shanty to cool off. I suggested that she go there and wait, as a surprise. I told her they really needed to make up, since they belonged together. She bought every word. Then all I had to do was keep a look out from my back door for her to arrive at the shanty, slip out of the café, and walk across the ice to the shanty, and take care of her."

"I didn't see your car," Paige said, almost to herself. "Is that how you got here today?"

"Yes. Bless the ice. It makes the trip a lot shorter."

Paige's head hurt just trying to understand what Jolene was telling her. "Ilke just stood here and let you shoot her?"

Jolene shook her head. "What part of this aren't you getting? She kept trying to get away, and I went after her, pulling her back inside. The second time was when I saw this woman, on the other side of the bay. I hit Ilke over the head with the electric lantern and went to grab the woman."

"Did you catch her?" Paige said, fearing that she too was dead.

"Yes. Never got a real good look at her face, though, because she had a big red scarf over it, and it was tied pretty tight. I was pressed for time, so I bound her up and locked her in here with Ilke. Ilke couldn't have untied her, since she was half dead, but somehow, when I came back later, the woman was gone. She'd broken the lock off the door, although, I admit, the wood was not as strong as it is now. Quin was so appreciative that I discovered his hut had been broken into while he was gone, especially when I told him I'd made it more secure." She smiled proudly. "He can't even hold a hammer."

"Then how did he build this ice shanty?"

"What makes you think he did? He ordered a kit and got a carpenter to put it together for him."

Paige's mind reeled. Every explanation only led to more questions. "Are you the one who tampered with Aurora's brakes?"

"If I had known she wasn't the one who saw me last year, I never would have done it. I love kids. You know that. I love Mike like a son. Quin and I would have had dozens of kids by now if it wasn't for all the interference."

Paige tried to buy herself some more time to try to think of a way to escape. "Have you always been in love with him?"

Jolene dipped her head, and Paige thought she might be crying. "He would have noticed me, if you and Ilke and his grandmother and his parents didn't all get in the way."

Taking a deep breath, Jolene looked straight at Paige. "Mrs. Dillon got away, but I'll find her someday. No one says no to me and gets away with it. Quin's Grandma Marissa knew that." She snorted. "His parents were the first to try to keep us apart. But I showed them."

Revulsion and fear swept over Paige. She knew Quin had been an orphan and felt sorry for him. Now it seemed his parents might have been murdered. What had Paige heard about that? A car accident? Perhaps with brakes that had been compromised?

Jolene narrowed her eyes. "I see you have figured that out. So did Marissa, at the end. That was too bad, because until then I had a cushy job working for her. But it all worked out. Quin had to come back to run the hotel, and I got to open the café with the money Marissa had left for her devoted assistant. Poor thing hadn't had a chance to change her will before she died."

Her anger sent new chills through Paige's already overloaded nervous system. She began to have difficulty breathing and Jolene stopped talking for a moment to stare at her. "People just don't appreciate me. It was brilliant, the way I mummified Ilke's body. And I owe the whole thing to your beloved uncle. He's the one who told me about it."

Paige was shaking. Had she done away with her uncle as well? "What did you do to him?"

"Oh, nothing, really. I planted some drugs among his things the last time I saw him. I knew they'd be found when he got to customs. The country he was going to does not take drug trafficking lightly. He's probably in a prison somewhere, rotting away."

"Why would you do that?"

"To keep him from coming back to Tamarack with any more of his assistants. They are too tempting for the men around here."

Jolene's eyes narrowed. "And now the only loose end is you."

Paige drew as far away from Jolene's outstretched hands as she could. "This is crazy. I will be missed right away."

"Crazy?" Jolene's voice rose on the word. "Is that what you think? Do you think I'm doing this in a fit of rage?" She jerked Paige close and stared down into her eyes, her own glittering so frigidly Paige wondered how Jolene could have warm blood in her veins. "I've been thinking about this for days. Ever since your sonny boy told me he'd be at Aurora's today.

"And now, it's time for you to go." With a strong push, Jolene sent Paige into the hole.

The icy water surrounded her, shocking her so badly she was unable to breathe. She went under, still able to see the light from the lantern, and popped up, gasping for air. But the light suddenly went out. Jolene had closed the hole, leaving her barely enough room to get her nose above the water line.

She remembered what Noah had said about the chances for survival in water that temperature and knew she was about to die, leaving her child an orphan. Numbness began to overtake her.

Chapter Twenty-four

Nate skidded to a stop in front of Paige's house and Wally was out the door sliding on the snow before he'd turned off the engine. She ran up onto the porch and started knocking on the door. When no one answered, she banged harder.

"Maybe she hasn't come back from Plattsburgh yet," Nate said. "What are you so worried about?"

"Didn't you see her car? It's around the side of the house. She's home. Unless something happened."

Nate grabbed Wally's cell phone off the seat of the car and hit redial for Dover. He waited anxiously for someone to answer.

"Nate," Wally shouted. "Look over there. Is that a car?"

Without waiting for him to answer, Wally slid and slipped all the way down to the shoreline. As she got closer, she saw that she was right. There was a car—Noah's.

In a fog, Paige heard banging. Her name was shouted, but it seemed so far away. She was drifting toward icy unconsciousness. She struggled again with her gloves and managed to get one off, loosening the rope enough to get her hands out. But she felt herself sinking and she couldn't kick her feet since they were tied together.

Suddenly one of her feet brushed up against something. She spun herself in the water and realized she could stand. Quin must have set up his hut over the shoals which lay a short distance from the shore.

That tiny bit of control helped her to get calm and try to think. She couldn't stay in the icy water. No matter how long she could stand, she would die. Frantically she began pushing on the cover of the hole. If she could open it she could use the rope attached to her feet to pull herself up. She'd seen Jolene tie it to the side of the hole, presumably so she wouldn't float away.

But it was so heavy she couldn't budge it. She was losing feeling in her feet and her hands. Maybe it didn't really matter at all. She was floating, lighter than—

A banging sound woke her and she heard more shouting. "Paige! Where are you?" The voice kept calling her, but she couldn't cry out. Only her nose was above the freezing water.

Then she heard a scratching sound just above her. Don't dig, she thought, that's silly. Just open the cover. Why don't you open it? She drifted off again.

"Paige!" The cover was suddenly yanked open and a hand reached out and grabbed her jacket, pulling her up and out of the water. She was barely conscious, but she knew when she leaned against him that it was Noah. Balto was with him, licking at her hands, although she couldn't feel it, she could only see his frantic tongue.

Noah lifted her free of the hole, put her on the couch, and began to peel off her coat and her boots. He struggled to get the rest of her clothes off, finally seizing a knife and cutting them away, down to her underwear. Then he grabbed a blanket to wrap around her.

"How did you find me?" she asked, shivering uncontrollably.

"Wally called and told me to go stay with you as soon as you got home, and to keep Jolene away from you and Mike. I came over here and saw your car, but you weren't around."

Paige was having trouble processing what Noah was saying. "How did Wally know about Jolene?"

"I'm not sure, but she said something about pockets and keys and dehumidifiers. Enough talking now, we've got to get you out of here."

Noah finished wrapping her and took out his cell phone. "Hang on a sec," he said.

The call to the rescue squad took only a moment. "They're on their way."

"You should be proud of your dog," Noah said, while briskly rubbing her arms. Paige got the sense he was continuing to explain to help her stay awake. "I came straight over here to look for you, and when I got there I saw Balto. He was whining and pacing around. I was admiring the picture you painted and saw that the rope in it was gone from the side of Quin's hut. Then I saw Jolene running away across the ice."

Paige was so numb she didn't feel the rubbing at all. She could only tell that Noah was putting his coat over her because she could see it.

"When she left Balto ran down to the shore and started to bark to wake the dead. I followed him out here. He went straight to the hole when we came through the door."

"Is she okay?" said a voice. Wally and Nate rushed into the hut, crowding out the disappearing daylight from the door.

"You got her!" Wally said. She immediately took off her coat and threw it over Paige.

Nate added his on top. "What can we do?"

Noah grimaced, tucking the jackets around Paige. "We've got to get her out of here."

"She was going to kill me," Paige said, "like she did Ilke."

Noah's eyes were enraged. "Don't worry, we'll get her." He picked Paige up as if she were weightless. "Ready?"

He carried her to the open door and through it into the dusk. The wind was blowing hard and knifed right through the coat and blanket. Paige was beginning to get some sensation back. With it came searing pain.

Noah leaned into the wind. Paige could hear Balto panting alongside them as his nails clicked along on the frozen lake.

On the shore, an ambulance was waiting. Without assistance, Noah got her onto a stretcher.

"Mike?" Paige asked weakly, while she was being transferred.

"Don't worry. We'll take care of him."

"We've got to get her to the hospital," said Noah, bundling her up even more. Paige heard Dover's voice giving directions.

"You have to catch Jolene," Wally said. "She tried to kill Paige."

"She did kill Ilke," Paige said, fighting off her shivers. But it was no use.

Dover leaned close and nodded. "I know. I'm only sorry we didn't know sooner."

"What do you mean?" asked Wally.

"They found her," said Dover. "Mrs. Dillon. An officer out in Arizona spotted her and picked her up. She said she ran away because of something that happened. I'm positive it had to do with the murder, based on what she told me. She had a picture. Apparently she's a photographer, and she faxed it to me. It showed Jolene dragging Ilke into the ice shanty. And she said she was dragged in there too but escaped."

"Why didn't Mrs. Dillon call the police?" Wally asked, her voice filled with indignation.

"I don't know. But we'll find out. And we will find Ms. Valley."

He got into his police car. "There's a bulletin out for her."

Paige couldn't stay awake anymore. She was too cold and in too much pain. Noah looked down at her, where she lay with her head cradled in his lap, and promised her she'd be okay.

The radio squawked and Dover answered it. "Good," said Dover. "Mike has been picked up. He's safe."

"I'll bring him to you after we get you checked in," Wally promised.

Paige nodded. Then she succumbed to the darkness.

"I guess we didn't need this piece of evidence, after all," said Wally. She and Nate were standing in Paige's kitchen watching a police officer take pictures of the key that had fallen between the stove and the cabinet.

"I can't believe it's actually there," said Dover. He looked at Nate and then at Wally. "But from what I hear, I shouldn't have doubted you. I still don't understand how you knew it would be."

Wally felt she didn't deserve Dover's admiration. If she'd only thought of it sooner, Paige and even Aurora might not have been hurt. "As I said before," she explained, "she had no pockets. Jolene, I mean. On the day we drove up here, Jolene greeted us when we arrived. I thought she was self-consciously drying her hand on her dress to shake Paige's, but when I thought about it, and the missing key, I realized she might have just come out of the house and was trying to hide the key but realized she had no pockets. Then she did something to the napkin in the basket of muffins, and it must have been that she threw the key into it to hide it."

"But why didn't she take the key with her when she left?"

"I don't think she could hide it in the basket once it was empty. Or maybe she planned to, but when she fell against the stove, the key fell into the gap. I heard something metallic when it happened, but I didn't really think about it. I was just worried she might have hurt herself."

Dover held up the key in an evidence bag. "If you are right, Jolene Valley's prints will be on this and possibly Ilke Hedstrom's as well. Between that and the photograph provided by Mrs. Dillon, plus the confession to Dr. Griffin, we should have a solid case."

"Will you be able to prove anything about those other murders?" Wally asked.

"Maybe. We'll certainly investigate." Dover's face was grim. "I didn't know Quin Wyatt's parents very well, but I knew his grandmother. She was an old dear. If Jolene really killed her, as well as the Wyatts, I'm going to see that she pays."

Wally looked at her watch. "Are you finished with us? We'd really like to take Mike to see his mother."

Dover had barely nodded when Wally zoomed out the door.

The reunion between Wally and Paige's mother, Marion, when she arrived in Tamarack two days later to take care of her grandson and her hospitalized daughter, was a warm one. Marion, who was as tall as Paige, nearly knocked Wally over when she saw her, and the two women were in tears seconds later. When Wally and

Nate got ready to go back home, Marion promised to stop off to see them on her way back to Arizona. They wanted to spend more time talking, but this wasn't the time. As soon as they were sure Paige would be okay, the Morrises headed south.

Since Wally and Nate had left home in such a hurry, they had a lot of catching up to do when they returned home late Thursday. They'd arranged to have most of the family come for dinner the next night to hear the whole story and make sure they both were okay after their ordeal.

Chuckling at the way the world had of righting itself, Wally let herself into the kitchen with her groceries. After all that had gone on, today was just a normal day. Sammy poked his head into the bags she'd put on the floor and checked out all the purchases while she hung up her coat. Any person looking in wouldn't think that the poor dog had been ripped out of his home recently and sent elsewhere, while his family ran to help in upstate New York.

He'd gone to a good home though. Wally had been quite surprised at Debbie and Elliot's eagerness to have Sammy stay with them, even though it meant getting someone to come in at lunchtime to take him out.

Oddly, when Wally and Nate had picked up Sammy, Debbie and Elliot had been whispering to each other in a way that made Wally wonder if something was up. Maybe tonight they'd find out.

"What do you think it is?" asked Louise, as she watched Wally preparing dinner a while later. Louise had come in for a news fix and wasn't leaving until she'd heard every detail of the ordeal in Tamarack and speculated about what else was going on. "A baby?"

"I don't know. And I'm not asking. When they're ready,

they'll tell us. Meanwhile, don't you want to know what happened to Paige since we left? I got an update from Paige's mother this morning."

Louise helped herself to a baby carrot in a nearby bowl. She'd brought over chocolate babka from the bakery for Wally to serve after dinner because Wally hadn't quite managed to get everything together. "The vet?"

Wally understood her friend's sentence fragment. "Noah stayed by Paige's side for days, although she was pretty much out of it."

"That's good," said Louise. "He seems like a nice guy. I don't know why you ever suspected him."

Pretending she didn't hear that, Wally continued. "I hope things will work out for them. They both deserve to be happy."

"The girl?"

Assuming Louise meant Aurora, Wally told her that Aurora's mother had gone back to Tamarack. The psychiatrist who examined Mrs. Dillon suspected an emotional break from her ordeal with Jolene and thought that was why she ran away and never reported what she saw. Paige had expressed hopes that their relationship could be mended. It was obvious there was healing to be done.

Louise picked up another carrot. "And the hotel owner?"

"Quin left town. He told Paige he couldn't stay there and watch as the police gathered evidence that Jolene had killed not only his fiancée, but also his parents and his grandmother. Do you blame him?"

"I guess not." Louise refilled her coffee cup and topped up Wally's. It made Wally smile to be home relaxing with her best friend for a change. It was also nice not to have major problems to worry about.

She'd been pleased to see that somehow, while she was gone this last time, the situation between Ruthie and Kallie had stabilized, and both girls ran up to her when she came in and even hugged her at the same time. It was a step, she told herself, in the right direction. If she could keep Kallie moving forward, there was hope yet.

She was glad she'd stepped in and talked to Kallie's father, especially after she heard the horror story that was Jolene's life growing up. That Jolene had become possessive and controlling was not such a surprise, once she was arrested and it came out that her father had left when she was six, never to return, and her mother had committed suicide when she was a teenager, leaving her in the care of a cold and cruel grandmother. Not that it excused her behavior, but perhaps it explained a bit of it.

The way the police understood it, from the information they obtained from a psychiatrist they'd called in, Jolene had always been obsessed with Quin Wyatt. When his parents forbade him to see her, she had tampered with their brakes. After college, she moved into her grandmother's house in Tamarack, after the old lady succumbed to cancer, and she became close with Quin's grandmother. Jolene thought there might be a chance for her with Quin then, but Marissa suddenly fired her. Some months later, Marissa was found dead of carbon monoxide poisoning. A faulty heater had been blamed.

Louise was wide-eyed as Wally explained the story. "She's a mass murderer and no one figured it out?"

"The murders were years apart," Wally said. "But, yes."

"The uncle?"

"Ted is on his way back. It turned out that it was lucky we started looking for him. He'd been put into a Mongolian jail and the key had been thrown away because illegal drugs, courtesy of Jolene, were found in his equipment when he got there. When the friend Nate contacted alerted the authorities that Ted was missing and they found out why, the State Department called in some people to straighten it out and he was released."

Wally started taking dishes out of the closet so she could set the table. "Any other questions?"

Louise shook her head. "No, nothing. Except what's going on with the kids? The whole neighborhood is waiting for them to start having children."

"I sincerely doubt the whole neighborhood even cares what Debbie and Elliot are doing," said Wally. She looked out the back door into the driveway. "For now, the 'neighborhood' will have to content herself with Jody and Charlie. Rachel and Adam just drove up."

Wally was by the car helping everyone to get out before Louise could respond. Jody, who was four, and Charlie, who was six months, had enough paraphernalia to fill the trunk of the car. Rachel and Adam were left to carry it in, while Wally held Charlie and Louise marveled at how Jody had grown. One would think she was the proud grandmother.

Nate had come down the driveway from his office in the barn and he scooped Jody up for a big hug, then reached over to give Rachel a kiss.

Once inside, Rachel looked at Wally in a way that made her feel as if she were under a microscope. "I told you I'm fine," she said. "Ask Louise."

Louise nodded. "She's great, but she's dying to know what your sister and her husband are hiding."

"I am not," Wally said. "They'll tell us whenever they're ready."

Rachel laughed. "Don't ask me, I don't know either. But here they come, so maybe we'll all find out."

"Ooh, I can't wait," said Louise. Both Wally and Rachel turned to stare up at her.

"What?" she said. "Am I not a part of this family?"

"Of course you are," said Nate. "But let's give them a chance to tell us in their own time."

Debbie came into the kitchen and looked from one person to another. A big smile spread across her face. "We have some news," she said. "Maybe you should sit down."

As if they had been playing a game of musical chairs and the music stopped, everyone scrambled to take a seat. No one spoke for several moments.

"Where is Uncle Elliott?" Jody asked.

Debbie came over and hugged her niece. "He's outside."

"Shouldn't we wait for him?" Nate asked.

"He's bringing the surprise. I just wanted to make sure you were ready."

Thoroughly puzzled, Wally held her breath. She watched as Debbie went to the door and signaled her husband.

As if in a dream, Wally saw Elliot walk up the back stairs and through the door. He was cradling something in his arms. But it didn't make sense.

Suddenly it did. As Elliot set the bundle down onto the kitchen floor, it unfolded itself into a tiny yellow Labrador retriever. The puppy was adorable, with dark chocolate eyes and a dark brown button nose, and it looked as if she was wearing a biscuit-colored onesie. The babysitting for Sammy that Debbie and Elliot had been doing was indeed practice, but not for a baby.

* * *

Paige was sitting up in bed when Noah came into her room. Unlike Ted's room, it did not look out on to Lake Champlain. It was just as well, she'd thought, since the lake was the last thing she wanted to see as she recuperated from nearly freezing to death in it. The view she had, of the nearby woods all full of snow, was chilling enough.

She looked over at her visitor. He seemed uncomfortable standing there. "Come in," she said. "I'm much better. They wouldn't have released me if I wasn't on the road to recovery."

Noah came and sat in the chair beside her. He peered closely at her. "You are looking much better. Maybe you don't really need these." He raised his hand and showed her the bouquet of flowers he'd brought.

"Oh, but I do," said Paige, gratefully accepting them. "And thank you. I'll ask my mother to put them in some water when she comes upstairs."

"Where are Wally and Nate?" Noah asked. "I didn't see them when I came in."

Paige carefully put the flowers aside and smoothed the comforter. "They went back to New Jersey."

"Really?"

"Yes. Wally said I was in good hands and they could go home without worries."

Noah seemed surprised. "Is your mother going to stay with you?"

Paige nodded. "She'll be here until I can take care of myself. It shouldn't be long, really, before I'm back on my feet. Probably early next week, according to the doctors, then she'll fly back to Arizona."

"Then whose hands . . . ?"

Paige wondered if she was about to make a mistake—did Noah really think of her that way?

She took a chance. "Yours."

"Mine?" Noah's puzzled look slowly disappeared. He came to sit on the side of the bed and gathered her into his strong arms, holding her close. "Mine." He smiled. "Yes. That's good. Wally is absolutely right."